Praise for TTM anthol

"Usually I like a few storie ... I liked every story in this boo ... e, and while many tug at ... u zombies or horses or magic ... n poetry for those who love that. This would make a perfect Christmas gift for the readers on your list, especially those who don't have time to sit down and read a novel." **~~Arkansas Reader**

"Anthologies can be tricky things. In most, one writer usually stands out more than the others. In this anthology, they must have chosen only the cream of the crop! Each and every short story was well-written, finely tuned, and imaginatively crafted. The poetry was superb. I can only hope that these talented writers will do another anthology together, perhaps on one theme." **~~Emily J. Henderson**

"If variety really is the spice of life, then this collection of short stories encompasses a delightful olio. The talented writers supplied me with suspense, inspiration, thrills, reconciliation, retribution, spite, forgiveness - the best and worst which the human soul can display. There truly is something for everyone encapsulated within this collection. The more stories I read, the more I wanted to read. I reveled in the individual voices which each author gave to their characters, closed my eyes and saw the settings which were artfully painted, heard the conversations and background sounds, and was transported, becoming a voyeur." **~~L. Hunter**

"What happens when you open up a writing competition and provide the entrants with a broad topic? You unleash lots of creativity and end up with a collection of work that reflects the attitudes and abilities of a wide variety of people. Elements of Time is a compilation of short stories, peppered with a few poems, all penned by winners of one of the many short story contests sponsored by Accentuate Writers. Newbies to seasoned writers are represented in this collection, each with a story to tell." **~~Elizabeth Grace**

Elements
of the
Soul

Bubba Goes
National
by
Jennifer Walker

RENDEZVOUS
RENDEZVOUS

Bubba to the
Rescue
Jennifer Walker
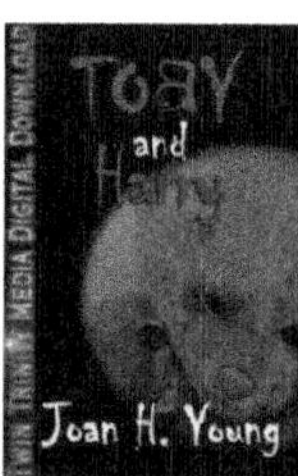
TWIN TRINITY MEDIA DIGITAL DOWNLOAD
TOBY
and
Harry
Joan H. Young

ELEMENTS OF DIMENSION

Primitive Fabric
Summer Bowl Fillers
Designs by

TWIN TRINITY MEDIA DIGITAL DOWNLOAD
Jennifer Walker
The
Fire

Twin Trinity Media
LLC

Elements of Life

Birth, Life, Death

An
Accentuate Writers
Anthology

Authors:

John Morrison
Katherine Shaye
Robert L. Arend
Lindsay Maddox
Kim Kevason
Sarah F. Sullivan
Nancy Smith Gibson
Jo Brielyn
Eric Patterson
M. Lori Motley

Poets:

Catherine A. MacKenzie
Lisa Lee Smith
Jo Brielyn
Lucinda Gunnin
L.L. Darroch
Joan H. Young

Foreword:

Rissa Watkins

Elements of Life: Birth, Life, Death

An Accentuate Writers Anthology

Library of Congress Control Number: 2012944441
ISBN-10: 0984209573
ISBN-13: 978-0984209576

First Edition
10 9 8 7 6 5 4 3 2 1

Authors: John Morrison, Katherine Shaye, Robert L. Arend, Lindsay Maddox, Kim Kevason, Sarah F. Sullivan, Nancy Smith Gibson, Jo Brielyn, Eric Patterson, M. Lori Motley

Poets: Jo Brielyn, Catherine A. MacKenzie, Lucinda Gunnin, Lisa Lee Smith, L.L. Darroch, Joan H. Young

Editors: Michelle Devon, Lynn Hunter,
Proofreaders: Max Neram, Kaira Jackson
Foreword by: Rissa Watkins
Illustrations / Cover: Farah Evers Designs http://FarahEvers.com

Wholesale ordering available
SAN 858-737X

www.TwinTrinityBooks.com
www.AccentuateWritersForum.com
Michy@twintrinitymedia.com

Published in the United States.

Twin Trinity Media
PO Box 1135
League City, TX 77573

Life, Birth and Death:
Through the Eyes of a Leukemia Patient

Rissa Watkins

When diagnosed with leukemia, your life as you've known it is over. You see the death of what you knew before. All the things that were so important suddenly aren't, and you face a shift in perspective.

But life begins anew and you start a different life, one that involves challenges and treatments that are all unfamiliar. It's scary, but you learn it doesn't mean a death sentence to be told you have this horrible illness. It just requires a new way of thinking.

Then comes the birth of hope. I had my first glimmer of hope when I was told they found not just one but five bone marrow donor matches for me. Bone marrow donation gave me a chance for a new life, a rebirth from treatment and possibly a cure.

Now, over a year later, with all signs of the cancer gone, surviving isn't my all-consuming focus. You realize living your life is just as important as keeping it. If you stay hiding in bed, what was the point of all those painful and sickening treatments?

Life, death, birth... they aren't always found in typical ways and, much like the stories in this anthology, don't always follow standard patterns. Much like life, these stories can surprise you. They evolve to fit the circumstances. You have to be open to the changes and be ready to embrace the challenges as they arise.

Most of all, you have to cherish every moment.

Foreword Author:

Rissa Watkins was born with the soul of a writer. Her father, who taught English to unruly high school students, also taught her the love of the written word. It is a love that lasts a lifetime.

She honed her craft telling tall tales as a child. She was first published at the age of ten with a book titled The Revenge of Remington Steele. Rissa garnered critical acclaim from her fellow fifth graders. Her four week run at her elementary school library was her first literary success.

Rissa has completed her first novel, Dying to Find You. *A sucker for punishment, she is now working on her second novel.*

Rissa lives in the Arizona desert with her husband, son and rescued dog Mocha. When not huddled over her keyboard, typing furiously, she likes to cook Thai food and other culinary treats. She is a budding gardener who has turned her black thumb into something more Chartreuse.

Rissa can be found online at RissaWatkins.com. Stop in to see what else she is crafting and feel free to leave a comment.

Table of Contents

Life, Birth and Death, Rissa Watkins

Signed, Tallulah Granger

by Katherine Shaye

Perception is a funny thing.

Often, we remember things differently than they occurred or forget them entirely, depending on what input our brain registers. Yet, despite the faults, our brains hold the only full record of the lives we lead and the people we become.

"You'll lose who you are. It will take away your life. Eventually, it will be pointless to live on another day."

That's what I heard when the good doctor explained my diagnosis. Later, away from the glare of fluorescents and the smell of latex, when I lay tucked in my own bed and the safety of my husband's arms, Jeremy would tell me what the doctor actually had said: "You'll start to lose your memories. It will progress in stages. Eventually, it will be difficult to live normally day to day."

The diagnosis: early-onset Alzheimer's. I spent nine months subsequent to my diagnosis in a drunken stupor, unsure whether my blackouts were a product of inebriation or degeneration. Turned out, alcohol didn't do much for my chronic memory issue.

After fifteen missed meetings at work, I lost my job. Seven police escorts back home because I was lost and could not find my way meant the end of my driving career. And the day I left a pan on the burner long enough to start a kitchen fire was the last day I spent home alone.

After what my husband not so fondly referred to as 'the lost months', we—and I use that term loosely—decided to check me into St. Juanita's Treatment Center for the Recollection Impaired. At thirty-four years old, I was the youngest inmate by a two-decade gap.

While Jeremy filled out my commitment papers, I chatted with the woman who would become my de facto roommate of sorts, by which I mean she would regularly fall asleep in my bed, having forgotten her room assignment had been changed four years prior at her request.

"And what's your name, dear?" Even though she meant nothing by it, her patronizing tone grated on me.

"Callie." I hoped my terse response would send a message. It didn't.

"That's a beautiful name. My granddaughter has that name."

"You don't say." I feigned enough interest to seem polite. "And you are... missus?"

Beaming with geriatric glee, the old woman filled in the blank with, "VanGuard. Patricia VanGuard, dear, and what's your name?"

Confused, I stuttered a bit in my response. "Uh, it's Callie. Callie Waters."

I wasn't sure whether to laugh or not. When I turned away, I caught the eye of the janitor across the lobby. His face creased in a wry smile. The look seemed to say, 'Yes, this is the standard fare around here. Get used to it.'

Mrs. VanGuard clapped two wrinkled hands together. "Oh, lovely, lovely. My granddaughter's name is Callie. It's such a beautiful name. And what is it they call you, dear?"

The urge to chuckle died in my throat. I could see it. This would be me in a few years. Hell, it might be me in a few months, unable to retain the simplest information, introducing myself to people I already knew, over and over and over and over and...

I had opened my mouth to scream when Jeremy caught my attention. "You all right, hon?"

Patricia was shining her happily clueless grin around the room, having already abandoned our almost conversation. "Yeah, me and Old Lady Rivers here were having a delightful chat about my future."

Jeremy eyed me with the same reproachful stare he reserved for his kindergarteners. My response to it was on par with their five-year-old reactions. I crossed my arms, glared at the floor and sulked.

My new friend, Patty V., came to visit me my first night. Her withered voice woke me from a dead sleep when she screamed about strangers in her bed. I watched two orderlies sedate the screeching Mrs. V. and drag her, limp and confused, back to her own room.

Welcome to your new home.

Three months later, Patty's three-in-the-morning wakeup calls were just another crooked painting in the funhouse of my life. It had all become part of the routine, the daily ritual that was supposed to keep me happy and healthy and make it easier to remember things. While on my way down the hall for my eleven o'clock with Dr. Merrick, I thought the strict schedule stole more of my sanity than it saved.

Dr. Merrick opened the door before I knocked. The smile he greeted me with was warm, as always, wide and nonthreatening. It was a look cultivated to soothe nervous patients wondering who he was, where they were, and why they'd come down this hallway in the first place.

When I didn't immediately turn and run, Dr. Merrick toned down the forced geniality and let more of himself seep into his expression. He was still the kindly forty-something psychologist, ready to listen to all my problems, only with a little more of his inner geek thrown in, some innate shyness fostered in high school and never fully dislodged. It was almost endearing.

I ignored civility, pushed past him, and took my place in the patient chair. He followed my lead, took his post behind the desk and waited for me to start.

"You got a girl at home, Merrick?" His naked ring finger already told me there was no wife. An unmarried doctor at forty; it lent more credence to my geek theory.

"I fail to see how that information is going to help today's session," Dr. Merrick said, his eyes centered on mine.

He was big on eye contact, always intent on making sure I knew he was listening the way a good doctor ought to. The focus also kept his attention from straying to places like my neck or my breasts. I couldn't fault him for it. I was the only woman under sixty he saw all day.

"Perhaps my brain is waiting for the right information to latch onto. Maybe if I learn something interesting enough, I'll be compelled to hold onto it despite all the brain rot. Tell me, are you getting it good behind closed doors?"

A faint blush rose in the good doctor's cheeks, and he used the excuse of cleaning his glasses to avoid looking at me. "Must we always start this way? We ought to talk about you. These sessions are supposed to be helping you cope."

"And helping you finish that book. What's the working title again? *Alzheimer's: Psychology of the Demented*?" I faulted and resented him for the book; no way was I going to end up case study #624 in some hoity-toity medical tome.

"*Psychology of the Afflicted*, actually, and my research is always secondary to patient care. Now, would you like to talk about your latest incident with Mrs. VanGuard? The orderlies informed me that things were a little... exciting last night."

Flashing back to the incident in question, my hand shot up to the three marks Patty's nails had scored into my neck. "You know, I'd really rather not."

If ever there were a time to forget, that was a memory

I would have gladly released. Like I needed another constant reminder of what my life had become.

I ducked a few more of his probes into my psyche until he gave up on conversation. He spent the rest of our session prodding me into his favorite games: How many words can I forget in five minutes, at what point in a story will I lose track of how it began, etcetera.

I left the meeting feeling as miserable as when I entered. His nonsense about helping me cope was shit.

Jeremy awaited me in the common room with lunch. Same as every other day, one thirty on the dot. He came between his morning and afternoon classes, the next step in the schedule.

"Any troubles today?" he asked. He handed me a homemade sandwich.

"None I can remember."

Jeremy forced a smile at my sarcasm, but the slight pinch between his eyebrows told me I'd upset him. We ate for a few minutes in silence while I worked up an apology. There were days I felt he took my disorder harder than I did.

"I'm sorry," I said. "I don't mean to be so blunt about it."

Jeremy was slow in his response, finishing the last of his sandwich and wiping his mouth before he spoke.

"Yes, you do," he said, with a knowing weight behind the statement.

Those three words summed up almost every fight in nine years of marriage. They almost all began with my need to be snarky and sarcastic rather than deal with feeling.

"It's the only way I can handle it, okay?" We were talking about the dissolution of my entire life, not some bad day at work. I had a right to embrace humor as a defense mechanism.

Jeremy didn't back down. We stared at each other, having the same fight we'd had a thousand times before without words. I blinked first, my attention falling to the table.

"I hate even thinking about it, never mind talking about it." A quick glance back at Jeremy told me this concession still wasn't enough, not that I should have expected it to be. I'd blown him off too many times before.

With a steadying breath, I started in. "You can't imagine how bizarre it is to be able to remember the subjects of all my fourth grade book reports, but still get lost trying to find the bathroom, to have perfect recall of obscure song lyrics, and yet some days..." I paused so the words wouldn't sound as choked as they felt, "...some days not be able to recognize your face."

Jeremy reached for me, but I pulled back, determined to finish what he had insisted I start.

"It's like I'm skating on a pond with giant pieces of the ice hacked out. It's sturdy and thick until all of a sudden, there's nothing, and I'm falling."

Turning to the window, I hid my eyes. The angry accusations they shot weren't for Jeremy.

Outside, the trees waved to me, tossed back and forth in a blustery wind, shedding leaves like tears. They were storm winds, the kind that exuded violence in every wisp.

"Callie?" a voice behind me asked.

I turned to find Jeremy had finally arrived for his visit. My watch read two fifteen. "You're late," I said, chiding him. "You know how persnickety they are about my schedule."

Jeremy's gaze fell to the floor with far more sadness in his eyes than I'd intended to invoke.

"Sorry," he said. "I'll do better."

My name is Callie.

At least, I thought that was my name. That was what everyone called me, and it sounded familiar enough.

"It's time for lunch, Callie," someone said. Instinctively I shrank back from the squishy woman bearing down on me. Her sugary smile felt insincere at best.

"I'm not hungry," I said, pushing further away from her grabby hands.

"Are you sure?" The woman kept her speech pattern slow, regarding me as something fragile. "Sometimes I think I'm not hungry, but when I start eating, I find out I was wrong. Why don't we go down to the common room—"

Her thick fingers reached for me again, and I jumped away. "No, I'm not hungry. Please go away now."

"All right now, Callie, stay calm." The woman's eyes flicked to something past my shoulder, her hands gesturing in subtle movements. There must have been someone else behind me. I felt corralled.

Summoning every ounce of speed I could manage, I darted toward the nearest door. When the woman came forward to stop me, my shoulder slammed into her, and she tumbled to the floor.

My fingers closed on the doorknob in time for someone else's fingers to close on my opposite wrist.

"Hey," I said, whipping around.

There were three of them, all saying my name in the same pacifying tone, all reaching their grubby hands for me.

"No," I shouted, "leave me be."

They were too close. I needed air. More hands grabbed for me. I couldn't see past their pale uniforms. My name still rang out in that placating chant. Swinging my free arm, I struck out at everything. "Let go."

One of them bit me right in the neck. It was sharp and stinging, and it made my head fuzzy. I couldn't focus. In my head, I was still yelling, still fighting, but in reality my limbs were full of lead.

Someone shut off the lights.

My fingers were the first to regain sensation. I wiggled a few of them, curious about what caused their tingly swollen feeling. It was like wearing Mickey Mouse gloves full of bugs.

"Well, this is new," I mumbled.

"Callie?"

My eyes snapped open at the familiar voice, and I turned toward the source.

Dr. Merrick sat beside my bed, his fingers in a steeple before him emulating some television doctor with bad news.

"How long was I gone?" I asked.

"You were drifting most of the afternoon. They had to sedate you after you attacked the nurse who tried to bring you to lunch." He pulled one hand back to check his watch. "That was about seven hours ago."

Dr. Merrick leaned his elbows on his knees and brought his face closer. Anxiety creased lines in his forehead.

"How long have you been watching me?" I asked, my voice thick with insinuation.

He ignored my question and remained in strict professional mode.

"While violence isn't necessarily unusual in cases like yours, this incident seemed to arrive quite abruptly. Is there anything in specific you think may have incited the outburst?"

The pins and needles crawled up through my arms and chest as more of me woke up.

"Sitting vigil for all of your sedated patients can't be standard procedure. It happens too often. You'd never find any time to work on that fancy book of yours."

As usual, he refused to rise to my bait. "Callie, it can only help you to open up to me. It's all right to be angry, but if you don't find an outlet for all that emotion, it will manifest in ways you may not have control over."

"Is this a special visit just for me, doc?"

Merrick pulled both hands down his face and then folded them in his lap. "I hold unscheduled sessions with all patients who are sedated for traumatic incidents. Since this was your first, I thought it wise to make my services available to you as soon as possible. Now, again I ask: Is there anything you have experienced that seems to be increasing your stress?"

I sat up and rubbed the tingles out of my neck with a stiff hand. "I don't know, Merrick. I can't remember."

Television was taxing. Too often while watching a program, I lost track of the storyline and never recovered it. I usually sat in the common room staring at the wall instead.

The noise of the janitor emptying trash bins trickled over from my left, bags rattled, buckets clunked, and then his footsteps padded toward the door. He stopped in front of me on his way out.

His face was youthful and handsome, the kind that found its way into trouble wherever it could. Shouldering one of the trash bags wrapped in his fist, he nodded at the door.

"Come on," he said.

Stepping outside the security locked doors felt fantastically rebellious—even if I only went a few feet. After ditching the garbage, the janitor joined me in leaning against the wall.

"You looked bored," he said. "Thought you could use some fresh air." He held out a grimy hand. "I'm Clint."

"Callie."

The hand disappeared into his pocket and reemerged with a flask.

"You want a taste?" he asked.

I made no pretense of modesty. "Please. Please. Please. I haven't had a drop in the seven months I've been here."

I swiped the flask and knocked back three slugs in quick succession. The savory burn of the liquid scorched my throat.

"Damn, woman, I said a taste." Clint confiscated the flask—not without effort—and brought it to his own lips. I watched with a jealous eye while he downed the last.

Disappointed, I turned my attention to the forest beyond the back fence and enjoyed the light reprieve the alcohol provided me.

"Why do they put this facility way out here in the middle of nowhere? You would think if any of the crazies wandered off, it would be easier to find us in the city."

Returning the flask to the folds of his dirty coveralls, Clint smiled. "Well, I haven't been here long, but as far as I know, they haven't managed to lose anyone yet. Folks are too old to scale the fences, I guess. Or they've already forgotten what's on the other side."

Though unintentionally so, Clint's words stung. Beyond the fence line, the tree branches curled like fingers and beckoned. My feet answered their call without my conscious consent.

"Callie, whatever you're thinking, it's not a good idea," Clint called from his post on the wall.

Instead of responding, I quickened my pace.

Wind rustled my hair and my feet pounded faster, driving me straight at the fence. Curses streamed out behind me while Clint's hurried footsteps joined my own. The fence was less than two feet away.

Scrabbling up it slowed me, but I was up and over before Clint could stop me. I took my first tentative steps into freedom.

Then a hand closed over the scruff of my shirt collar. Clint's breathing heaved behind me. "What are you doing?"

I turned my head enough to see Clint's body half spitted across the top of the chain link fence, one arm straining to hold onto me.

I put dejection in my tone and pulled out sad puppy eyes. "I'm not trying to run away. Where would I even go? I just want to... I don't know, look around or something."

When he opened his mouth to speak, I was positive a 'no' rested on his tongue.

"Fifteen minutes," he said. "And you don't leave my line of sight."

I nodded my agreement, and Clint hauled the rest of himself over the fence.

Walking along, I wondered how much of this experience my brain would record. I wondered if the thoughts, the images would be among those that came back on occasion or if they would slip away forever, bits of sand in the wind. I wondered whether I had any gut instinct that could lead me home again if I drifted away out here in the woods. With Clint breathing down my neck, I knew there was no way to test my curiosity.

He stayed right behind my shoulder while we walked, close enough that we bumped arms every few paces. He mumbled a few apologies but didn't back up. His tension was too amusing not to mess with.

I froze, causing Clint to run into me.

"What was that?" I whispered.

Clint surveyed the area. "I didn't hear anything."

Eyes wide, I pointed in a vague direction. "It came from over there." He took a few steps forward, peering through the trees at nothing. I tiptoed backward and scooted behind the nearest tree.

"I don't see any— Callie? Shit, where'd you go? Callie!" Clint's voice called out to me, shrill with panic.

I waited for another anxious yell before I leaned out from behind the tree, grinning.

Sweat had broken out across his forehead. "That's not funny."

My grin widened. "Oh, come on. It's a little funny."

Clint sucked in a slow breath and shook his head. "We're going back now."

As soon as he turned back, I darted behind another tree. I crouched to the ground.

"Damn it. What'd I say?" His footsteps thundered around the immediate area. "Enough of this, already. We need to go back."

Crawling, I made my way in a wide arc to a spot opposite where I'd been. His cursing and crashing drifted away from me.

I chuckled to myself when the sound of feet echoed nearby. A man's voice called out, hunting for someone. Hunting for me. The thought clutched at my chest like an icy fist. I had to get away.

Still on hands and knees, I scrambled through the underbrush, tree roots and bush branches scratching at any exposed skin. That close to the ground, I smelled the rich earth mixing with the tang of blood from my palms.

Huddled on the ground, I listened for the voice. When all I heard was wind in the trees, I decided to take my chances. I sprang to my feet and sprinted forward.

More branches tore at my face and chest, but I didn't slow down. In the distance, the man's shouting was indistinct, still searching. I had to keep running.

My lungs protested, burning with the strain. Desperate to slow down, I chanced a brief glance over my shoulder and, in my distraction, slammed into a tree. The jolt stole the last of my oxygen and knocked me to the ground. With my final tendrils of energy, I rolled onto my back.

Panting, I stared through a break in the trees at the sky with fluffy clouds streaming by in a stark white parade. I brought a hand to rest behind my head, thinking how pleasant it was to watch clouds on a nice day. I'd never felt so relaxed... or tired. I closed my eyes for just a minute.

Yelling voices woke me. It was too dark to see much beyond the beams of light swinging above me. My bed felt like a box of rocks, and my chest ached, but I felt a cool breeze from what must have been an open window. Fresh air filled my nostrils, and I breathed deep.

Some sort of dust flew up my nose, and I sneezed several times, rolling over to cough a little. My noise centered the lights in my direction.

Footsteps brought the light beams closer until they all hovered over my face. I squinted against the glare. A man with glasses leaned in close enough to block most of the brightness. He barked a few orders to the others then asked me how I felt.

I shrugged. "I feel fine. How are you?"

Dr. Merrick was the first to break our silent staring match. "There's this theory about dogs dying of old age. Supposedly, they reach a point where they accept their fate and abandon their families to go die. Alone."

I fought the urge to roll my eyes and compromised by glaring out his office window instead. "You're comparing me to a dog? Some mongrel that wants to die? You know, if I were suicidal, this wouldn't be helping."

"Not suicidal, Callie. Desperate. I think you would rather run away and die on your own terms. At least that way, you'd still have control. But if you stay and force yourself to deal with this, you have to watch yourself lose control. Worse yet, you have to let others watch you."

I wrestled with that comment, replaying it in my brain. Each iteration made me angrier still. "I was barely a hundred feet from the building. If I couldn't remember the way back, maybe I deserved to stay lost." I shot up from my chair, a surplus of energy making me restless. "Everything is still slipping. Day by day, more pieces of my life are melting away, and I don't know how to fight it."

Dr. Merrick watched my pacing with rapt concentration, causing an idea I should have ignored to pop into my head.

I ran fingertips back and forth along my collarbone. Some might have called it a nervous gesture, if it hadn't been so slow and deliberate. Not entirely sure what I was doing, I made my way around the desk.

"Callie..." Dr. Merrick's voice was unsteady.

"You said you wanted to help me." My fingers moved to the buttons of my shirt.

Pushing back in his chair, Merrick let his eyes follow my fingers. "I do, but this won't—"

"Yes, it will."

It had to. I needed it, a memory so searing my disease couldn't wash it clean. Remorse was the most resilient of emotions. Even now, I felt it boiling up inside me alongside thoughts of Jeremy, his face, his voice, his scent. None of it would stay with me. Happiness disintegrated too easily. I needed something deeper, more painful. My thighs brushed against Merrick's knees.

His hands were quick and closed over my wrists before I was too close. He halted my motions. It wasn't an outright denial. I pushed forward.

"Give me this," I said, fighting his weak resistance. "Give me a moment I can't escape. Make something stick."

I watched him consider it, saw the debate play behind his eyes, but his resolve held. My opportunity slipped away.

"This isn't what you want."

Two inches separated my hands from his face, an impassable distance. I stared across it at the man who wasn't my husband.

"My life stopped being about what I wanted a long time ago."

With that, Merrick stood, decision made. Escaping around his desk, he grabbed the phone. My hand shot for the cord but a glint of silver on the desk caught my eye, and I snatched it up instead. It would be a substitute for the emotional pain Merrick had denied me.

"Make sure they send a nurse up with security," I said. The words drew Dr. Merrick's attention up from the phone buttons, his eyebrows drawn tight. My skin was already pale with the pressure of the letter opener's tip. "You know, 'cause I think I'm a bleeder."

Dr. Merrick launched himself across the desk, but not quick enough to stop me. The metal pierced straight through my forearm, and an exquisite moment of frozen time seized me; everything beyond my arm flickered into nonexistence.

Before the pain, a sick satisfaction came from seeing

the metal implement protruding from right below my elbow. Perverse yet profound, I thought, and utterly unforgettable. One side dripped coppery liquid onto the carpet, reigniting my senses.

I fell into Dr. Merrick's arms when dizziness took me. My arm throbbed with the ebb of the initial shock. Someone dimmed the lights. Someone else shouted. Then a frantic voice whispered in my ear.

"Jesus, Callie. Why?"

I only smiled, eyes focused on my bloody arm. "The pain, Merrick. How can I forget the pain?"

Jeremy explained it to me again, but the logic continued to elude me.

"Straight through my arm?" I asked, examining the matching puncture wounds on both sides. He nodded, and I found myself warming to the idea.

If I couldn't find amusement in it, then it would only depress me. I had stabbed myself. "Did I happen to mention why?"

Jeremy didn't share my fondness for the situation. His entire body curled in on itself, his eyes flicking around the room to everything but me.

"Dr. Merrick won't disclose anything that happened in the meeting. He said he's filing the report to his higher ups and transferring you to another therapist."

"What?" I jerked my head up.

"What did you expect? You took a knife to your arm in the middle of your session. It obviously wasn't going well."

"Letter opener," I said, the pinched skin of my incision reclaiming my attention.

Jeremy finally looked in my direction. "Wh—"

"It wasn't a knife."

He expelled a mouthful of air in what could have been a laugh if there'd been any humor to it. "Does it really matter?"

To me it did. A knife suggested planning and

forethought, skills I didn't quite possess any more. The letter opener felt improvisational, almost archaic in its inefficiency. It was a perfect allegory for me, unable to operate in consideration of any other moment but right now.

In a sudden movement, I pushed to my feet. "I need to talk to Dr. Merrick. Surely, we can work this out," I said and started for his office.

"Callie." More than hearing my name, Jeremy's tone stopped me in my tracks. When I turned back to him, he leveled me with a flat stare. "Is there something we should be talking about between you and him?"

His eyes searched mine, seeking relief from the pain I saw behind them. That ache reached out enough to say my answer, one way or the other, could break him.

I wanted to say no, but a wild storm of guilt thrashed around in my stomach and held my tongue. It came with no explanation, waves of it pounding into me without cause.

"I— I don't know. I can't remember." It was a cheap shot, appealing to the disease, but I needed an out.

Jeremy sensed my reluctance. Years of fighting to get answers from me told him I held something back.

"That can't always be your excuse," he said, his voice tired. "It's not fair to me."

My sarcasm lashed out on instinct. "Well, I'm sorry my debilitating disease is making your life difficult."

The words shot from my lips, little barbed arrows waiting to tear up flesh. I didn't stay to watch the damage they'd inflicted.

When I arrived at Dr. Merrick's door, it was propped open. Inside, he was busy packing, and my light knock startled him. He didn't invite me in.

From the threshold, I gestured around the disheveled office. "All this because of little old me?"

Merrick moved to the bookshelf behind his desk and emptied its contents into a large box. "This is a change I've needed to make for a while. The timing has little to do with you."

While I leaned in the doorway and watched him work, I tried to replay our last session in my head. As usual, the harder I tried, the emptier things became. "I'm sorry I don't remember what I did."

I felt like an addict, apologizing and swearing that it was my last binge, the last time I'd black out and lose control. Only it wasn't some drug I could walk away from with enough will and determination. "You can't leave yet. What about my routine?"

"As long as you keep your sessions at eleven, I'm sure it won't matter who's on the other side of the desk."

Another book clunked into the box.

"I'll open up."

Dr. Merrick's gaze drifted up from his packing. "Excuse me?"

"If you stay," I said, "I'll be more cooperative. I could contribute a lot to that book of yours. I'm an early onset case. We're only like, what, maybe five percent of the Alzheimer's population. That's pretty rare."

His eyebrow crept toward his hairline. "Are you trying to bribe me?"

A coy smile lit my lips. "I'm asking you for help. Real help. I want to hold it together for as long as possible, to be better for Jeremy, to be," I glanced down at my arm, "less destructive."

I walked down the hallway with a sense of déjà vu. It felt familiar, but I knew I'd never been down it before. If I had, I would have noticed the artwork sooner.

Five frameless paintings hung along the wall. I stood in front of the center one, captivated.

"This one looks angry," a voice to my left said, startling me out of my trance. The man who stood next to me maintained a respectful distance, his eyes turned to the art like mine.

"It's more frightened than angry," I said. "You see how the strokes are short, almost tentative. The artist is depicting intense emotion here, but she's uncomfortable with it."

In my peripheral vision, I saw the man's mouth curl into a soft grin. "Something she's always struggled with."

My head snapped to my new companion. "You know the artist?"

Again, the man grinned as though enjoying a fond memory. "We've met."

"Wow, I would love to meet Tallulah Granger." I glanced at the black signature scrawled in the corner of each picture. Even *it* seemed imbued with a fearsome passion. "You couldn't introduce me, could you?"

At that, the grin wilted. "She's uh— on vacation at the moment. No one really knows when she'll be back. She hasn't been home much lately."

"That's a shame." We lapsed into silence.

Down the hall, an animated old woman waved at me. "Afternoon, Callie, dear," she said, before wandering off abruptly. I raised a hand at her retreating form.

"Do you know her?" my art friend asked.

"She's my grandmother." My head cocked sideways. "I think."

He nodded at this, the grin creeping back up to his lips. "So you're Callie?"

That was how my grandmother had addressed me. It must have been true. "Yeah, I guess I am. Who are you?"

The man introduced himself as, "Jeremy," with a small at-your-service nod.

Jeremy seemed like a nice name. "Well, Jeremy," I said. "I don't know if you've noticed, but that painting over there on the end looks a whole lot like you."

Dr. Merrick had his notepad out. I'd consented to it as part of my new open attitude toward his book. His restless pen skimmed across the page, but his eyes never left mine as we spoke.

"Why choose a strange name? I thought the point was to remember the important parts of your life."

I paused, trying to think of the simplest way to explain. "It doesn't mean anything to me."

The pen stilled, Merrick's eyes narrowing behind his glasses. "I'm not sure I understand."

"The name 'Callie Waters' is too ingrained with discontent in my mind. When I look at Tallulah Granger's work, I see something I can connect with, but at the same time, I don't recognize it as my own. It doesn't remind me of myself, or my situation. The paintings are a way to have a piece of myself without remembering what I've lost, what I'm losing..."

Dr. Merrick didn't interrupt the silence I left at the end of my explanation. We sat in the quiet, waiting to see what happened next. Three and a half minutes ticked away.

"Tallulah Granger," he mused. "Interesting."

Noticing we'd delved into my favorite subject, I was eager to join in. "I just love her work. Don't you?"

About the Author

Katherine Shaye is an aspiring novelist and avid people watcher, most likely to be found sitting on a bench in a park, mall, or airport simply observing life around her. She spends her days living in a co-op with ten other fascinating individuals, and her nights hard at work on an urban fantasy series.

She credits her early interest in storytelling to her chronic fear of the dark. While lying in bed every evening, unable to sleep with the shadows creeping around her, she would make up stories to distract her mind from the things that go bump in the night. As her stories grew too large for her head to carry, they needed somewhere else to live and thus began her writing. At age twelve, she received her first literary award for a poem entitled "I Hold in my Hand," which spurred her interest in writing from hobby to passion.

Now, more than a decade later, she spends almost all her free time in libraries and used bookstores, hoping her work will someday line their shelves. You can check out some of her current misadventures at:

http://sauceoff.wordpress.com/katherine-shaye/

Lost and Found

by Jo Brielyn

I grieve the loss of part of me
That's gone, ne'er to return.
Though, why it left is still unclear.
I fear I'll never know.

I used to laugh and live so freely.
Now, sadly that's not me.
I long for it, I search for it.
Yet still it's out of reach.

But in its place is compassion
And a faith I never knew.
For losing that beloved piece of me
Has brought me something, too.

I learned life is a gemstone
Not to be tossed carelessly about.
But, rather, to be shared in love,
Not merely survived alone.

I was created for a purpose -
To love, to share, to grow.
By living life with this in mind,
New meaning I now find.

So, while I may still question
Why I'm unlike I was before,
I see sometimes the old must fade
Before new growth can begin.

Late Night Walk

by Lisa Lee Smith

Far as I can tell
we travel to distant places
and just end up looking
for smiles we almost recognize
on faces we already know
framed by familiar colors of hair
to shake loose our empty, tired spirits.

Your presence is unyielding
to the transparent rain
and belies the disfigured heart
of a worn-out life
while my affinity for bitter gall
and dusty, antiquated books
still evokes your perfectly breathless laughter.

Remind me to tell you
how it is that I got here
and why it didn't satisfy me
any more than it would an affectionate fly
determined to cling with consternation
to either side of the screen door
and be famished whether inside or out.

Hard to really see
between the blurring lines
but your memory is
the clickety-clack
of heels and toes on cold cement
and fading the farther away you go.
What a resplendent pace we kept up, don't you think?

Stealing Life

by M. Lori Motley

"Whoops. Sorry about that, old man." The whisper drifted out of the ground and into the burgeoning dark, answered only by a sigh of wind in the trees above. A dark figure huddled between the fresh walls of earth and bent the fingers of the hand he held back into a normal position. Twisting his body and rising up to his knees, he held the ring so it caught the light from the streetlight just outside the gates to the cemetery.

"Michael and Regina–1947," he muttered and his forehead creased in a frown. An engraving meant less money, but he took what he could get. He slipped the ring into the front pocket of his jeans, eased the silk-lined lid back over the body and hefted himself out of the grave.

Martin whistled a few random notes into the darkness and grabbed the spade that leaned against the neighboring gravestone. His Uncle Gary was maintenance for Shady Lawn Cemetery, which served five counties and was one of the biggest in the state. While he spent most of his time righting stones toppled by kids and picking up trash, he also ran the backhoe that dug graves. He lived in a trailer behind the offices and spent ninety-nine percent of his off time, and probably half of his on time, stinking drunk.

Sunday evenings, he'd sober up enough to eat dinner with Martin and his mom.

"Boy needs a masculine influence," Gary would say, grabbing chicken with his fingers. He had come to dinner every Sunday after Martin's father died, when Martin was four years old.

"That kind of influence, you don't need," Martin's mom would say after Gary left. "He's your father's brother, family, but not a model of what a man should be. You steer clear of his ways."

She'd peer closely at Martin when she said this, and he would nod. He was smarter than that.

Uncle Gary was good for one thing. As soon as Martin reached his fifteenth birthday, he offered to throw some work Martin's way. Late night grave filling interfered with his time at Stinky Jay's, swilling down Pabst and cracking jokes with the waitresses. Two hundred twelve dollars per week at the laundry in town went as far as Martin's mom could stretch it, but any extra money helped.

Gary gave his nephew twenty dollars for every hole he filled, and it was enough to keep their heads above water for a while. When his mom came home from her yearly with Doc Patterson, sat Martin down and told him about the cancer, it just wasn't enough any more.

The spade dug into the fresh-turned pile of earth and the boy tossed the dirt down into the hole.

"Bye-bye," he whispered, "and thanks for your help," he added, pausing a moment in his shoveling to pat his pocket. The hole slowly filled with damp earth. By the time Gary came reeling home from Stinky Jay's, the job was done. Martin took the twenty his uncle offered, and helped him to his cot in the dark trailer.

It was after midnight when Martin let himself into the house. His mother snored lightly in bed, her green quilt clutched under her chin. Martin leaned over to kiss her forehead and laid the twenty on her nightstand. The gold ring was deposited next to two small crosses on gold chains and a pair of earrings in his father's old cigar box, which lay tucked at the back of Martin's sock drawer.

The following morning, Martin met his mother in the kitchen, holding her head and sipping black coffee before heading off to work.

"You got that math quiz today," she said, glancing up at him with tired eyes. "You studied last night, right?"

He nodded even though it was a lie.

"You slept okay? How're you feeling?"

She looked at him for a long moment before replying. "I slept." Then she sighed, and her shoulders slumped. "Doc Patterson says I need more of that prescription. The damn cancer mestat... metsa... Huh. I can't even say the word, and it's killing me." She let out a harsh bark of a laugh.

Her tired gray eyes looked up at her son. "No use hiding it from you. You're old enough to know."

Martin's lip shook and he looked away, fighting the tears that welled up. "I'll drop out of school... get a job."

"You drop out of school, sonny mine, and I'll skin you alive," she countered, scowling at him. "You'll need that education." She sipped coffee, and her face softened. "Thanks for the money, and make sure to thank your Uncle Gary for giving you the work."

He watched her lumber up the street clutching the twine handle of the bag she carried her lunch in with one skinny hand. He rushed off to school ten minutes later and passed the day in a haze of boredom and worry, failed a math quiz and forgot to write down his English homework.

As soon as the three o'clock bell rang, Martin bolted out the door to walk his regular course down the main street of town, scanning shop fronts for Help Wanted signs. Mr. Cortez at the market let him deliver old Mrs. Anderson's weekly shopping and gave him five bucks.

He passed Murray's Pawnshop last before turning

down the barely-paved road that led toward home. He glanced into the dim store and could just make out Murray sitting at the back, reading a magazine with his half-moon glasses pushed down his nose. Murray didn't ask questions. In such a small town, Martin figured he probably didn't need to ask questions to figure out what was going on anyway.

"Got two tonight, Marty," Uncle Gary called as soon as his nephew stepped into his trailer at Shady Lawns. "You want me to do one and you do the other?"

"I could do both if you want. I... I could really use all the work you can throw my way, Uncle Gary. My mom..."

Gary lit a Camel and drew deep. "The cancer again, huh? That doctor's gonna have a nice shiny Mercedes outta your mother's hide soon. God bless her poor soul."

Martin scowled. "Do you think you can give me the work?"

Gary stood up and stretched.

"Yeah, I guess I can afford it." He scratched his stomach and squinted his right eye against the smoke that curled upward from his mouth.

The first grave held an old woman, rouged and powdered, with her gray curls set neatly. A brooch with pearls and a sparkling cocktail ring from her right hand disappeared into Martin's pocket.

"My mother needs these more than you do," Martin whispered as he lowered the lid of her casket again. He filled the grave quickly, the spade biting into the earth.

Martin almost cried out when he lifted the lid of the second casket. The woman it held was middle-aged. The planes of her face reminded him of his mother, and he could imagine her neatly combed hair was the same familiar shade of graying brown. His jaw clenched involuntarily, and he raised a filthy hand to bat away the moisture that had gathered in his eyes.

A simple gold bracelet and a pair of earrings joined the brooch and ring in his pocket. Instead of climbing out of the grave and starting his work, Martin leaned back against the hard earth wall and stared at the woman's face.

"Hey," he began softly, "what got you?"

He tipped his head sideways and waited. An owl hooted in the woods nearby and roused him from his thoughts. He worked feverishly to fill the hole. A blister on his palm broke on the wooden handle of the spade, but he didn't notice. The job done, he returned the shovel to the shed and went home, not bothering to wait for his uncle to get back.

The jewelry from his pocket joined the other pieces in the box before he crawled into bed. The next day was Saturday, and he decided to visit Murray in the morning. His eyes slipped closed, but his mind kept clamoring, "Eighty bucks? Ninety? How much time will that buy you, Mom? How much?"

Stepping into Murray's Pawnshop was like walking into a cave: dim and cool. Soft glows highlighted some of the more impressive pieces for sale: jewelry, a stereo system with four speakers, and a silver coffee pot. Martin clutched the jewelry deep down in his pocket as he walked to the rear of the shop.

Murray perched on a sturdy folding chair in the back of the shop, his belly spilling over his gray pants and lying on his thighs. He pushed his spectacles onto his forehead as he looked up. A wide grin spread across his face.

"Marty!" he called out, and immediately descended into a fit of coughing. He took a nip out of the flask he kept behind the counter and sucked air in sharply. "What do you got for your old friend Murray today?"

Martin pulled the jewelry out of his pocket, laying it out on the glass countertop in a pile. Murray's fat fingers moved over it like a carrion bird's beak over a carcass.

He separated the chains, slid the cocktail ring over the tip of his finger and held it up to the light.

"Not bad, not bad at all," he muttered to himself. He set the ring down and examined the other pieces in turn. Squinting up at the boy across from him, he barked out, "Fifty, take it or leave it."

Martin scowled. "I'll take seventy, and you'll still be getting a bargain."

Murray's laughter transformed into that same hacking cough. His hand sought the bottle again, he drank and the bottle disappeared back under the counter.

"You're getting smart, Marty, my boy. I'll give you sixty, and we both walk away happy."

Martin just nodded, and the jewelry vanished from the countertop like magic. He took the crumpled bills the man slid across to him and folded them into his pocket.

Murray's cough followed him out of the shop.

Sixty bucks wasn't enough to stop his mother's slide toward death. Blisters broke and reformed on Martin's hands until permanent calluses covered his palms and fingers. While his uncle swilled down beer, Martin dealt with death and dirt in the midnight hours. Exhausted and fraught with fear and sorrows too large for his adolescent mind to carry, he grew more sullen and withdrawn.

His mother didn't get up in the mornings to go to the laundry any more. She clutched the green quilt and tried to smile when Martin came in with cups of tea and toast. He set his rough hand on her forehead, smoothing away the constant creases of pain and worry as well as he could.

Lying in his bed late into the night, staring at the moonlight play across the ceiling, he found himself praying for someone to die—someone other than his mother—anyone.

A family killed in a house fire on a Saturday night

meant Martin could refill his mother's prescription for pain meds, which at least let her sleep for a while.

"At least you'll be with your family on the other side," Martin whispered to the father, a hook-nosed man with a gold wedding band and a cheap watch. "If there is another side.

"At least you didn't suffer," he said to the mother. Her pale, curly hair twisted through the chain around her neck and Martin finally had to rip it off with a tuft of hair still entwined. "Or at least not for long."

A surge of heat and a quick suffocation as smoke filled your lungs was nothing compared to the slow rake of pain upon pain until the body couldn't fight off the disease any more and succumbed.

The three little girls in their half-size, white coffins gave up heart-shaped birthstone pendants. An eternally smiling Barbie doll lay against the littlest one's chest. Her face was a twisted mess of burns.

"Closed casket," Martin murmured, and thumped the lid to the coffin shut again.

A bad car crash on I79 and he could keep the electricity on for another month. A grandfather had a coronary in the supermarket, and Martin stocked up on Campbell's cream of chicken, the only thing his Mother would even try to eat any more. An immigrant shop-owner was shot in a robbery, and Martin went home with a small sapphire on a chain, planning to cash it in for part of the phone bill.

He didn't get the chance to visit Murray's Pawnshop the next day. Martin woke in the morning and stumbled blurry-eyed into his mother's room only to find her still and cold, her forehead smooth of any pain wrinkles, her lips parted slightly instead of pressed together to stifle moans. He sank down on the corner of her bed and enveloped her hand in his. He held it, tears tracking silently down his face and then, at last, stood up and went to call the doctor, coroner and his Uncle Gary.

The funeral passed in a blur of handshakes and

condolences from people Martin didn't know. He stood next to a sober Gary by the door to the viewing room at Shady Lawn's service building and tried to keep his gaze from straying toward his mother lying in the coffin at the far side of the room. At last the trickle of people from town and the laundry dried up, and Martin and Gary were alone.

"May she rest easy. You come and stay with me, eh Marty?" Gary said, clapping an arm awkwardly around his shoulders.

Martin knew he never would. His mother had always told him not to look up to Uncle Gary, not to be like him. He didn't plan to end up that way.

When Martin didn't reply, Gary dropped his arm and walked out, lighting a Camel as he went. Martin drifted to the front of the room and sat on the folding chair closest to the casket. He sat there and stared, sometimes at his mother's still face, sometimes at nothing. He sat there and time slipped away into early evening and on toward dusk.

The soft thud of the director's shoes on the tile roused Martin, and he looked up. The man offered a practiced look of sympathy. "We need to make preparations for burial. Perhaps you should go home; try to get some rest."

Martin nodded and got to his feet. With one more glance at his mother's still face, he turned and walked out. He breathed deep of the night air and looked upward to see the first stars twinkle in the deep blue depths of sky. From the maintenance shed on the edge of the property, he heard the backhoe roar to life.

At a quarter past ten, Martin knocked on the door of his uncle's trailer, not really expecting an answer.

"Went to Jay's," a scrawled note on the table inside read. For a brief moment, Martin considered closing the door and heading back to the house to go to sleep, but he couldn't.

Martin grabbed the shovel from the storage shed behind the trailer and headed toward his mother's grave. He stood at the foot of it for a minute, peering down into the darkness at a scant gleam of moonlight hitting polished wood. He crouched, and then eased himself over the edge of the grave into the ground.

The damp smell of soil filled his nostrils as it had dozens of times before. But as he took a deep breath, his hand on the coffin's latch, he imagined a whiff of vanilla musk, his mother's favorite perfume, drifting over him as well. He swallowed hard, his eyes tightly squeezed shut against the hot sting of tears.

Another deep breath and he flipped open the latch and eased the lid upward to expose his mother's face. A lock of hair had fallen over her forehead and he reached in to brush it back.

"There," he whispered. "That's better."

Martin took another breath, his lip quivering.

"Hi, Mom." He dashed a hand across his eyes. "I miss you already... so much. I tried, ya know? I tried to help."

He couldn't stop the tears. The reality crashed into his mind like an ocean wave and swamped him, spilling out of his eyes and splashing against the smooth coffin lid.

Fumbling in his pant pocket, Martin pulled out the gold chain and teardrop sapphire he had taken from the shopkeeper's body. He leaned forward and clasped the chain around his mother's neck, arranging the pendant against the collar of her blouse.

"I wish," he said in a strangled whisper. "I wish I could've given you everything you needed. I wish it would've been enough."

Sobs choked his voice and turned it into a keen of sorrow. His face transformed into a mask of agony, of heartbreak.

"Mommy..." he sobbed, one shaking hand reaching down to touch her cheek.

Martin dropped the lid of the casket back over his

mother's still face and scrabbled out of the grave, digging into the dirt with hooked fingers. He grabbed the shovel and thrust the blade into the mound of dirt. Hefting it, he turned and forced himself to throw the soil down on top of his mother's coffin. The shovel bit into the pile again and again as he filled the grave, blinded by tears. When it was done at last, the skin on his hands torn open and bleeding, Martin simply dropped the shovel to the ground and walked away into the night.

About the Author

By day, M. Lori Motley is a divorced, homeschooling, self-employed mom. By night, she escapes reality whenever possible to tweak the fantasy worlds that grow in her mind. She began writing fiction with a scintillating tale of a giant cow that ate a city when she was six. Since then, her writing experience has grown to several published short stories, dozens of un-published ones, six novels in various states of completion and some rather awkward poetry that no one seems to understand but her. Learn more about her published works and current projects at www.MLoriMotley.com.

Dream Dancers

by Lucinda Gunnin

I dreamed
of dancing girls and endless delights,
shopping sprees and power supreme.
Your story was more earthy,
feral and strong,
silent.
An easy distance developed,
Respect and fear, a trembling knee and wavering tongue.
Unexpectedly, we danced.
A soft song in our minds
Shared by just we two.
We danced, and we knew.
The fantasy shared,
we wrote it together
testing the waters,
feeling our connection.
Never letting the fantasy slip
into reality.
Months go by
without a word,
leaving me wondering
how we feel about each other
until I see you again
and we fall back to the fantasy
with no intruding real life.

About the poet:

Lucinda Gunnin is much more inclined to write prose than poetry, but when inspiration strikes... she still sometimes ignores it. Poetry was her secret vice in high school, the writing she tried not to admit to doing. She still prefers reading it to writing it.

Old Photographs

by Lisa Lee Smith

I'll sing with
long-lost ghosts
who whisper
pasts of hope;
I'll dwell on
shadow and stone
saving time
behind my eyes;
I'll fritter away
my moments
for visions of wonder
and regret;
I'll watch the
dusky, indigo light
while dreams
renew my life;
I'll breathe from
her ageless soul
and silky ashes
in western winds.

Birth & Death in Shadow Cove

by Nancy Smith Gibson

All the natives of Shadow Cove were a little bit... well, strange. The story passed down through generations said the village was settled well over two hundred years ago by a small band of people who had escaped punishment for having special gifts—magic, one might call it. The Church said those talents had been bestowed upon them by the devil himself. Fleeing certain death, the people who had been blessed or cursed—depending on your point of view—pushed farther and farther west, until they finally settled in a remote cove in the Ozark Mountains and let time pass them by.

Until the last fifty years or so, those who lived in Shadow Cove were descended from those twenty families who found safety in that remote area. Oh, sure, occasionally a brave young man ventured beyond the cove, sometimes as far as Springfield, or even St. Louis or Kansas City. Before long, he'd find himself an outsider—or worse, suspected of witchcraft—he would return to Shadow Cove, often bringing a bride with him. So we would have new genes infused into the community from time to time, but still and all, our children were born with talents unknown to folks outside our cove.

Then civilization found us. The state officials said, "We're building this highway to make it easier for you to get places."

The county folks said, "We'll build a road from your village so you can get to the highway."

New things came into our lives: electricity, phones, TV, and eventually, outsiders.

About ten years ago, the developers discovered us. Suddenly, Shadow Cove became the 'in' place to have a home in the quaint village time forgot, away from the hectic lifestyle of the city. We became the chicest, trendiest place to live, and the outside world descended upon us in numbers. Soon we had a drug store, a market, an antique shop, and places that fixed things we'd never had before. We had doctors and dentists, a veterinarian and a farm store, schools and computers—all sorts of people, places and possessions we never wanted or needed. The problem wasn't things, exactly; it was the people who came with the modern world. We couldn't keep our mystical gifts hidden while we worked, shopped and went to school with outsiders.

Whenever a problem arose that might endanger our secret, it became a practice to have a meeting of native-born Shadow Cove people. We would talk it out until a solution was found. Japeth Truelove called a meeting to discuss the problem with Ethan Porter and his new bride. Japeth was generally the one who called the meetings because he had the biggest house. It could hold everybody, or at least as many as usually showed up.

The people straggled in. When Aunt Ethel Gowen arrived, she announced someone was going to die at that great big new house they were building on Whippoorwill Road.

"How can anyone die if no one lives there yet?" Susie Conner asked.

"All I knowed is I seen the ball of golden light just a-hoverin' over that there house, so someone is gonna die," Aunt Ethel answered peevishly.

Susie Conner knew full well that Aunt Ethel was always right, so no telling why she questioned it. But that was Susie, questioning everything. All that was forgotten when Alma Porter and Raenell Corms came in red-faced and upset. "That boy'll stay in trouble 'til he's dead. See if he don't," Alma said when she took her seat.

"You do have yer hands full with that'un," Raenell agreed.

Of course, everyone wanted to know what Johnny had done that time. "He's walkin' home from school an' one of them town kids was pickin' on him. I guess he'd had his fill of it and you'uns know he can ne'er hold his temper, so Johnny turned that boy into a toad. Anythin' Johnny don't want to face or gets mad at, he turns into a toad," Alma explained, as if we didn't already know about how Johnny was.

"Land's sakes," sputtered Japeth. "What did you do?"

"Well, at least he brought the toad home. I don't rightly know what I would ‘a done if he hadn't. But leastways we had the toad, so I went next door and fetched Raenell.

"We took Johnny an' the toad out in the road an' I made him turn it back into a boy again. Raenell put a memory spell on the poor lad so he won't remember what happened. Johnny swears there weren't nobody else around to see what he did."

She fanned herself with the fold-up fan she had taken from her pocket.

"That boy is grounded for so long he may not get out of his room for a year and a day, and his pa will prolly tan his behind tonight. We've talked and talked to him about turning everythin' into a toad.

"The cow kicked him one night when he was milking, an' he turned the cow into a toad, an' we didn't find out until the next morning. I'll tell you he was in real trouble that time!" Raenell reached over and patted Alma on the knee in sympathy. "If that toad a' gone off in the night we'd a' lost a good milk cow."

She shook her head.

When the last couple of people arrived, the meeting

started.

Japeth said, "As you know, Ethan Porter married a town girl six months ago."

"That nephew of my husband's don't think things over any better than my Johnny does. Act first, think later," Alma muttered.

"Nevertheless, he did, and that's done. As you probably also know, she's in the family way, 'bout four months along, as near as Ethan tells. Aunt Zoe says, well, why don't you stand up and tell us, Aunt Zoe?"

"Well, you-uns know I kin tell who has the gift, a'cause I can see this glowin' light around them's head: The brighter the light, the stronger the gift." Murmurs of agreement came from the assembly. "I done seed that girl, Ethan's wife,"

"Bitsy," someone called out.

"Yes'um, Bitsy. I done seed that Bitsy at the farmer's market the other day, and her belly was glowin' to beat all, an' her not very far along yet. That baby is goin' to have some kind o' gift, let me tell you."

"So why are we having this meeting?" Tom Bundle asked, irritated at having to stop work on his farm for the meeting.

"You just think about that, Tom. Just think about what that there doctor and them nurses are goin' to say if'n that little baby comes out doin' magic of some kind. You think we're goin' to keep it a secret then?"

"That little baby ain't goin' to come poppin' out doin' no magic." Tom crossed his foot up on his knee. "Y'all are makin' somethin' out of nothin'."

"I wouldn't say that," said Molly Huckleberry, one of the oldest people in the room, and sister to Zoe and Ethel. "When Rueben Stone was born, stuff started flyin' all over the room. Jest small stuff, mind you, him bein' just born. He didn't get to moving big things until he was older, but still, you couldn't miss what was goin' on."

"We can't take a chance on that happening," Japeth said.

Alma spoke up. "I remember, when Ethan was born, the electricity started goin' on and off in their house. It weren't 'til later he learned to fix electrical stuff. That's his gift, you know, workin' with electricity."

"Has Ethan talked to Bitsy about any of this?" someone in the back asked.

"I have," Ethan said. He edged through the crowd into the room. "I know I put it off, but I did finally get around to telling her about me having the gift, about everyone from Shadow Cove havin' a special talent, and how our baby would, too."

"What did she say?"

"She just laughed. I don't think she believed me. She said, of course I was special to her and to my ma, and of course our baby would be special and smart because it is ours. I can't figure out if she thought I was just funning with her or if I was a little touched in the head, but she wasn't taking it seriously. I'm afraid to push it any more. If she really does think I'm crazy, she'll leave me and go back to her parents. I don't want that. I love her."

He looked despondently at the floor.

"No, we can't have that," said Japeth. "If nothing else, this baby has to be around others with gifts."

"So what can I do?" asked Ethan.

"We'll have to think on it. But one thing's for sure; this baby can't be born in the hospital."

Over the next few weeks, small groups of Shadow Cove inhabitants met to make plans for the upcoming birth. Both a sonogram and Alma Corms said it was going to be a boy for Ethan and Bitsy Porter.

Aunt Ethel's prediction came true when the workman putting up the TV satellite dish on the new house on Whippoorwill Road died when he slipped and fell off the roof, and Johnny finally got ungrounded when he promised not to turn anyone else into a toad.

The women planned their part of the birthing day while the men who, except for Joe Whitecloud, had less to plan said they were ready for their role in the charade.

Finally, everything was ready; all they had to do was wait.

Everything was ready at Ethan and Bitsy's house. The nursery was painted and furnished. The crib was waiting for its occupant to make his appearance in the world. Bitsy was, as she said, ‘as big as an elephant', and glad the wait was about over. The doctor had said "any day now," and Bitsy'd had a few mild contractions, off and on.

"Bitsy, honey," said Ethan one day, "my mother, my aunts and a few others put together a little baby shower for us, and they want us to come up there for an hour or two to open presents and have a cup of punch."

"I don't feel like it, Ethan. I just want to sit here with my feet up. I feel too bad to go anywhere," said Bitsy. "Tell them either to bring it all down here or else save it until after the baby is born."

"Sugarplum, that would hurt everybody's feelings. They've decorated and all. It would only be for an hour or two. We'll come right back home. You can sit in the big easy chair at Momma's. You'll be comfortable, I promise."

So Bitsy, being the naturally sweet person she was—Ethan did pick a nice wife, even if she was an outsider—gave in, and they went to Ethan's mother's house. It was a pretty spring day. Bitsy even commented it was a lovely day to be out and about, and she was glad Ethan had talked her into going. When they arrived, there was a crowd of men and women, and the house was decorated with balloons and streamers, both inside and out. The men congregated on the wide front porch, while the women went inside and played a couple of baby shower games, and Bitsy opened presents. Just as the party started, a gentle rain started to fall.

"That'll be good for the growing things," Raenell said, a smile in her voice.

When the gifts had all been opened and 'oohed' and 'aahed' over, it was time for punch and cake. Bitsy said she really wasn't feeling well and thought she would pass. Janie Whitecloud, Joe's wife and the midwife for Shadow Cove, said she knew just the thing—a cup of herbal tea. She always gave her pregnant ladies this herbal tea, she said, and it would make Bitsy feel better in no time. Several of the younger women in attendance agreed, saying it had made everything so much better for them. About the time Janie brought the cup to Bitsy, the sky opened up and a deluge of rain fell. Had Bitsy walked out onto the front porch, she would have seen a strange sight: Joe Whitecloud chanting softly, and several men, at Joe's direction, burning various leaves and sticks and saying odd phrases.

But she didn't. Walk out onto the front porch, that is. She sat and drank the soothing tea. Soon she felt as relaxed as could be. But then, the first real hard contraction hit her.

"Ethan," she called out, "Ethan, it's started. I need to go to the hospital!"

"Sure thing, honeybun. I'll get the car," he said, just as if he were really going to do it.

Just then, Japeth Truelove rushed in the front door.

"The bridge has washed out! It must have been raining like this up on the mountain for some time. The creek went up over the bridge, and it gave way and washed downstream. We're stuck here for a few days."

As soon as he said that, another contraction hit Bitsy, stronger by far than the last one. "What are we going to do, Ethan? This baby is coming! We've got to get to the hospital!"

Janie Whitecloud spoke up. "Don't you worry none, Bitsy. I've delivered lots of babies. You're in good hands with me."

Bitsy's patience was at an end. "You hear me, Ethan? I need to go to the hospital now! Right now! Get me to the hospital!" she yelled. Then her water broke.

"No time," Janie said. "It's coming quick."

She took Bitsy by the arm, and surrounded by the other ladies of the community, the mother-to-be was ushered into the guest bedroom, where everything stood in readiness. The bed was covered in layers of white sheets and Janie's equipment was placed with precision on the dresser. Diapers and blue baby blankets awaited the new arrival. The women helped Bitsy undress, put on a soft cotton gown, and climb into the bed.

"Here, Bitsy. Drink some more of the tea. I promise it will help," said Annie Corm, Raenell's daughter-in-law and a new mother herself. Bitsy managed a few more sips before the next contraction hit. After that, there wasn't time or need for more tea. The baby boy soon made his appearance into this world and was washed, dressed, and swaddled, then handed to his mother.

"Hello, Thomas Ethan Porter. I'm glad to meet you," she said. She ran one finger over the soft blond fuzz on his head.

The wee baby in his mother's arms stretched in newfound freedom, squinted and blinked before he looked into her face and pursed his rosebud mouth.

"Hello, Momma. I'm glad to meet you, too."

Shadow Cove was generally a peaceful little town, but sometimes things happened that were, well... different. Some were happy events, such as births, but others, well, you be the judge.

Alma and JoeDon Porter had three sons: Jed, Josh, and Johnny. Johnny was ten years old and, sometimes, when he was angry, he would, as mentioned before, turn a person or an animal into a toad. Until recently, no one had figured out how this would be helpful to anyone, including Johnny himself, at any time in the future. Alma had tried, without success, to break him of it.

Josh took after his father and had the gift to help plants and crops grow. At least that was what people told him, but he didn't believe it. He was sixteen and thought he was almost a man and should have a magic talent all his own, like the other people descended from the original settlers of Shadow Cove. He didn't think getting things to grow constituted a gift. People who didn't even have magic could do that. He wanted something special, like his brothers.

Jed Porter's gift was winning at cards. He didn't even have to think about it, didn't count the cards or anything, he just won every time he played, no matter what the game. Pretty soon everyone in Shadow Cove quit playing with him. There was no fun in knowing Jed would win before a hand was dealt. It started when he had been a little tyke and had played Old Maid or Go Fish, and continued through his teen years when he learned canasta and poker. Some urged him to learn bridge, so he could make a name for himself winning tournaments, but he tried it and said it bored him even worse than the other games, so he didn't play it again.

When he had turned twenty-one, Jed had proposed to Emily Truelove. They had planned their wedding and life together. Jed really and truly wanted to give Emily a nice house to live in, but he couldn't afford one on the salary from the hardware store. He asked Japeth Truelove, Emily's daddy, to call a meeting so Jed could get permission to get the money by playing cards to build a new house. Jed wasn't too sure of the morals of it, since it involved taking money from others, and he didn't want to be shunned. When everyone had gathered at the Truelove house, Jed laid out his plan.

"I want to go to Las Vegas and win enough money to build a house for me and Emily by playing poker," he explained.

"I seen them tournaments on the TV," said Joe Whitecloud. "You go play in one o' them tournaments and work your way up. You might can be famous and win a million dollars."

"I don't want to be famous, and I'll settle for a lot less than a million dollars," Jed replied.

"Yeah, Joe. He don't need to be calling that much attention to himself. It'll be hard enough, winning every hand and not have people pointing him out and takin' his picture and everything. No tournaments."

Joe grumbled at his suggestion being turned down, but finally everyone at the meeting agreed it was okay to go to Las Vegas and win enough to build a nice house for Emily, if he would stop there and come home. It wouldn't be like winning money from poor working folks; he would be winning from the casino, and the casino could afford it. And it wouldn't be like cheating anyone; it would just happen.

The next few days, Jed prepared for the trip. He packed a suitcase, asked for time off work, and recruited his best friend, Eban Conner, to go with him. He wanted Eban not only for the companionship, but because Eban's gift was the ability to fix cars. He sort of tinkered with them, and they ran perfectly. He had even been known to pat a car on the dashboard, talk to it kindly, and it would straighten right out, whatever was wrong with it. He said one should never talk ugly to a vehicle.

"Would you work good for someone who talks bad to you?" he would ask. "A car or a truck, like a horse, will try its best to do what you want if you treat it right."

Jed thought it would be good planning to have a car fixer along, just in case his old pickup broke down.

When they arrived in Las Vegas and checked into a hotel, Jed found a poker game. Eban wandered around looking at all the lights and people. He played a slot machine every once in a while. Playing slots was definitely not Eban's talent, so he stuck with the penny and nickel slots, where he won a little every once in a while but lost more.

Jed started out with a low-stakes table. He didn't know much about playing poker, but he knew he was going to win. Somehow, he said, he just knew which cards to keep and which to discard for new ones. Soon enough, he had won every hand. He quit, because a crowd had gathered around him to watch him win.

He went to find Eban, who was playing the penny slots. When he sat by Eban, he said, "Play that one over there. It's fixin' to pay off."

Eban did, and it did. Eban won sixty-three dollars. When they realized Jed could tell which machines were close to paying off, they walked around looking for those. After a while, they quit doing that and went to a big buffet for supper. After supper, they went upstairs to their room and went to bed.

The next day went about like the first one had. After breakfast, Eban played the slots, and Jed played poker. He started at a table that had higher stakes than the one he'd chosen the night before. Of course, he won every hand. When he drew a crowd, he quit and went to play some other games.

He had heard the word blackjack before, but he hadn't known what it meant until that day. Jed stood around and watched for a while and then picked a table to play. He discovered he won as easily at that game as he did at poker, but he became bored after an hour or so and left the blackjack table to look for more games.

Jed noticed there were two men who seemed to follow him from place to place. His father and uncle had warned him that the casino was liable to think he was cheating, winning every hand the way he did, and told him to find some way to lose some money occasionally. Jed returned to the one place he was sure he could lose by not picking the winning machines, the slots. He lost a couple of hundred dollars in a dollar machine, and then he went to look at some more kinds of gambling games.

He was terrible at craps and lost some money there before he found the roulette wheel. After standing and watching other people play for a few minutes, he discovered roulette was like poker. He could tell which square to put his chips on to win. Jed stayed there winning for over an hour before he became bored with roulette and moved on.

The two men had left him when he lost at craps, but two more watched when he won repeatedly at roulette. They followed him when he went to find Eban and sat at the next table when they went to lunch. He signaled Eban to not talk about his winning. He was afraid Eban would say something about Jed's gift, and the men were close enough to hear what they said.

After lunch, Jed said, "Let's look around this town a little, walk down the street and see the sights."

He cashed out some of his chips to have money to buy presents for Emily and his mother. When he and Eban were on the sidewalk, he explained how two men were following him when he was winning.

"They're looking for how I'm cheating, I reckon."

"They won't catch you doin' that, fer sure" said Eban.

"Well, don't say anything about my talent for winning where anybody can hear. Better yet, don't say anything about it at all."

They went in a couple of other casinos where Jed found some slots that were about to pay out. He also played blackjack for a while and won. At another hotel he sat in on a poker game and won several thousand dollars.

Before they went back to their hotel, they went shopping. For Emily, Jed bought a pretty bracelet with charms and all sorts of sparkling stones. For his brothers, he bought shirts, and for his mother, a pair of earrings.

When they returned to their hotel, Jed played a few hands of poker, winning each one, of course. When he got up from the table to go meet Eban for supper, the two men approached him.

"Would you come with us, sir?" one of them asked.

"Why? Is something the matter?" Jed asked.

He ran over in his mind what he would say: *I'm a good poker player. I'm lucky. My stars are in the right place today. I'm not cheating!*

He wasn't sure about the last one. He didn't know if just knowing came under the heading of cheating or not.

They worked their way across the crowded floor and stood in front of a man in a suit and tie.

"Sir, we wish to congratulate you on your wins. We are upgrading your room to a suite, and your stay with us will be completely free of charge. We want you to feel welcome here, so welcome you will not feel the need to leave here to gamble at other casinos."

He reached in his coat pocket and pulled out two slips of paper.

"Let me give you these two tickets to tonight's show and," he reached into another pocket, "these coupons are good for dinner in our restaurant for you and companion of choice. We hope you will continue to enjoy your stay with us each time you visit Las Vegas."

Jed found Eban and told him the good news. After they moved their few things to the luxurious suite, they went to supper—except it was called dinner there—and then to the floor show with beautiful women wearing little clothing and a famous singer performing songs they had heard many times on the radio. When it was over, they played a while at the slots. Jed made sure they lost at the quarter machines and won at the dollar ones, so the men who were following them again saw they lost sometimes. All in all though, they came out way ahead.

The next day was supposed to be their last full day in Las Vegas. They had agreed to play all day and leave first thing the next morning. Eban was way ahead, thanks to Jed pointing out the slots that were ready to pour out money, so he amused himself winning and losing. He would still take home a good bit more than he came with. Jed alternated between roulette, poker and blackjack. Just before noon, Eban came by to see if Jed wanted to go to lunch.

"Tell you what: I'm doin' so good, let me play another few minutes and then let's check out and head for home. I'm sick and tired of sitting here. I think my butt has gone to sleep. I want to go home and get some exercise."

"I agree with you, buddy. This gets boring after a while. I'll go up to the suite and pack us both up. I'll be ready to leave when you are. I'll bring our bags back down to the checkout desk and wait for you there."

Eban went upstairs to get ready to go home.

It's time to tell you about Eban's other talent besides fixing vehicles: He never met a lock that kept him out of anything. A padlock would open when he tugged gently on it. A door opened whether it was locked or not. He never thought about keys or key cards or anything like that. He just walked up to doors and opened them.

When he stepped off the elevator on the eleventh floor that day, he was thinking about all the money they had won and all the sights they had seen, so he wasn't paying much attention to where he was going. He and Jed were staying in 1118, but Eban didn't notice when he approached 1116 that it was the wrong room. He turned the knob and, as usual for Eban, the door opened easily. When he walked into the room, the first thing he noticed was a naked man and a naked woman—well, really he noticed the woman first—going at it on the sofa. All parties were surprised, to say the least.

The naked man was the first to speak. "What the hell do you think you are doing? Get out of here!"

"Sorry! Sorry! I got the wrong room!"

"How the hell did you get in?"

"The door wasn't closed all the way," Eban responded as he retreated out the door. "Sorry!"

Eban went to the right room—he checked the number carefully this time— and quickly packed for both of them. He ferried their bags downstairs via the elevator and sat in the lobby by the checkout desk until Jed arrived.

It wasn't long before they were on their way home, richer than when they arrived. The assistant manager, Mr. Brown, had come out and tried to persuade them to stay a little longer, but Jed said he had business he had to take care of back at home. Mr. Brown gave Jed a business card, and then told him to call that number the next time he wanted to play, and the suite would be free. Jed took a few hundred dollars of his winnings in cash and the rest in a check, which he had the casino mail to him back at his home address. He said he would be nervous carrying all that money on him.

Soon they were on the road back to the Ozarks, laughing and talking about all they had seen and done the last few days.

"I reckon they didn't want to you leave Las Vegas, good buddy," Eban said. "They was treatin' you real nice."

"I figure that's because they thought if I kept playing, sooner or later I'd lose everything I won off them," Jed replied. "That's what happens to most people."

"Yeah, but you ain't most people."

"That's true enough."

"Well, your gift got you and me fixed up, money-wise, but my gift 'bout got me in trouble," Eban said.

"In trouble? What happened?"

Eban told him about accidentally walking into the wrong room and seeing the couple on the couch.

"Boy-oh-boy! That was some sight, I bet," Jed said.

"You better believe it. That guy was mad as all get out."

"I guess you'd better be more careful if we ever go somewhere again. You mighta got beat up or something," Jed commented.

"Yep. I will be. That fellow looked tough, all right."

"How tough can a naked guy look?" Jed asked, and chuckled.

"Pretty tough, good buddy. Pretty tough," Eban said and laughed.

They ate supper that night at a café that served home-style cooking. A television was on in the corner of the room, up high where everyone could see it. Eban watched it while he ate his meatloaf. Suddenly, he stopped, put down his fork and said, "Quick, Jed, turn around and look at the TV."

Jed looked up at him, then jerked his head around to

look at the television, his brow furrowed in confusion at Eban's urgent request.

"See that man?" Eban said. "That's the man I walked in on in the room next to ours."

"So what is he doin' on TV?" Jed asked.

"That thing at the bottom says 'famous mobster murdered'," Eban answered. The sound was turned down. They couldn't hear what had happened, so they finished their meal while they speculated on what might have happened. Later that night in the motel room, they watched the news and learned that Salvator 'Big Sal' Cambiani was found shot in his hotel room. The Las Vegas police were pursuing clues as to the identity of the killer.

"Gosh," said Eban, "I wonder if that woman he was screwing did him in, or if someone else did it. I'm glad whoever it was didn't walk in when I was there, or I might be dead, too."

The next day, Jed and Eban continued on to Shadow Cove. They arrived to happy welcomes from all their friends and family, who were regaled for several days with stories of the sights in Las Vegas.

Jed received and deposited the check from the casino, and while he waited for it to clear, he and Emily picked out a five-acre plot of land down the road from both sets of parents. They looked at house plans in earnest. When the check cleared, they bought the land and contacted the contractor about starting the house. The wedding was set to be held in four months. With all the friends and family living in Shadow Cove, and with all the magical powers possessed by those involved, it wouldn't take long to get everything put together for a beautiful wedding ceremony and to get a house built.

However, one day about two weeks later, Cousin Ruth Fine called to say two strangers had checked into her bed and breakfast. Now, of course, it wasn't unusual for strangers to check in at Ruth's. Since there was no hotel or motel in Shadow Cove, the bed and breakfast was the only place for out-of-towners to stay, after all, and everyone who stayed there was a stranger. But these were stranger strangers than usual, Ruth said. They looked and talked like they had stepped out of that television show, *The Sopranos*. The strangers talked real funny and wore Hawaiian shirts. No one in Shadow Cove did that, not even all the people who lived in new houses and condos that had sprung up all over since the outside world had found them years ago.

Cousin Ruth decided she just had to use her gift, which she generally ignored the best she could or else it would drive her bonkers. You see, Cousin Ruth could hear things real well—really, really well. Ruth said her momma told her the story passed down in the family was this gift came from mothers listening for their children: listening to hear what they were up to, if they were in danger or hurt or scared or sick in the night. Since all the generations down to Ruth had big families—Ruth was one of nine children—it made sense. Ruth didn't have any children, but she still had the gift, which she tried to hold back on, except when it was needed, or else she would be bombarded with voices all the time.

Ruth could hear the neighbors in their houses maybe a mile down the road if she tried hard. So it wasn't hard for her to hear what the two strangers said upstairs in their rooms at the other end of the house, while she sat in her back parlor. What she heard, she didn't really understand. She knew the men weren't there for anything good. They were talking about 'hits' and, at first, she thought they were talking about baseball. But she soon decided that 'who ordered the hit' was Mafia talk for killing someone.

When they came downstairs and asked her if she knew where they could find Jed Porter, it upset her so much she could hardly talk. She managed to say, "He works at the hardware store on Main Street."

She knew it was Wednesday, which was Jed's day off, but she thought if she sent them down there, it would give her time to call the Porter house and warn him the two Mafia men were looking for him.

They also inquired about the tall, skinny, dark-headed man who was Jed's friend. Ruth thought about lying but didn't think she could get away with it, it being such a small community. She answered, "That would be Eban Conner. He has a garage out on Pine Tree Road."

They asked the directions to there, and she told them. She didn't know what else to do.

When they left, Ruth went immediately to the telephone and called the Porter house, but no one answered. She tried Eban's house, which was where his garage was, and had the same phone, but he didn't answer there either. Wherever they were, they were probably together, like usual. By the time Ruth got someone on the phone, it was all over but the shoutin', as people say around Shadow Cove.

A half-hour later, having gone by the closed garage and the hardware store, the two strange men showed up at the Porter farm, where Jed and Eban were working on Jed's daddy's tractor in the yard by the equipment shed and the barn.

"Here they are, the two big men in Vegas."

When Jed and Eban looked up, they saw the two strangers. The short, balding, fat one wore a red shirt with white flowers all over it. The tall, skinny one wore a green and blue Hawaiian shirt, and he twitched constantly. His eyebrows raised and lowered, one eye blinked, and he moved from one foot to the other. They both held guns pointed right at Jed and Eban.

"Farm boys, huh? Who'da thought a farm boy would be able to take out Big Sal," said the short, fat one.

"A perfect disguise, a perfect disguise," said the twitching one.

"A good disguise, but not perfect. We should'a known they were pros from how this one," he waved his gun at Jed, "was winning at cards. No one wins like that without a trick up his sleeve, or a card." He chuckled.

"Too bad you ain't gonna live long enough to teach me how you did it."

The skinny man laughed while he jiggled his gun.

"We didn't kill anyone," Jed said.

"No. Not anyone," echoed Eban.

"Sure you did. The camera in the hallway caught you going in his room, staying just long enough to plug him, and leaving. You both checked out right after that and high-tailed it back here."

"But that was a mistake," stuttered Eban. "I went in that room by accident. Our room was next door, and I wasn't watching where I was going."

"So how'ja get in that locked door?"

"It wasn't quite closed. I just pushed it open."

"Nah. Big Sal would never leave a door like that. Try again," the fat one said. "Maybe you have a maid in on it who fixed it for you, that it?" He turned to the thin man. "Maybe we need to check the maids on that floor when we get back to Vegas."

"Yeah. Check out the maids."

"No! It wasn't the maid," Eban blurted out. He didn't want anyone hurt because of his talent with locks. "I'll tell you the truth. I have this gift, this talent. I can open any door just by turning the knob. Nothing is ever locked to me. It's... well, it's magic."

Both the men broke into laughter. "Magic, is it? Well, that's a new one. I never heard that one before."

"No, never heard that one," parroted the skinny man.

Suddenly, the fat man was serious again. "What we want to know is who hired you for this hit. Was it out of New York or Chicago? Or maybe Dallas? Just tell us who paid for taking out Big Sal."

"But I didn't kill him! I promise he was still alive when I left the room!"

"Sure, sure. Who hired you?" he asked in a soft voice that was scarier than if he had yelled.

"We didn't kill him," said Jed and Eban together.

The fat man in the red shirt pointed his gun at Jed

and said, "Okay, if that is how you want to play this. I'll count to three, and if you don't come up with a name by then your buddy here gets it." He extended his arm. "One. You'd better come up with that name. You don't want to see your pal here die because you won't tell. Two—."

But he never got to three, because suddenly, there was this *poof* sound and the gun fell to the ground. The fat man disappeared. In his place sat a big, fat toad.

"Johnny!" yelled Jed and Eban at the same time.

"Johnny, get out of here!" Jed hollered.

"Did'ja see, Jed? Did'ja see? I turned that sucker into a toad. I'm not lettin' any goon hurt my brother. No, sir," Johnny said. He had stepped out of the barn. "Do ya' want me to turn the other one into a toad, too, Jed? Do ya'? Huh?"

At that, the twitchy skinny guy's eyes rolled up into his head, and he fell on the ground, dropping his gun as he went down, out cold.

"Grab that toad, Johnny," Jed said when he went to kick both the guns away from where the skinny man was in a heap. "Don't let it get away."

Johnny took off after the toad, who was hopping this way and that. Johnny caught it once, but it wriggled out of his grip and hopped into the barn, with Johnny, Jed and Eban right behind it. Looking for a way to avoid capture, the toad made an unfortunate choice: It hopped into the stall with Bessie, the cow Johnny had, a few weeks earlier, turned into a toad. Bessie, having spent an entire night as a toad, was now understandably skittish at seeing one appear at her feet. Determined to get rid of the intruder, she kicked the trespasser against the stall wall and then stomped it until it was flat as a fritter.

They all looked at the flattened toad. Finally, Jed said, "Johnny, take Bessie down to the end of the barn and tie her up to the post, then come back here."

"Yessir." Johnny did as he was asked and returned to where Jed and Eban stood looking at the dead toad.

"Turn him back into a man, Johnny."

"But he's gonna be dead, Jed, like the toad. Squashed and dead."

"Yeah, I know. Do it anyway. Eban, you go call the sheriff and have him come out right now."

When the sheriff arrived, Jed explained how these two men, who he and Eban had never seen before, showed up accusing them of having killed a man by the name of Big Sal in Las Vegas when they were there three weeks before. They hadn't done such a thing, they said, but shortly before the murder, Eban had accidentally walked into the wrong room and saw Big Sal and some women having sex. Jed and Eban had left Vegas shortly after that and returned home. The two strangers had arrived and threatened to kill them if they didn't tell who had hired them to kill Big Sal.

"They were standing there, threatening us with guns, when suddenly, that man out there in the yard clutched his chest and fell down, dropping his gun. I guess he had a heart attack."

The ambulance arrived just then and the EMTs put the tall, skinny, nervous guy on a stretcher and started for the hospital, which was thirty miles away. Later, the EMT said the man woke, babbled something about toads and then died before they reached the emergency room.

"The other man," Jed continued, "got scared when that happened and ran into the barn. Maybe he thought someone had shot the skinny guy. I don't know, but he ran into Bessie's stall for some reason. Bessie, she's one nervous cow. She didn't like a stranger getting in the stall with her. She kicked him, he fell down and she stomped all over him. I got Bessie out of the stall, but it was too late."

The sheriff said it was the wildest tale he had ever heard. After he checked the identities of the dead men and talked to the Las Vegas Police Chief, he came back and told Jed and Eban they were in the clear. Skinny—whose name was Jerome "Jitters" Moran—had indeed died of a heart attack. The other man—Perolli "Pizza Man" Gambino—had died from a head injury and being stomped by Bessie. They were both members of the mob whose leader had been the late Salvator "Big Sal" Cambiani. Big Sal's killer had been caught: It was the woman Eban had seen in the room that day, who was angered when she found evidence in his suite that he was seeing another woman besides her.

After all the excitement died down, Jed and Eban both swore they would never, ever, go back to Las Vegas. Johnny bragged about saving two lives with his talent, and even his mother had to admit it was one time turning someone into a toad was the right thing to do.

About the Author

Over the length of her abundant life, Nancy Smith Gibson has met many people with unusual gifts, some of whom are related in "Birth and Death in Shadow Cove". Yes, some of the people in the story are her relatives. Others are pure fiction.

Wouldn't it be fun to have a talent like some of these characters? What would you choose if you could?

Watch for more stories about Shadow Cove in future anthologies from TTM.

All These Things

by Catherine A. MacKenzie

They say your memory's the first to go,
but mine's still here,
and who are 'they' anyway?

I know my bones are decaying,
and my body's weaker than before,
but my memory's still here.

I look at my children
and my grandchildren,
all adults now,
and wonder where the years went.

Was just yesterday
when I was young like them,
but now I'm here where my parents were
and where my grandparents were
when I was the age my children are now
and my grandchildren,
and I never thought I'd age this old—
this fast.

And now it's time to downsize
and nearly time for me to go,
and I have all these things I cherish
and hold dear,
things I cannot take with me,
things my children don't want,
things my grandchildren don't want,
and how did I get this old
with my mind still strong,
with all these things that mean so much to me,
these things I can't give away

because they're worthless except to me,
and I can't throw these things away
because they're my memories:
my past,
my life,
and my parents' past,
and my grandparents' past.

These things are me.

And where have my parents' memories gone,
and my grandparents' memories?
Who holds those?
Is it only me?

My children don't care about memories
and things that aren't theirs,
they don't seem to care about the past,
nor the future.

So is it just me?

Am I wrong
to cling too much
to what I know is fleeing
and fleeting
and soon to be gone,
wanting to grasp
and hold tight
to my life
and my past
and my memories
that no one wants but me?

The Pact

by Lindsay Maddox

"Here's the deal," Sophie explained, smacking a wad of gum in her seemingly ever-moving mouth. "You will sign this pact, guaranteeing you friends for life. I mean, seriously, life. Thick and thin, we'll be there."

It was fall and the first day of our junior year. I had never been one to make close friends with classmates, and it was obvious Sophie was clued in to this fact. Truthfully, with the trauma I had experienced the past summer, the idea of a built-in group of friends was tempting.

Sophie was the queen of the junior class, the alpha dog, if you will. She easily fooled adults into thinking she was the sweetest, most innocent girl in our entire class, but one look at her scandalously stocked underwear drawer would prove otherwise.

"Who else is in?" I asked, still confused about why I was even being considered for this new clique. I wasn't unpopular by any means, but to be seen even talking to Sophie was astounding, based on my average position in the high-school hierarchy.

"I'm still so sorry about Dave. Are you okay?" she asked, ignoring my question. Her tactic worked to catch me off guard.

"I, um, I...," I stammered and blinked my eyes rapidly to avoid the onslaught of tears that threatened to seep from them.

Sophie put her arm lovingly around my shoulder, and the tears I had tried to hold back refused to be contained any longer.

"I don't understand why he had to die, Sophie. I feel like I'm missing a piece of myself."

"Shhh, Emma." Sophie's voice was soft, motherly.

She handed me a tissue.

"This is why we need each other, all of us," she whispered. "We need to look after each other when everything in our lives seems to be crumbling apart."

She led me to the grassy knoll on the far end of the school campus where three other girls sat and waited for us. I knew them as the popular girls, the girls who would barely bat an eye at me if I so much as tried to say hello.

"Emma," Sophie said, "meet Belle, Ashley, and Jane. They're going to be your new best friends."

I sat with them and talked. They told me deciding to do this with them was the mature thing to do, that only the smartest girls were included. They reiterated the idea that, if I joined, I would be guaranteed friends for life.

I had known it was wrong. I had realized even then I was being sucked into their cult-like manipulation. Yet, I had let myself succumb to peer pressure. I was hurting, lost, and had thought I needed them.

I was so naive.

"So, what made you want to sign the pact?" I asked Jane a week later during lunch.

"Same reason as you," she shrugged. "I need friends now, more than ever. People who love and cherish me."

"Yeah, I understand that," I replied. "Is everything okay at home?"

"Home? Yeah! It's great," Jane said, sarcasm dripping from each syllable. "You know, because watching my mom drink herself into a stupor every night and then proceed to yell at me about why I'm a worthless piece of trash really makes for an amazing home life."

"I'm so sorry, Jane."

Though we had not been friends even two weeks prior, I pulled Jane in to hug her tightly.

We really do need each other, I thought. Jane sobbed into my chest.

I came to learn throughout the week that each person involved in the pact had a similar story, seeded in pain and emotional trauma.

Belle, always the top of the class and successful at anything she tried, was constantly berated by her parents if she gave what they thought was less than 110%. Nothing was ever good enough for them.

Ashley's parents had recently announced they planned to divorce. Her dad had cheated on her mom for seemingly the hundredth time, and apparently, her mom had finally reached her breaking point. Both parents were fighting tooth and nail for Ashley to live with them and were pressuring her to decide between them. Mind games and manipulation ruled her world, and she was tired of it.

Whatever the reason for the pact, it was blatantly clear we were all hurting badly.

"Where's Sophie?" I asked Jane the following week at our same lunch spot. "She's been out two days in a row now and school just started."

"She called me last night," Jane replied. "Sounds like the flu."

"Yuck. I hope I don't get it."

The bell rang and I stood, shrugging my backpack on. Jane grabbed one of the straps and swung me around to look at her.

"What's going on?" I asked, concern rising in my throat upon seeing her pale face.

"Emma, have you started on your part of the pact?" she whispered.

"No. I don't really have any way to—" I began.

"You need to get on it now," Jane interrupted.

"What's the rush?" I asked. Although I had signed the pact, I had assumed it was more of a suggestion than something we were required to do.

"Sophie is mad that we haven't held up our end of the deal. She says she's been working at it and expects us to, you know..."

"Fulfill the pact," I muttered, completing her thought.

"Exactly."

"Have you, um, started?" I asked.

"Yeah, I have. Belle and Ashley have too."

My throat tightened, and the cafeteria suddenly felt smaller than before. I turned my back on Jane and walked swiftly outside for air.

I can't do this! I screamed in my head. It was so dumb. I found myself wondering why I had ever signed the pact.

When I arrived home that evening, the reason was blatantly clear. Mom was in the living room, knees to her chest, swigging a bottle of wine and clutching a picture of my brother in her hands. I quietly passed, knowing she wouldn't pay any attention to me.

"Emma?" her voice croaked.

"Yeah, Ma?" I asked, taken off guard.

"Do you know what today is?" Her eyes were bloodshot and wary. I could smell the wine on her breath even from across the room.

"It's Friday," I replied.

"It's September fourteenth, Emma!" she screamed, leaping from the couch and bounding across the room toward me.

I cowered away, afraid she was going to hit me, the way Jane's mother hit her.

"What kind of a sister are you?" she continued.

Dad walked into the room.

"What's going on?" he asked, glancing between my mother and me.

"Your daughter," Mom said, pronouncing the word as though it were something truly despicable, "doesn't know what today is."

"Honey," he replied quietly. He took her by the shoulders and leading her back to the couch, "It has been three months, please, give her a break."

I can't believe I forgot, I thought, realizing exactly what day it was.

"He died!" mom screamed. "Three months ago, on the fourteenth, Dave was killed! How could you ever forget that?"

"Mom, I've had a lot on my mind today. It just slipped my thoughts."

With nightmarish clarity, I remembered June fourteenth. I remembered coming home from the last day of school to an empty house, taking a long nap, and still finding myself alone. I remember the sun setting and the eerie silence that fell over the house. On that day, the stillness stung my ears, making the sudden ring of the phone sound like cymbals that crashed in my head.

Tears saturated my cheeks and dripped silently from my chin while I stood in the living room and listened to my mother's near hysterical cries.

"You should be crying," she seethed.

I grabbed my car keys on the way out and left the house. Tears still poured from my eyes. I backed out of the driveway and headed down the road. I didn't know where I would go, but it didn't matter; I needed to get away.

My cell phone rang, cutting through the silence of the car. I assumed it was my dad calling me to come back. Without glancing at the Caller ID, I answered.

"Sorry, dad, I can't come back tonight. I just can't. I'll be—"

"Emma? It's Jane."

"Whoops!" I chuckled through my tears. "Bad day at

my house, as I guess you can tell. What's up?"

"There's a party tonight at Sophie's. She wanted me to tell you that you are expected to be there. Really, though, you'd want to come anyway, right?"

"After the episode I just experienced? Yeah. Yeah, I'll be there."

That evening, I took one slow, nervous step after another to Sophie's door. I had never been to a party before. I knew two things would be involved on this particular night: First, there would be alcohol; second, I would be expected to work on my end of the pact.

Sophie opened the door before I had a chance to knock. She looked somehow different, her face more round than usual.

"Wow, Soph. Are you okay?" I asked.

"Yeah, got over the flu and then started eating everything in sight! No big deal," she replied. "Come in! We've been waiting for you!"

I had taken barely two steps inside the door when Belle handed me a drink.

"This will help calm your nerves for tonight," she whispered and winked.

I took a tentative sip and chugged the rest. I needed calm nerves, but more than that, I wanted to forget about the miserable confrontation with my mom. Ashley handed me my next drink, and before long I didn't have a care in the world.

"Easy, lady!" Jane giggled when I stumbled over to her and sat on her lap. A camera flashed somewhere nearby.

"I jus' looove you so mush," I slurred, trying to focus my eyes on her face.

"Hey Em-ma," Sophie's cheery voice sang out while she walked toward me, a boy from our class on her arm. "This is Jacob. I think you two would get along really well."

"He's key-yute," I attempted to whisper to Jane, but

based on the giggles surrounding me, I could tell I wasn't as discreet as I had thought.

I lifted my arms up toward Jacob and he helped me to my feet.

"You smell delishhh," I said, burying my face into his chest. "Les go somewhere quiet. 'Kay?"

Sophie, Jane, Ashley, and Belle all gave me a thumbs-up when I glanced back at them on the way to the guest bedroom. Once inside, I clicked the door closed behind me and pushed Jacob back onto the bed.

"Well, hey there," he smirked, obviously pleased by my forward behavior.

"Hi, I'm Emma," I smiled, straddling his torso between my thighs.

A tiny voice in the back of my head cried, Don't do it, Emma, you idiot!

I was too drunk to care what that know-it-all had to say. The pact was clear. I wanted to fulfill my part of it.

As swiftly as my alcohol-numbed fingers would let me, I unzipped and unbuttoned my pants and then Jacob's, sliding them to the floor. He was raring and ready to go before I even stood.

"Wow. Hi, soldier," I said, and I giggled. "That was fast."

"Well, it isn't every day I get to be with a hot girl like you." He blushed.

"Shh! No silly lines. You're already going to get in my pants."

"It wasn't a line, Emma. I'm totally serious."

Based on the wide-eyed expression on his face, I completely believed him.

"Did you bring condoms?" he asked.

"No." I giggled again. "That's the dude's job!"

"Shit," he muttered.

"No worries, I'm on the pill," I said, but I lied.

I'd like to say our sexual rendezvous was exciting and adventurous, something to look back on one day as one of those, wow-that-was-so-stupid-but-really-fun type of memories. Somehow, this one didn't make the cut. That was probably because it took less than five minutes before he exhausted his manly supplies and crumpled onto the bed satisfied.

"Whatever happened to ladies first?" I teased. I rolled onto my back and lifted my legs and butt into the air.

"Oh, crap, sorry," he said, and he blushed again. "Uhm, what are you doing?"

"Trying to make sure your swimmer men get to my eggs," I replied, a deadpan look on my face.

His face turned immediately pale.

"Wha—what?" he croaked.

"Dude, I'm just kidding!" I laughed. "But the look on your face was priceless."

The next morning, I woke on the floor of the living room amidst empty bottles and cups. I squinted against the blinding light pouring through the window and groaned. Hangovers, I quickly realized, were no fun. I forced myself up off the floor slowly, my head pounding and my limbs stiff from sleeping in such an awkward position. I made my way to the bathroom, unsure of whether I was going to throw up or simply empty my bladder.

The door was locked. I tapped on it lightly.

"Anyone in there?" I asked in a hushed voice.

I heard the toilet flush, but it didn't mask the sound of vomiting.

"Are you all right?"

"I'm fine," Belle answered. "Who's out there?"

"It's Emma, Belle. Let me in, okay?"

The doorknob clicked, and I walked in. Belle repositioned herself in front of the bowl. I grabbed a hair tie out of my pocket and pulled her vomit-crusted hair away from her face.

"Drink a little too much last night, B?" I smiled.

"I wish," she replied, pointing to the counter.

There, perched on the edge, was a positive pregnancy

test.

"Wow, Belle, you're, you—," I stammered.

"I did it. I fulfilled the pact. I'm the first. Mommy and daddy would be oh-so proud." She grinned slightly. "You'll take care of me right now, right?"

"Of course, Belle. That's all a part of it. We're in this together. But, we just signed the pact a week ago. How are you already pregnant?"

"Sophie told me about the pact over the summer, and I decided to get a head start. I guess I'm an overachiever at everything I do."

I helped her undress and step into the shower and peeled off my own clothes as well. She was weary and weak. I washed her hair and face while she held onto the walls.

"Did you and Jacob, you know...?" she asked while I turned off the water and wrapped a towel around her shoulders.

"We did," I replied solemnly, leading her into the nearest room. "Looks like I may be joining you soon."

"I'll take care of you then, Em," she whispered, before she curled up in the covers and fell asleep.

It took a while for what I had done to sink in. I couldn't entirely blame it on the alcohol, although that certainly was a factor.

One by one, my pact friends announced their pregnancies. Belle was first, followed by Ashley, then Sophie. All were due in the beginning, middle, and end of the following May; all had started trying to get pregnant over the summer.

That left Jane and me. We had both done the deed the night of Sophie's party, and again at another party two weeks later. The second time, though I didn't tell anyone, I had used protection. Though I knew I might have gotten pregnant with Jacob, I thought it couldn't hurt to protect myself just in case.

That was strictly against the pact, and I risked facing some serious backlash from my friends.

Pact Rule #1: *Try everything in your power to get pregnant. No protection, no abstinence.*

Jane called me in mid-October in hysterics.

"I'm pregnant, Emma!" She laughed and sobbed into the phone.

"Wow, Jane, you too," I muttered.

"You should find out soon, right? I mean, we had a similar cycle and all. Oh, my God, Emma. I'm so scared!"

"Calm down, Jane. Take deep breaths."

"My mom is going to murder me," Jane said. "Aw, screw her. At least now she can't push me around. Everyone knows you can't abuse a pregnant chick."

I sat silently while she giggled and cried, snorted and sobbed about her news. I looked over at my calendar and realized she was right. I would have a positive pregnancy test if I were pregnant now.

"Em! Take a test now!" she yelled, snapping me out of the trance I had fallen into.

"Um, yeah, okay," I mumbled, fumbling my hands around beneath my mattress to find the pregnancy test I had hidden weeks before.

"Pee on it, girl!" Jane said. She sounded excited.

I wondered to myself how one girl could encompass so many emotions in one phone conversation.

"I'll call you back," I said.

"No! Do it while I'm on the phone. I want to be the first to know. After all, you were the first person I told," she replied.

I pulled out the stick, arranged myself on the toilet, aimed, and fired—a difficult task with my nervous hand shaking. I set the stick down on the counter and waited.

"What does it say?" Jane asked.

"I don't know yet, silly. Chill your pants. It says to wait three minutes."

I paced the bathroom floor and chanted in my head, Please don't be positive, please don't be positive, please don't be positive.

The three minutes passed far too quickly.

"Three minutes!" Jane squealed. "What does it say, Em? Tell me!"

I picked up the test, closed my eyes and inhaled deeply.

"It's—," I began.

"Yeah? Yeah? It's what?"

"Positive," I sighed, opening my eyes and focusing them on the stick.

"Oh, my God, Emma! Do you know what this means?" Jane shrieked. "It means we have all fulfilled the pact. Best of all, it means we will be due around the same time!"

I didn't share her enthusiasm, but I pretended I did. After a lengthy conversation about baby-related topics, I finally ended the call.

I had broken another rule, but couldn't let Jane know.

Pact Rule #2: *Do not lie about being pregnant.*

At school, the pact friends and I met at the same grassy knoll we had been meeting at every morning since the day we signed our lives away. Jane shared our news and everyone cheered for us, giving us hugs and congratulations. Belle and Ashley commiserated with each other on how miserable they felt, and Sophie said she was glad she hadn't been hit with morning sickness yet.

The first few months went by quickly. I didn't have to worry about seducing random guys any more and also didn't have to worry about making myself look pregnant. I repeated the same symptoms that Belle and Ashley had complained about, and even pretended to dislike certain foods and smells. I was actually pretty impressed and a little frightened by my ability to lie so easily, especially to Jane, who I had grown to love like a sister.

Then things got tricky. The first three girls were obviously getting more round in the middle, and classmates had begun to notice. Rumors spread like wildfire. Soon, it was divulged that our little group was involved in a pregnancy pact.

We became known as the Skank Squad.

It was mid-January when things took a whole different turn in our group. To appear a little more than four months pregnant, I wore a small fake belly beneath my shirt. I hid my non-pregnancy well, but it was only a matter of time before I was discovered. After all, I would have to give birth eventually.

"I was kicked off the basketball and soccer teams," Belle sighed, her six-month pregnant belly poking out from beneath the too-small shirt she wore. "Not that it matters, my parents kicked me out, too."

"You can come live with me at my dad's place," Ashley said, wrapping her arm around Belle's shoulders and giving her a kiss on the head.

"And we're here for you, too," Sophie smiled, wrapping her arms around Belle's waist.

An uncomfortable feeling washed over me, and I realized my period was threatening to start. I knelt and fumbled in my backpack, relieved when I found a quarter hiding at the bottom. My shirt had lifted up on my back and I tugged at it to pull it back down when I stood.

"I need to run to the bathroom before class," I said, gathering my belongings.

Sophie gave me a look I couldn't decipher, but as soon as I had noticed it, she had changed to her normal cheery expression.

I hurried to the nearest bathroom, afraid I would end up leaking through my clothes if I didn't get there in time, which would inevitably blow my cover of being pregnant. I dug the quarter out and fumbled with the machine.

"Damn it, work!" I yelled, though I knew this particular machine always took an extra jiggle or two before it dispensed.

I was so immersed in trying to get a tampon, I didn't hear the bathroom door open and close behind me.

"What are you doing?" Sophie's voice was like ice.

"I, uh, I'm..." I stammered, trying to think up a valid reason why I would be buying a tampon.

"You were never pregnant, were you?" she scowled, walking toward me.

I don't exactly know why, but Jane's words suddenly flashed in my mind, Everyone knows you can't abuse a pregnant chick.

She was right. I couldn't shove Sophie out of the way to escape. She was most definitely pregnant. Staring at her, just steps away, a hand on one hip and a look of complete hatred in her eyes, she suddenly looked even more pregnant than Belle and Ashley.

Out of nowhere, a loud **pop* reverberated against the bathroom walls. Horror filled Sophie's eyes. She looked down at her soaked shorts and the liquid pouring down her legs and pooling onto the tile floor. Soon after, the bathroom door opened and Jane, Belle, and Ashley appeared.

"Oh, my God! Sophie, your water just broke!" Jane screamed, fumbling in her backpack for a phone. "I'm calling an ambulance!"

Sophie leaned against the sink, stunned.

"Sophie, this is serious. How far along are you?" Belle asked.

She hesitated. "Six? A little less than six months."

"That's really early, Soph. Just stay calm, we'll get you to the hospital," Ashley said.

The girls led Sophie out to the front of the school and moments later, an ambulance arrived. Sophie said nothing about me or the fact that I was lying to them all. Instead, she smiled faintly and said, "See you guys at the hospital, okay?"

Once the ambulance had driven off, Ashley, Belle, and Jane dissolved into tears.

"There's no way her baby is going to make it!" Jane sobbed, rubbing her own barely protruding belly. "That's just too early."

That evening, Jane and I were the first to arrive at the hospital. Cautiously, we entered the delivery room and stood behind the privacy curtain. There was no sound. No baby, no talking, nothing.

"Sophie?" Jane called softly.

"Yeah, right here. Come on in!" Sophie's cheery voice replied.

We stepped around the curtain and saw a normally well-kept Sophie sitting in bed looking positively bedraggled. Her hair was pulled back into a messy, knot-filled ponytail. Dark circles had appeared under her eyes and red spots peppered her cheeks. She smiled wearily at Jane and shot me a reproachful glance.

"Sophie, what happened?" Jane asked, glancing at Sophie's belly. Beneath the blanket, it still looked swollen. "Did you have the baby?"

Tears welled in Sophie's eyes. "Yes."

"Is she okay?" Jane whispered.

"She's gone," Sophie mumbled through her tears.

Jane rushed over to hug her. I took a tentative step toward the bed, unsure of whether or not Sophie even wanted me there.

"Don't come any closer," Sophie demanded.

Jane stepped back and glanced at Sophie and then me.

"What's going on?" she asked.

"Why don't you tell her?" Sophie sneered.

My mouth was suddenly dry. A lump grew in my throat, threatening to block my airway. I knew this was going to happen eventually, but that didn't make me feel any more prepared to face it.

"Tell me what?" Jane asked, anger replacing the concern she had previously worn on her face.

"I—I'm so sorry, Jane. I should have told you sooner. Please, forgive me," I pleaded with my friend, dropping my eyes to the ground in shame. "I'm not really pregnant."

Jane's anger turned to pure hatred. The sweet friend I had known the past several months was replaced by a furious enemy.

"How dare you," she spat. "Get out, Emma. Get out of this room. Get out of my life. I cannot believe you would do such a thing to me—to us!"

"Jane, please, let me explain—" I began, but Jane cut me off.

"There isn't a single excuse you could give that would make this okay. You lied to me. Get out of here."

A nurse entered the room.

"What is going on here?" she demanded. "Sophie needs her rest. She's been through a lot today."

"It's fine. I'm going," I replied. "She should stay. Sophie needs her."

I left the room and walked swiftly down the hall, wanting to put as much distance between myself and the predicament I had put myself in as possible. My heart broke with each step, realizing that I had lost my best friend at a time when she needed me most. I turned down one hallway, then another until I stopped short. I had reached the nursery.

A couple was standing at the window, gushing over a baby girl with dark, curly hair in the front row of bassinettes. Tufts of dark curls peeked out from beneath her pink hat and her skin was a beautiful milk-chocolate color. She was simply gorgeous.

"Can you believe she's finally here?" the woman asked her husband. "We have been waiting so long for this."

I wondered if they were an aunt and uncle or possibly a friend of the baby girl's family.

"I know," the husband said, pulling his wife into his chest. "We just have to wait out the first forty-eight hours and hope Sophie doesn't change her mind."

Upon hearing those words, everything clicked into place in my mind.

"She's gone," Sophie had said. She didn't say her

baby had died, she had simply said she was gone.

Sophie was pregnant months before everyone else.

The realization hit me like a semi-truck to the gut.

I have to tell the others.

This task proved more difficult than it seemed. I couldn't reenter the hospital room and out Sophie then and there. After she was released from the hospital, it was already well-known amongst the group that I had lied, and I was sure to be quite thoroughly blacklisted.

Sure enough, the next day at school, I received my first taste of the pact backlash.

Bright pink fliers covered the walls and lockers of the hallways. In large, bold font, they read: Back off guys. Emma is into chicks!

Beneath that was a picture of me on Jane's lap the night of the first party. It was doctored to look like I had my hands touching her inappropriately. I rolled my eyes and grabbed as many fliers as I could before realizing my attempts were futile. People were piling into the halls, reading the fliers, and breaking out into fits of laughter. I quickly resigned myself to thinking I'd wait until college to start dating.

"You shouldn't have lied," Belle's smug voice came from behind me. "Serves you right!"

"You should talk," I scowled, turning to face her. "I lied about being pregnant, but at least my lie only affects me, not anyone else. Unlike yours."

The arrogant look on Belle's face dissolved immediately.

"What do you mean?" she asked quietly.

"I know what really happened with your pregnancy," I said.

"How did you find out?" she whispered.

"I have my ways."

"I know it was a mistake," Belle pleaded. "Please don't tell Ashley about me and her dad.

I tried my hardest not to let my jaw drop to the floor.

"Wait—what?" I asked, incredulously.

"I mean, technically, I'm pregnant with her half-brother. That's messed up," she said.

"With her father?" I asked.

"That wasn't the secret you were referring to, was it," Belle said, and I could see her cringe.

"Uh, no." I chuckled. "I was talking about you hiding in the pantry chugging beers at the party two weeks after you found out you were pregnant."

"Oh, crap."

"Help me take down the rest of these lovely fliers, and I'll forget this conversation even happened," I reasoned.

"Sophie will kill me, but—" she paused. "Okay, deal."

The damage was already done, but I felt a slight twinge of accomplishment when we each dropped an armload of fliers in the recycling bin.

"Promise me you won't say anything to Ashley or the others?" Belle pleaded.

"Belle, nobody wants to talk to me. Even if they did, your secret's safe with me."

She smiled and gave me a quick hug.

"I'll never forget you taking care of me the day I found out I was pregnant," she said. "I don't know if you realize how much that meant to me."

"That's what friends do," I said, and I smiled. "They look out for each other."

As soon as the words came out of my mouth, echoed from Sophie months prior, I knew I couldn't divulge Sophie's secret. What did it matter anyway, if she decided to give her baby up? That little girl's parents were obviously excited to bring her home and love her to pieces. In the end, that was all that mattered.

It was several months before I talked to Belle again. Despite our friendly hallway rendezvous, I was still the pact-breaker and ultimate bad friend. That was why I was shocked when my phone rang two months later, and Belle's name came up on the Caller ID at three o'clock in the morning.

"Belle?"

"Yeah, Emma, it's me. Jane needs you."

There was a palpable sense of urgency in Belle's voice, one I hadn't heard since the day I received the call that Dave had died.

"Your brother and his girlfriend were in a really bad wreck," my dad had said. "It doesn't look good for Dave, Em."

"Are you there?"

Belle's near-panicked voice dissolved the memory of Dad's call.

"I'm here. What's wrong, Belle? What happened?"

"Just come down to the hospital. Now."

Without hesitation, I leaped from my bed and threw on the first outfit I could find. I scribbled a quick note to my parents and made my way as fast as I could to the hospital. Horrific images flashed through my mind, and I wondered how bad the situation was.

Jane was only about seven and a half months pregnant.

Had she been in a car accident? Did she lose the baby? The questions piled up in my mind, one upon another. Each unanswered question created a new, more dreadful scenario in my mind.

At the hospital, I ran from the parking lot to the emergency room where they told me Jane had been transferred to the delivery ward. My heart galloped in my chest with each step I took toward her room. It wasn't until I stood outside the door that something occurred to me: What if Jane doesn't even want me here?

It was a painful realization, but one that I brushed away quickly. Belle had called and told me to come. Jane could turn me away, but she needed to know I cared.

Slowly, I entered the room and stood facing the privacy curtain, much like Jane and I had when we visited Sophie months prior. I cleared my throat, unsure of what to say. I heard feet shuffling on the other side.

"It's probably her," Belle's voice whispered.

"Emma?" Jane croaked.

"It's me, Jane. Can I come in?"

"Yeah." She sighed.

I stepped around the curtain and drew in a sharp breath, cupping my hand over my mouth.

"What happened, Jane?" I asked after I had regained my composure. "Who did this to you?"

Bruises and gashes covered every visible inch of her skin, and her face was puffy and swollen. I stepped forward and grabbed an icepack off the tray beside her. Taking a seat on the edge of the bed, I gingerly placed the ice on the side of her face that bore the meanest looking bruises.

"It was my mom," she whispered, looking down at her fingers intertwined on her lap. "I had hidden the pregnancy real well, and then I just couldn't any more. She got pissed and beat the shit out of me."

"Oh, Jane," was all I could manage. Tears choked my throat and blinded my eyes.

"So far, my little boy is okay, though," she said, flashing a weary smile. "Still kicking away in there."

"Listen, Jane," I said, staring into her eyes. "I am so sorry. I—"

"Shh," she interrupted. "It doesn't matter, Emma. I know you didn't mean to hurt me. You didn't put the crazy idea of getting pregnant into my head, and last I checked, you didn't knock me up, either."

"Well, I dunno, there are some pretty scandalous pictures of me on your lap at that party last September," I joked.

Jane gave a short laugh and clutched her ribs.

"Don't make me laugh!" she said, smiling and wincing at the same time.

"Let me take care of you," I pleaded. "Come and live at my place. My parents would understand. Heck, it may even help my mom to be able to take care of someone."

"I would really like that, Emma. Thank you."

I stayed with Jane all night, tossing and turning on the uncomfortable cot in her room. At seven in the morning, I sat up and stretched my sore muscles. Jane was fast asleep, so I decided to head out and find some coffee. I took one step out of the door and nearly tripped on the person sitting beside it.

"Sophie!" I gasped. "What are you doing out here?"

"I just wanted to see how Jane's doing before I headed to school," she replied. "But I didn't hear anyone talking in there and didn't want to wake her up, so I was waiting."

"Yeah, she's out like a light," I said. "I want to kill her mom for what she did to her."

"I know," Sophie scowled. "My sentiments exactly."

"I was going to hunt down some caffeine. I know we're not exactly best buds any more, but you're welcome to join me if you want."

Sophie hesitated for a moment and then nodded.

"Yeah. I'd like that."

We were silent while we walked down the hall, found the cafeteria, and sat down with our hot coffees in hand. I had no idea what to say to her and I guessed the feeling was mutual.

"I- I'm sorry," Sophie mumbled.

"Huh?" I asked, thinking I must have heard her wrong.

"For what I put you, put everyone, through. The whole pact thing was so selfish."

"Why, Sophie?" I asked. "Why did you start it?"

"I was already pregnant when school started," she confessed. "I didn't want to be the only person in our class pregnant, and I thought that maybe if there were several of us pregnant at once, then the focus would be less on me and more on the entire group."

"Why us, though? Why Belle, Ashley, Jane, and me?"

"I knew you were all vulnerable," she sighed. "I figured you'd all be the most likely to go along with it, and initially, I was right. I really should have known you wouldn't do it. Your brother always told me how smart you were."

Her words pierced my heart. I wasn't expecting her to bring up Dave in our conversation. At least not yet.

"I know we had just started dating, but Dave meant a lot to me," Sophie explained.

"I'm jealous that you were the last person to hold his hand, to see him smile. You were there to hear his last breath," I muttered, holding back the tears of hurt I had been keeping from Sophie since the previous summer.

I glanced up at her through the tears in my eyes and saw tears streaming down her face as well.

"Sophie?" I asked, my voice cracking. "Can you do me a favor?"

"Anything," she said, her voice as choked up as mine.

"Can you please come over and tell my mom about your little girl? She would love to know that a part of Dave is still living. I know it means the world to me to know my baby niece is being so loved by her family."

"Y-you know about that?"

"I saw her at the hospital the day you had her," I explained. "I did the math. I knew you were pregnant before the rest of us, and I knew you and Dave were serious. Plus, her dark skin and curly black hair sorta gave her away."

"If I'm being totally honest, Emma, she looked a whole lot like you. She was beautiful. I'm really going to miss her."

"You did the right thing, Soph. Dave told me how much your parents hated you dating a black guy. I can't imagine they were too thrilled with you being pregnant with his child, either."

"No, they were pretty pissed," she admitted.

"Well, now she has a family that loves her to pieces and can provide for her. You did what was best for her."

In the end, Sophie kept her word and came over to tell my parents about their granddaughter. My mom gushed and sobbed over the pictures she brought, sent to Sophie by the baby's adoptive parents. Eventually, years down the road, we were all allowed to meet her, but simply knowing she was out there was an immense source of comfort to our family.

Jane came to live with us and, just as I suspected, my mom immersed herself in healing Jane's wounds and pampering her. When Jane gave birth to her little boy, she decided to keep him and love him the way she wished her own mother had. She and I moved out together and eventually went our separate ways, but I never forgot the bond we shared.

Belle eventually told Ashley about her baby and their friendship deteriorated rapidly. To make matters worse, Belle's parents prosecuted Ashley's dad for statutory rape. Needless to say, there was little trust left between the friends when it was all over.

The pact affected all of us in so many ways. For Ashley and Belle, it was painful and destructive. For Jane, it helped free her from her mother. For Sophie and my family, it gave closure and hope to a sad time in our lives. The pact may have been created under selfish pretenses, but in the end, it gave birth to change. For that reason alone, I will be forever grateful for that time in my life.

About the Author

Author, humorist, web designer, mommy extraordinaire, Lindsay Maddox has had her works featured in all of the previous TTM publications. She is the creator of Silly Mom Thoughts, a humor parenting blog where she shares the adventures of raising four small kids (including twins!). You can find out more about Lindsay by visiting http://lindsaymaddox.com.

Bits and Pieces

by Lisa Lee Smith

She'd end me and herself
—of that she assured me—
in her hysterical fury at someone else.
Fortunately for him
and perhaps for us all
he was elsewhere, sleeping it off.
Half of me didn't believe her raspy voice
and I rested my head
against the cold comfort of the glass
while I waited to find out
if fear would become necessary.
I thought about the way
people chuckle when they call babies ugly
as if they don't even understand the beauty
of new life and all its potential.
I thought about the time
a fresh egg was splattered
all over our picture window
just after sunset on Halloween
but she never caught the pranksters.
She cleaned the mess so thoroughly
you'd have believed the whole thing never happened.
The street lamps and front porches sped by
while she gripped the steering wheel and
crossed back and forth
over the yellow lines
as they glowed in unnatural light from
the car, the 7-Eleven, the brilliant senselessness
of wondering if she'd ever make the left turn for home.
I stared at the dark, familiar overpass ahead
as if I had not already crossed it a thousand times
before that particular midnight.

I'm Not Ready to Go

by Catherine A. MacKenzie

I feel you there in the night,
I sense your presence
as your breath blends with mine,
and I scream in the darkened silence
that I don't want to go.
"I'm not ready yet."
Will I ever be ready?
Is anyone ever ready?

I pray you to leave,
to depart to places unknown,
to take: someone else's daughter,
someone else's wife,
someone else's mother,
someone else's grandmother—not me!

I'm too young.
I have more living to do.
Doesn't everyone?

This life has sped by too fast and there are still many more things I want to accomplish and places I want to go and people I want to meet and more grandchildren's cheeks I want to kiss.

I don't know how I reached here so fast—the end of my life—done, complete, finished. But I'm not done, complete, finished. There's too much living left in me. When I am ready, I will go willingly, but right now, this is not the time.

Please leave.

I'm not ready to go.

Not yet...

Lifelines

by Robert L . Arend

Rachel Barnes smoothed the antiseptic carefully over the top surface of her hands, scrubbed between and around her fingers and rinsed. She gently toweled her skin dry.

Enough.

She hid her hands in plastic gloves and crossed the hall into the operating room.

"Good you could join us, Barnes," Dr. Benjamin said, his voice flat and cold. "You're late."

"Sorry, Doctor," Rachel replied. "I had trouble getting a cab after lunch."

"Lunch at the employee cafeteria not good enough for you?" the surgeon teased, in an obvious attempt to back away from his earlier irritation.

The anesthesiologist, too busy checking his intravenous line and the patient's vitals, ignored her. He nodded to signal the surgeon the patient was ready.

Rachel's job was to irrigate fecal matter away while the other tech suctioned. The surgeon needed to remove three feet of bowel and then resection. Three hours passed before the patient was ready to be moved to recovery.

All but the surgical techs pulled their gloves off. Rachel turned her back to the others before removing her own. Careful to keep her hands closed and close to her body, Rachel turned back, walked stiffly to the waste can and dropped her gloves in.

"Rachel, can you take the bowel to the pathologist?" Dr. Benjamin asked, lifting the container from the table.

Before she had time to think, Rachel stretched forth her open right hand to slip the handle from the surgeon's hand into the grasp of her own.

"What the hell?" Dr. Benjamin murmured. He snatched the laboratory container back.

Rachel hands instantly became fists.

"Open your hands, Rachel," the surgeon ordered.

When she hesitated, Dr. Benjamin put the container on the floor, gripped her right wrist in one hand and pulled her fingers open with his other, revealing her unwashed skin.

Rachel pulled away and fled the operating room.

Rachel Barnes studied each picture of herself. Her eyes zoomed in on the palms of each open hand.

The first picture was of baby Rachel, reaching for the camera lens: the lifeline, bold and deep, curving along the palm of the toddler's right hand.

Photo two was of twelve-year-old Rachel, haughtily stretching her right hand toward the holder of the camera to collect money, won in a bet with her father over whether she could raise her C in American history up to an A: lifeline retreated about a quarter of an inch from the base of the thumb.

Then there was tech-school-graduate Rachel, both palms up, hands resting on a table and each to a side of her freshly received Certified Surgical Technologist Certificate: lifeline half of baby Rachel's.

Finally, married Rachel: lifeline even less.

Divorced Rachel examined both of her thirty-eight-year-old hands. She could barely see the faint, quarter-inch lines on both.

She handed the pictures to her best friend Tiffany.

"I never noticed until Bill and I went to Atlantic City on our honeymoon," Rachel told Tiffany. "I went into a palm reader's shop on the boardwalk. She said she had never seen lifelines so faint and short. She told me nothing in my life will provide lasting happiness, that my life is just a brief stop, to learn tolerance and patience, before abrupt return to the spiritual realm—and she charged me thirty-five dollars for that."

Tiffany handed the pictures back to Rachel.

"Let me see your hands," Tiffany said, mystified.

Rachel carefully removed her black gloves.

Tiffany turned her friend's hands over. "My god, Rach, when's the last time you washed your hands?"

The undersides of her hands certainly were filthy and shamed Rachel. "I only wash the tops of my hands," she told Tiffany. "I wear plastic disposable gloves to protect the undersides when I shower or wash dishes." She started to cry. "I'm afraid to wash the lines...that soap and water will dissolve what's left of them."

"Is this why you were fired last week?" Tiffany whispered.

"I wasn't fired," Rachel said defensively. "I requested an accommodation under the Americans with Disabilities Act, and when they wouldn't give it to me, I quit."

Tiffany timidly frowned. "I don't think dirty hands qualify as a disability."

Both women were silent while pondering the open palms, their concentration broken only when the waitress asked if they wanted more coffee. Once their cups were full and they were alone again, the women looked into each other's eyes.

Tiffany looked away first. "I don't know what to say, Rach," she said. "Maybe this sounds silly, but have you gone to another palm reader for a second opinion?"

Tiffany tried to suppress a giggle.

"It's not funny," Rachel rebuked. "Show me your palms."

Tiffany warily flattened her hands on the surface of

the table. Rachel traced a finger, enviously, along her best friend's long and well-defined lifeline.

"You'll be alive long after I'm dead," Rachel said. She pressed her fingernail to gauge the depth of Tiffany's bold lifeline.

"Ouch," Tiffany protested, but when she jerked her hand away, the sharp fingernail nearly tore the line open. "Hey!" she exclaimed loud enough to cause heads to turn in adjoining booths. "I have to get back to work. I think you need to get some therapy."

Rachel watched Tiffany hurry to the checkout line, sorry she had scratched her friend, but the incident had shown her what needed to be done in order to stay alive.

"Such a deep, enthusiastically curved line, almost to the thumb's knuckle," Madam Trisha said, gently spreading the lines of Tiffany's right hand. "You love waking up in the morning. You love the work you do. You enjoy the nightlife. And, when you're ready to sleep, you embrace your dreams, too."

Tiffany was enthralled.

Everything Madam Trisha said was so true, she thought. "What about love? What about the future?" she asked.

"So many men have shared your bed and your body, all only briefly," the reader replied. "You crave sex, but are always disappointed. You want love, but, so far, shallow men; they quickly bored you. You have mostly been attracted to Leos, and you should have come to realize they only love themselves, none left over to give."

"So, I'll never get married?" Tiffany murmured, feeling a tear form.

Madam Trisha smiled. "Oh, oh, oh, be not sad. Soon, your soul mate comes for you. You will know him because of psychic memories from before this life. He is looking for you now, as you are for him. Soon you find one another."

Stunned, Tiffany almost forgot the true reason she

made the appointment to visit Madam Trisha.

"I have a friend," she began. "She was told by another palm reader that she will die young because her lifelines shrank to almost nothing."

Madam Trisha's mouth straightened. Angrily, she demanded, "Does your friend believe this?

Tiffany nodded, afraid to say more.

"Quack—that phony—that quack," Madam growled. "Tell me about your friend."

"She showed me pictures of her hands, from when she was very young up to a few years ago," Tiffany said. "Her lifelines were big as a child, but grew shorter and shorter as she grew older."

The flickering candle seemed to transfer a flame deep into each of Madam Trisha's gray eyes.

"Lines on palms change, just as our lives change direction. Lifelines do not declare how long life will be, but only the manner by which a person views his or her own life experiences. Short, faint lifelines usually belong to those who believe their lives will be short. They are generally those indulged and happy in childhood but unprepared for the struggles of the adult world."

"So I should tell my friend to ignore what she was told?" Trisha asked. She noticed Madam Trisha's anger caused the palm reader to drop the pretense of an accent.

"Yes. Tell her to come see me—free of charge," Madam urged. "It'll be the least I can do to make up for what that fraud told her. Where did your friend see the quack?"

"Atlantic City."

"Figures. Tell her to come see me. Tell her she could have no lifelines at all and still live to be a very, very old woman."

The charge was twenty dollars. Tiffany gave Madam twenty more.

Rachel waited an hour until she could feel the

euphoria provided by the oxycodone. She had stolen two pills from an inattentive nurse's medicine cart before that awful business in the personnel office.

That nurse was probably fired, but at least she'll have a lifetime to recover, Rachel thought, unlike herself: out of work and out of life.

She shifted the chair. She had showered and, for the first time in months, had thoroughly washed her hands. She opened those hands and was instantly alarmed by the clumps of peeling skin. Flaked and red-raw from wrist to palm, the tiny lines had finally been washed away.

She had never taken oxycodone before. She'd heard that some could become immediately addicted to the narcotic from first swallow.

What does it matter? she thought. *What life I had left has been washed away...*

The razor blade, from a tool used to scrape gunk off the glass cooktop, awaited her on the white tablecloth. The sharp thin edge seemed to shimmy and pop little sparks. The blade would either extend her life or end it.

Rachel thought of her mother. She thought of her wonderful father. Both were dead. She wondered if she would join them soon. They had given her so much.

Why couldn't they have given me lifelines like their own?

Still, she had been happy as a child. Perhaps she would have stayed happy and kept her lifelines had she never left home.

She clasped the blade between her fingers and sliced into her left hand.

The rain had turned into a deluge, the wipers barely able to clear the windshield fast enough to permit Tiffany to see. She had given up trying to call Rachel in order to concentrate on driving. Rachel wasn't answering her cell phone anyway.

She's probably asleep. Maybe I should just get off

the next exit and turn around and go home, she thought, before the car in the eastbound lane slid into her path.

Rachel admired her new lifelines: so deep, so long, so red.

She stood and staggered from the kitchen, holding her hands up while blood trailed on the floor after her. In the living room, she saw the light from the streetlight beam through the arched glass at the top of her front door. She struggled to breathe and crumbled to the soft pile of the carpet.

"I guess I know what it's like having an airbag explode all over you," Tiffany said to the EMT. He asked her a lot of questions, but she was sure she was only shook up and didn't need to go to the hospital.

An ambulance took the other driver away though, she thought.

A state trooper approached them with her handbag.

"Miss, I need to see your driver's license, registration and insurance, please."

She fell in love the instant she looked into the patrolman's eyes.

"Miss? Your driver's license, vehicle registration and insurance, please?"

She fumbled through her purse for her wallet.

"Can you find them for me?" she asked, handing him her wallet. "I'm so nervous."

Tiffany watched the trooper quickly locate the items and write the information on his clipboard. Rain dripped from the brim of his hat onto the report sheet.

Quite the professional, Tiffany thought, wanting to touch him, to kiss him.

The tow-truck driver leaned down. "Here's our business card, ma'am. We'll tow your car to the Ford dealership up the road for repairs, if that's all right with you. How do you want to pay for the tow?

Tiffany took her insurance card from the patrolman

and handed it to the driver, then returned her eyes to those of the state trooper. His eyes seemed frozen on her eyes as well.

"How will I get home?" she managed to say.

"I can radio a cab," the driver offered.

"Forget that," the patrolman said. "I'll see she gets home."

Tiffany felt her insides melt.

"What's your name, officer?" she asked shyly.

"Eric. Eric Stevens," he answered. He took his coat off and reached behind her to rest it on her shoulders. She wanted to fall asleep in his arms.

"Were you headed home?" Officer Eric asked after he started the engine of his patrol car. "If you were, you were driving in the wrong direction."

Tiffany remembered Rachel. "No, I was on my way to a friend's house—a girl friend's house. You know, if you don't mind, can you drive me there? Rachel's place is just off the next exit. I'd rather stay over there tonight than be home alone after what just happened."

"Sure," Eric said. He steered his patrol car from the berm onto the road, but his tone sounded disappointed.

Tiffany told him Rachel's address. "There's something I really need to tell her, anyway. She's not answering her cell, and I'm a little worried about her."

Eric nodded and turned onto the exit.

Rachel, honey. Go back... Go back...

She stood before her mother and father and reached for them. She hadn't felt so happy in such a long time.

It's not your time, Rachel. Go back. Go back.

Oh, Rachel, her mother said. *What have you done to your hands?*

Rachel hugged her father, but when he pushed her away, she saw her own blood drip from his shoulders.

Her mMother opened her hands and held them up to Rachel's eyes. *Look. Look. My lifelines vanished before I gave birth to you.*

Mother was sixty-eight when she died, Rachel remembered.

Pounding. Louder pounding. Something crashing. Rachel looked down and saw Tiffany. A policeman had kicked her front door open. She felt a tornado rip through her head, then nothing.

Tiffany glanced at the numbers outside the rooms while she hurried down the hall. She had not visited Rachel in almost two weeks, since her friend was transferred from the hospital to the crisis center. When she came to room 1218, she asked Eric to wait outside while she entered alone.

Rachel was in a chair in the far corner. A blanket covered her lap. Eyes closed, she was pale, and she made a rattling sound when she took each breath.

She's going to live, though, Tiffany thought, and she thanked God for that.

Rachel opened her eyes. Tiffany walked over to her.

"Tiff," Rachel murmured.

"I would have come to see you sooner, Rach, but they wouldn't allow visitors until today. So, I thought I'd stop by on my way home," Tiffany said. "The nurse at the front desk says you're doing better. She says you'll need a little more therapy. After what you've been through, I don't know what to say."

"I saw mommy and daddy," Rachel told her. "They're still alive, just not here. They were mad at me for cutting my hands."

Tiffany shivered. "Why, Rachel? Why?"

Rachel licked her dry lips. "Life, Tiff. To make new lifelines, to stay alive."

"What that palm reader told you was a lie, Rachel. I went to Madam Trisha's last month, the night we found you. If Eric hadn't used his flashlight to see through your door glass, saw you fall... Anyway, Madam Trisha wants to see you, to tell you lifelines have nothing to do with how long people live."

Rachel frowned, as though thinking about what Tiffany told her. She closed her eyes. "Too late for that."

"What do you mean?" Tiffany said.

Rachel slipped her arms out from under the blanket, turned her hands over and raised them.

Tears flowed down Tiffany's cheeks when she saw the ugly wounds, still red and angry from having been cut. "Oh, Rachel, how could you have done that to yourself?"

"Life," Rachel answered. "They may be ugly, but with lifelines like these, I'll live forever."

About the Author

Robert L. Arend has written articles for websites that include OpedNews.com and FireDogLake.com. His short stories "David and the Outside" and "Creation" were previously published by Twin Trinity Media in the anthology Elements of Dimension, *along with his poem "Astral Voyeur".*

Other of Robert's short stories have been and continue to be published in the short story/flash fiction/poetry anthologies of the Circle 8 Writers Group. More are to be published in future volumes of Twin Trinity Media anthologies as well.

Among the Redwoods

by L.L. Darroch

The trees speak in eloquent voices,
thousands of accumulated years beyond my meager human knowledge.
I am humbled standing in their whispering presence.

They rise tall against the onslaught of civilized expansion,
their girth increasing with passing centuries,
the history of the world pressed in their rings.

While they reach up to heaven's light,
children sprout to life at their feet,
grow up in their elder's shadows.

Fallen friends on the forest floor
give sustenance to feed the earth,
reborn in their woodland family - an unbroken circle of life.

I stand small beside them,
my mortal troubles dwarfed into insignificance by their majesty.
In moments of shared splendor I offer up prayers,

pleas for friends and family in need,
to find the healing life and wisdom
given freely among the redwood trees.

About the Poet

LL Darroch is a traveler and explorer both by nature and nurture. She treasures the people who have touched her life and the faith and heart that guides her. When she isn't absorbing the world around her, including the people and creatures that inhabit it, she is busy writing about it. She is also a craftsperson, nature lover and artist.

Children have always been a major part of LL Darroch's life. With stories and poems in nine books, three more soon to be in print, and many more in the writing stages, plus additional writings online, she is hoping to fill up at least one book shelf with her published work.

Join LL Darroch on her writing journey and visit her at www.darroch-meekis.webnode.com. Please be sure to sign the guest book and let her know you were there.

Naked

by Sarah F. Sullivan

The man and his wife were both naked, and they felt no shame. ~~ ***Genesis 2:25***

It has been said that when God opened the eyes of Adam and Eve, He gave Eve special perception. The needs of her husband, the pains of her children and all other minute details women inherently understand, all of these were made known to Eve, and she, in turn, passed her God-given perception to women after her. Eve's keen vision manifested in a variety of ways, but especially in the matters of men, or rather, of cheating men. And for a brave few, the gift of visualization extended to self.

We sat in a garden one evening not so long ago, and she told me a story, a story that had been told to her by someone else who had claimed yet another had told the story to her. It was a common enough story, or so I thought, one as familiar a story like that of Creation, or of so many similar themes:

He said/She said.
I heard you coming, so I hid.
Woman wanted to know good and evil.

Yet this story, as familiar as it seemed, was somehow different than those cautionary tales passed by oral tradition, told by one woman to another. It was familiar, but distant, and it needed to be told, to be shared.

It began in the garden. It was summer. The grass had outgrown its newborn softness, replaced by chafing brown edges fostered by the suffocating summer heat. The smells of the garden reached the porch, slowly rising in heavy waves from the earth. Mint, patchouli and sage all swelled up together in waves of potent fragrance. The sun settled in a pool of lavenders and oranges, and the ever-persistent cat had once more lain beneath the shade of the apple tree that refused to bloom.

She sat in the center of the garden, barefoot, on the limestone slabs still warm from the afternoon sun. The garden was the only quiet and comforting place for her any more. In some ways, her home had become a prison.

Less than two months after Mia's birth, Eva's husband had sat at their table, paper and coffee in hand.

"I won't be coming home after work this evening," he had announced to her. "I'll be staying with a friend."

Stunned, Eva had been able only to stare when he nonchalantly sipped his coffee, as if he'd said he was just going to the grocery store. She stammered, trying desperately to form words, "Wha—what are you... I don't—"

"Don't take it so hard. This has been coming for months. I know it's not the best timing, what with the baby and all, but I just can't stay sane if I live here," he snapped.

She confessed to me later that his sanity was the last thing in the world she was considering. She was a new mother, on maternity leave, and expected back to work in a few weeks. She wondered what she would do without his support.

His sanity? My God, how selfish!

She dumped his coffee down his pants. She felt women everywhere would agree that hers was an understandable reaction.

He screamed like some fearsome creature and staggered to one knee, clutching his groin desperately. She had half a mind to step on him, squish him like a bug. Instead, she threw his paper and briefcase out the front door, and then retreated to the next room to feed her daughter. He left and didn't come to collect his things until two months later.

His friend just happened to be twenty-two years old, blonde, big-toothed, big-boobed, and possessed a Cheshire-cat grin. She had the curvaceous body of a stripper and a name to match. Eva laughed in his face when he reluctantly revealed her name was Candy.

While he packed his things into the only suitcase he owned, he grumbled, almost under his breath, "It's not her fault. You shouldn't give her such a hard time."

"You know, you're right. I think I'll bring her a pie for so kindly and considerately fucking me... oh yes, and my husband, too."

He shrugged, shouldered his suitcase and practically ran down the staircase, nearly tripping on the last step. He always did that; the last step always seemed to trip him for some reason.

And for some reason, that thought nearly made her burst into tears—such a stupid thing, so stupid.

He married Candy when the ink on the divorce papers had barely dried. Needless to say, Eva hadn't attended the ceremony. Her former mother-in-law admonished her not to be selfish. It was the older woman's opinion that Eva should support him. He was, after all, Mia's father. She should do it for her daughter's sake.

"You can't hide her from Candy forever," she chided.

"No, but I can damn well try," Eva whispered, clutching her daughter close.

After her divorce and his remarriage, Eva began to spiral. She suffered from feelings of inadequacy, depression, frustration, and worst of all, complete and utter silence. She lived in a house with her daughter but without anyone to talk to. Her mother was halfway across the state, and for some reason, everyone except the girls at work seemed to side with the male-chauvinist-pig mentality that a man should do what he wants to be happy, regardless of who he hurts in the process. Never mind mama and baby at home.

Eva felt isolated.

Just to have something to do, to keep her occupied, she began to draw and paint. She said anyone who looked at those first sketches would have had her committed.

HATE

ANGER

ENVY

SIN

TERROR

FUCKING AFRAID

All written in red, black and purple oils, stroked madly across a canvas. She hadn't painted since college, but it felt like therapy. She would do it while her daughter slept, and gradually, she built up her skill.

After a time, she stopped painting words and moved on to objects. The object paintings weren't much better than the words had been, but were a little less direct. Nothing but sad, depressing images filled canvas after canvas, and it didn't seem as though she could paint anything else.

A year after the divorce, she invited a friend from work to dinner. They sat outside and ate on the wicker table Eva had moved from the patio to the garden. They talked, gazed wistfully at the flowers in bloom and compared gardening stories, until her friend noticed the paintings. Eva had been painting in the garden, and her portfolio rested next to the apple tree, closed up tight, a glass of water, still full and stained red, resting at the tree's base.

"Do you mind?" her friend asked.

"Go ahead," Eva said. She nervously drank her tea extra fast while her friend perused the paintings.

When her friend reached the end, she smiled. "You're not depressed, are you?"

Eva laughed and shrugged at the sarcasm.

"Have you ever thought of painting yourself nude?" her friend asked.

She hadn't. "No..."

"It's incredibly liberating."

Eva still blushed as she recounted the story to me years later.

"I'm sure it would be liberating... that one would need to be liberated to do such a thing," she told her friend. Inwardly, at the time, she thought it was the last thing on earth she'd ever do.

Her friend saw the doubt in Eva's eyes immediately. "I promise it is. All these things," she signaled around at all the work she'd seen, "they're helpful to paint, I'm sure... especially the hangman's noose." She grimaced. "But try painting yourself... and not in a depressing light. Paint yourself the way you are. Naked to the world, stripped to the core of your soul. That's the way he's left you, isn't it? Paint that. That's real."

Eva sat on the couch after her friend left, playing with the ends of a blanket her mother had crocheted. She considered her friend's suggestion. It was a thought, but a terrifying, silly one. She pondered it: painting herself nude. She felt her cheeks flush and was certain she had blush crimson. Shame overwhelmed her. She didn't understand why she should be embarrassed or ashamed.

"It's my body," she muttered. "I see it every day. Why should I be ashamed to look at it, to paint it, even if all the world should see it?"

After several moments, she paused, smiled nervously, and then announced to the empty room, "Damn all the world. Let them look."

So she borrowed a camera, loaded it and set it on the dresser directly across from her bed. It was the middle of summer, but somehow that fragrant breeze found her as her trembling fingers pulled her blouse over her head, and goose bumps erupted down her skin. After she had removed her clothes, she stood awkwardly still in the center of her room.

She felt as though every article of furniture was watching her in disgust.

Unnecessary nudity, she imagined the furniture might have whispered. She's not supposed to be nude unless she's changing. Get some clothes on!

The shame was overwhelming, and the warm breeze seemed bitterly cold.

She finally ignored the imagined whispers, took a deep breath, pressed the timer on the camera and lay down on the bed. The first several pictures revealed her anxiety. Her body was turned stiffly toward the camera, legs pushed together firmly, arms supporting her body as she lay on her side.

"That first flash felt like a gunshot," she mused when she retold the story later.

After the flash, she looked down at her body, imagining what the recorded picture looked like. She had to laugh. She looked and felt so utterly uncomfortable. A grimace was just fading from her face, her cheeks were bright red and her legs were still striving to push towards her abdomen to cover the lower half of her body. Finally, she reset the timer.

With each successive snapshot, she relaxed and allowed her legs to fall where they wanted, allowed them to leave her groin unprotected. She was conscious of her embarrassment, her post-pregnancy body, the stretch marks on her thighs, the potbelly that still remained, her full breasts, but she didn't look away from the camera. She kept contact. She kept firmly in mind that it was just her, that the core of who she was had not changed. She connected to the woman she was before—before her marriage, before her child, before the whole damn world fell apart—before she was so self-conscious and insecure in herself that she couldn't even take a picture of a naked body, let alone her own.

"I wasn't about to let that man take my confidence away from me," she mumbled in remembrance while she related the story to me.

Eva's heart palpitated in her chest when she submitted the roll of film for development by a private photographer. She was excited two weeks later when she grasped the large manila envelope that contained the developed photos, blushing while she ran to her car.

Eva did what she would have done if they were pictures of her daughter or of her friends. She sat in her car and excitedly tore into the packet. She looked at the pictures over and over and over, spending more than a half an hour there on the street. She looked at herself, not in the hurry of dressing, not in the harsh light of searching for new stretch marks and extra pounds, but just as herself. And she was beautiful.

She sketched herself that afternoon and didn't stop until after midnight. Every night after she put her daughter to bed, she tended to the painting. The end product was amazing. The painting showed a confident woman, dark head resting on her hand, the other hand gently resting on the curve of her hips, legs outstretched towards the end of the canvas, one gracefully falling over the other. The eyes that stared back at her made her eyes fill with tears. The eyes on the canvas showed confidence, but also the pain she had felt. Her painting had captured her husband leaving, her daughter saying "Da-da" and not hearing anyone answer. She had even painted her own self-hatred, her own redemption.

Ignoring the clerk's startled face, she brought the finished canvas to a store to be framed. He spluttered and stammered so that she couldn't help but smile graciously and say, "Yes, yes, it is me."

He turned beet red and nearly dropped the portrait in his embarrassment.

Once home, she hung the painting on the staircase, and it stayed there through her daughter's growth, through her ex-husband's attempt to return to their lives after Candy bore him a daughter, through her own attempts to love again, and through her failures to find love again. That face, that body, reminded her of the strength she didn't think she had. It was always there in the stairwell, the constant smiling face, her one comfort...

Until her daughter turned ten.

Eva was in the garden when the incident took place. She was happy, admittedly, for the first time in a long while. She was listening to the sounds of the geese seeking warmer countries; the cold north winds pursued them with every flap of the wing. Mia had padded out into the yard, barefoot. She buried her toes in the dirt while she asked the question, face red, eyes fixed on the ground.

Mia had grown up with the painting. She knew it was her mother. She even knew why her mother had painted it and why she had hung it in the stairwell. When Mia was still a baby, her mother's coworkers had expressed concern for her delicate, developing brain.

"What will she think when she finds out it's her mother... naked?" they whispered.

Eva calmly responded, "Well, God knows she's seen my breasts often enough. She sucks on them regularly."

Needless to say, many coworkers never brought their own children to Eva's house. She wasn't surprised. She hadn't expected everyone to understand.

"Why do you want it moved?" Eva asked, a lump rising in her throat as she looked at her daughter. She was surprised at herself. She felt as though she should scream and cry. She felt as though her daughter had punched her hard in the stomach. She felt as though her daughter had just confessed she didn't really love her.

Mia shrugged. "It's just that some of my friends might not understand. They might think it's weird or something."

"It's not their business."

"I know. But still. You can't just expect everyone to be okay with the fact that your naked body is in our stairwell."

"Well, where do you suggest it go?"

"Maybe your room?"

Eva turned away from her and quickly walked into the house as tears filled her eyes.

"Can you think about it please, Mommy?" Mia called after her.

Eva went to her room and paced, tears spilling over her cheeks with reckless abandon. She stared wildly around her room. The painting didn't belong there. There was no place for it. It belonged in the stairwell, where she could see it every day when she would go up and down the stairs, through the many ups and downs of her mood. She needed it there. It wouldn't be the same if it was locked in the bedroom. No one else could see it. No one else would understand. No one else would care.

For her daughter's sake, Eva moved the painting. It was like swallowing her pride, like hiding her confidence. She hung it over her bed, directly across from the doorway so it was visible from the hallway. She never closed the door, and she made frequent trips upstairs.

She knew that many of her daughter's friends had seen the picture, but most didn't ask about it. A few did, but her daughter shrugged it off.

"My mom's an artist," she'd say. "She does lots of things."

Even in its exile, the painting smiled.

About the Author

Sarah F. Sullivan's non-fiction work has appeared on Associated Content, Yahoo! News, Lincoln, Nebraska's Star City Blog and in Elder & Leemauer's compilation, "Authors of Tomorrow." Her fiction is forthcoming in Twin Trinity Media's The Best of Unsent Letters. She lives with her husband and daughter in Lincoln, Nebraska.

Breathe

by Catherine A. MacKenzie

She looks down upon him,
her husband of sixty-odd years
prone upon the sterile bed,
the crisp white sheet up to his chin,
his weary eyes closed
and muted mouth agape,
breathing heavy,
then shallow,
sucking in the air,
grasping at life
amid whispers of death,
a mind entombed within,
lost and floating,
floundering
and shrouded in mystery
as he lingers,
while she waits
and watches
and wonders
what a mind thinks
when it is gone.
After it disappears
where does it go?
Do we ever wake
to find our life gone?

About Featured Poet:

Catherine A. MacKenzie

Cathy enjoys writing poems, short stories and essays, some of which appear in various anthologies, including those published by Chicken Soup for the Soul, *Dancing with Bear Publishing, Twin Trinity Media and Rebel Ink Press. Her writings have also won several contests.*

Along with several short stories, she is currently working on a novel.

Cathy also paints, pastels being her favorite medium and her grandchildren her favorite subjects. Cathy lives in Halifax, Nova Scotia, with her husband, and they winter in Ajijic, Mexico, where several of her works have appeared in local publications.

Contact Cathy at: writingwicket@gmail.com. Check out her website at: http://writingwicket.wordpress.com/

Words Like Glass

by John Morrison

"Let's see. Seven cents on the bread. Sorry, that's up a penny since last time. Damn war. And oh, I'll have to have stamps on that sugar. Say," Mr. Sam asked while he bagged a few items, "why do you look so tired this morning, Rosa Mae?"

She reached in her handbag to retrieve ration stamps and her coin purse. Without looking up, she explained, "I had to cover for Jessie again last night. That gout had her down again, I guess. Seven offices, I did, and that's a lot of scrubbing in ten hours."

"Lordy mercy, Gal, it sure to high heaven is. Oh, here." His hand extended toward her while he spoke. "You can take this paper home with you; I'm through with it.

"Fed up, too; ain't nothing much different today. When old Roosevelt made Eisenhower supreme over all them allied troops, I thought that might make something happen, but not yet.

"You rest up this weekend now, ya hear?"

Walking toward the door without turning, she said, "I will, Mr. Sam."

Down the block and around the corner, she walked slowly between the rows of shabby, upper south side structures toward her own apartment. The air felt a little cool to her that summer morning but not fresh. Boxed in couldn't be fresh, not like the fresh she remembered from her last Chicago neighborhood, with real homes, paved streets, and sidewalks instead of the beaten earth walkway she sauntered along.

It wasn't like mornings when she was a barefoot girl in the open spaces of the Arkansas delta. These buildings were more like big, overused boxes with people stuffed and stacked inside.

Realizing two men across the way were walking directly toward her, her throat seized and chest froze in mid-breath. She tightly squeezed the sack, her arm cradled against it.

The chief petty officer was short with a red face, and the buttons on his jacket struggled a little at keeping in his stomach as he spoke.

"Evenin', ma'am, **ahem**. We're trying to find a colored lady who lives down here somewhere by the name of, **ahem* *ahem**, Claudella Young. Do you happen to know her or where she lives?"

Rosa Mae's chest loosened enough to squeak some airy words through a knotted path to her lips. "Mrs. Young passed away about a month ago, down at the St. Thomas Infirmary."

"Oh, **ahem**, well uh, we're sorry to hear that, ma'am." He pulled a pad and pencil from his jacket, before he continued. "Uh, do you know about any other kinfolk who we might be able to get a hold of?"

"The only family Mrs. Young has—"

He noticed a tear bead on her cheek, so the chief interrupted. "Awful sorry to hear about Mrs. Young's passing. Awful sorry, **ahem**."

"The only family Mrs. Young has, that I know of, is her son. He serves in the Navy. She had no word of his whereabouts for six months before she died."

The men exchanged a quick glance at each other.

The young lieutenant said, "Thank you very much, ma'am. We're sorry to have bothered you."

With a slight nod and a brief touch to the bill of their hats, they turned and walked away.

Rosa Mae stood like a statue while their figures diminished. Hearing a distant **ahem** brought her back to awareness after what seemed like an hour of being suspended in terror. She felt as still as one of the rusty garbage cans that lined the center of the dirt stretch between the buildings.

No morning sound of tenants stirring had been able to reach her awareness, and she realized she clutched the grocery bag too tightly. She relaxed a bit.

She cleared her throat, and she continued to walk toward the particular set of black metal stairs that let her ascend to her home.

> *Japanese Premier, Kantaro Suzuki, has announced Japan will fight to the very end rather than accept unconditional surren...*

"Keeps spittin' out Philco words," she only half said with a humorless chuckle.

She clicked off the radio.

The Reverend Taylor had spoken words last Sunday, she recalled: *"We have to remember now, our fighting sons are brave and loyal boys who are guarding our peace and our shores. We must be strong. We must be patient. The Lord is on our side, Brothers and Sisters. Amen. He's gonna bring them boys home. You wait and see."*

She wanted to try those words aloud for herself, only replace 'them boys' with 'Ray', but they formed like grit in her throat. Instead, she mumbled, "Church words."

There were a few dabs of Karo Syrup left on her plate from what she had dribbled over the butter beans. Before leaving the table, she dragged it onto a bite of bread and thought of how she missed the sorghum molasses her grandmother sometimes had boiled out back, down in the delta.

Back in the bedroom, she opened the linen drawer for a clean sheet and noticed the brown leather case at the back of the drawer. It was in its spot, and usually she ignored it. That time, she couldn't let it go... so she took it from the drawer, placed it on the bed, and opened it. It was the first time in all these months she'd touched it.

Her eyes quizzically studied the sleek lines and shine of what rested inside the purple velvet contours of a tailored bed. It was sleeping like a pampered king.

As she had seen her son do, she took it out of its case and slowly polished the horn with a cloth he had neatly folded beside the royal bed. She returned it to its soft slumber.

Opening the closure of a compartment inside the case, she saw a bottle that read 'valve oil', a partially used penny-box of wooden matches, and a cork lid from a liquor bottle. She picked up the cork and brought it under her nose. There was the faintest hint of odor, like walking past the open door of one of the nearby saloons.

A preacher. His daddy was a preacher... 'least that's what he pretended to be. Why couldn't he be one too, like I tried to push him? Reverend Raymond J. Wilson, my proud boy, evangelist of promise.

Ray's daddy had used his fine-sounding words not only to squeeze every dime from the flock, but also to convince his wife there was no truth to the stories about affairs with ladies of the church. She had pretty well believed him right up until the day he disappeared with one of those ladies and all the church's money.

There she had been, alone with a six-year-old child. Her man was not just gone; he was on the lam. There she still was. She was no longer in a real house. Her reversal of fortunes had brought her down to where a cleaning lady could afford shelter to raise her boy, fighting cockroaches for space.

Night after night, she would have to go out to search for Ray when he was a boy. At least she usually knew where to look: in the alley behind the saloons. The live music played inside would find cracks where it could ooze out to freedom. It found Ray, and whispered something important in his ear while he leaned back against the rough wall, hexed in the shadows.

Ray-Raymond-Raymond Jeremiah Wilson! Sometimes it would take a shout to pierce through.

But the young Ray broke the spell often enough to run errands for the old folks in the buildings, just because they needed something. Sometimes they would give him a coin or two.

He also would hang around Moody's filling station, picking up a penny or nickel doing Lord knows what or for whom. It had taken him nearly a year, but he had saved eight dollars and twenty-five cents for his first beat-up old cornet.

He had spent hours outside Tubby T's door in hope the old, drunk horn player would wake up long enough to show him a few more notes. Because Tubby T was enormous in size and blind, Ray had done lots of things to help him out, so he usually obliged.

Ray carried the horn's mouthpiece around in his pocket all the time, blowing through it as often as he could to strengthen the muscles in his lips into a well-defined embrasure.

Once, Rosa Mae spoke to the Reverend Taylor about the sinful path Ray seemed destined to tread.

"I've tried talking to that boy too, Mrs. Wilson," he had said. "It ain't no use. Besides, we can't all be preachers. Some's got to carry other loads. Now, some's just got to do the preachin', but others gotta do what's left. Just leave that boy do what the good Lord tells him."

More words... More words to strip pages of hope from the storybook Rosa Mae Wilson had written for herself. Then the war came with its threat of changing her ending even more.

Sitting on the side of the bed, the shiny trumpet

asleep in the open case beside her, she reached for it again. Not gingerly, as before, but jarring it from its rest with her firm grip, which began to squeeze and tighten more. Suddenly, she raised it above her head and released a cry, "Damn you, Ray!" bringing it down sharply, the bell hitting the edge of the case, putting a large dent in it.

She struck the case over and over. Noticing the newspaper lying on the bed beside the case, with a headline touting 'Peace Efforts Continue', she turned on it with her beating. "Damn you war!"

Her eyes fell toward her son's picture, its edge wedged under the wooden frame of the mirror mounted on the wall near the chest of drawers. She had received the picture in the mail after he completed basic training.

Look at you, all handsome in that sailor suit, shined up and smiling like you're on some kind of picnic!

She came up from the bed and lunged toward the picture. Not noticing her own grimacing image in the mirror, she cried out at Ray's image, "You selfish, no count... you're no better than a common, black-assed street nigger!"

While she sobbed, she repeatedly struck out at the picture until the mirror cracked. She hit and hit until the glass shattered, raining down to bite her arms on its way to the floor, falling sharply like the words that continually rewrote her life. She hit until, finally, she collapsed to her knees with blood from her arms spotting the pieces of glass and linoleum. She had energy only to cry.

Night slipped into the ghetto, offering a deep gray wash to the trash outside, that hid the dirt on the few ragged children still at play on the walkway with their sticks and tin cans. Still exhausted, Rosa Mae dragged herself to the window and raised it a bit.

It was Saturday, and the night people who had begun to emerge from their apartments caught her eyes.

They shuffled along in their colorful finery toward the faint sounds of music that drifted from the hellholes; the sounds that, through the years, she had fervently ignored. Lured like lost sheep, they followed its call to the edge of iniquity's cliff and jumped, one by one. Slowly she shook her head from side to side, while she turned toward the bed and stretched out on her back.

She stared at the single electric cord that dangled a bulb a few feet down from the center of the ceiling. She couldn't tune out the sound. Several bands could be heard from different nightspots, forming one abstract fugue that drifted through her window.

Maybe, as the first available diversion from what these times and this day had offered, she latched hold of what she heard and closed her eyes. Past the burn in her belly, there was a distasteful security in it, like the needed protection accompanying the return home of even a scoundrel husband.

She felt a little rested but didn't fully agree with what her body was doing. She only watched while it got up and moved toward the door.

It was fully dark when she reached the alley behind Moody's filling station. She thought about how long it had been since her trips down there to fetch Ray back home. The familiar smell of oil-soaked dirt beneath her feet rose to repel her. Yet, beneath the space where anger and disgust would rise over his inconsiderate behavior, the hint of a different current moved, tugging. He was her baby, and this strip of strewn bottles and wrecked car engines next to the rear of dives had been like a shrine to him.

Carefully and with purpose, she made her way to the back of the Narrow Escape, a cellar blues club below an abandoned two-story office building. The back entrance, at the foot of a sunken concrete stairwell, was never used. The door had been secured years ago, and junk had accumulated in front of it.

Someone, probably Ray, had placed a row of small,

scrap I-beams from the old foundry to bridge the sides of the stairwell. This created a vantage spot for sitting near and peering through the transom window above the door.

Rosa Mae watched her body commit an unnatural act when she stepped on the I-beams. She positioned herself for a panoramic view through the dirty window, to see and condemn what, like a sponge, her son had absorbed through and through, against God's and her wishes. She would stare it down with straight eyes, curse its encroachment.

It was already crowded inside. Most faces were strange, but a few she recognized, one from her own building. Most were smiling, a few were dancing, but many sat at the mismatched restaurant booths or folding card tables. Surprisingly, not all were drinking.

One table of four men played cards under a cloud of thick cigar smoke hugging the air above their game. People talked and laughed, and when the band finished a song, they turned toward it, applauded and shouted.

A man from the crowd approached Tubby T's chair at the front edge of the bandstand and said something close to his ear. The blind man leaned his chair back, reached in his pocket, and retrieved a few coins, which he placed in the outstretched hand before him. In return, he was handed a half-pint bottle of amber liquid. He released a big laugh, and then he unscrewed the cap and tipped it to his lips, tilting back his head until the bottle was upright. His head looked small above the bulging neck and massive body, and the contents of the bottle churned and bubbled as though resisting its drain into the dark throat of a whale. Without a breath, it was emptied, and Tubby T pitched it to the floor.

He picked up his horn again, and they started to play another tune. Rosa Mae listened without motion for a long time while the sound landed on ears hardened by time.

She looked at the faces of the players—piano, bass, drums and trumpet. She looked for sin. In its place was a gentle bond between partners that seemed to reach past everything else.

She heard exchanges of innovative musical phrases, counter-melodies and rhythms contributed by each player. She noticed glances and nods between them that even the blind man seemed to catch.

She had come to visit sin, to glare hard-eyed at it for having ripped the last page from her book of dreams. But her eyes were soft... and damp.

What she saw was Ray. What she heard were his meanings.

She saw his face as a little boy, tiny, eager. When he grew and changed so much, he didn't really lose that inside smile or the gleaming dot of light in each of his eyes, because she could see it now, like the folks through the dirty window must have seen it.

It hadn't been lost... he just had to look for the place it would fit in a world where most parts don't match, a place that, at least until the bandage curled up and fell off the next day, disguised the poverty and hardships, and the war that wouldn't end.

She felt empty and full at the same time.

"Son," after a while she heard herself speak aloud, as if Ray were beside her, listening, "it's all right. It's... it's all right, Ray. It don't matter if you're no preacher or not. You were born spreadin' promise."

The allied armies kept up pressure all
along the line yesterday...

She listened to crackly words from a radio with speakers brittle and torn by too many years. The Philco sat on her small kitchen table and spoke of war. She picked at the last of the black-eyed peas and pepper sauce on her plate.

There was a knock.

Her heart flinched and went still for a few beats.

When she moved toward the door, fear tweezed at her skin. While she slid back the night bolt, she heard a sound in the hall.

Too familiar. Too recent.

Ahem* *ahem

About the Author

John's writing collection through the years is small. His career in retail advertising offered an avenue of release for much of his creative urges. However, the occasional short story or poem worked its way into his thoughts in a way he couldn't ignore. Only then, would it wind up being toyed with on paper.

In 1997, he retired from JC Penney in Dallas. The next year, he and his wife, Jan, moved back home to Arkansas. After he lost Jan a few years ago, John joined a local writers critique group to help fill some time. He dug out some old stories, brushed them up, read them to the group, and received encouragement to make submissions.

Words Like Glass *was his first such attempt, entered in the* Elements of Life *anthology contest sponsored by* Accentuate Writers Forum. *To his surprise, he received the honor of having submitted the winning entry.*

One Soul Quivering

by Lisa Lee Smith

Like a bird in the hand
of other-worldly forgiveness
needing uncertainty
for the sake of free will
I'm crying out, "If you say so!"
but for now I am too wary
of the slippery rocks
to make my way across those pristine waves.

Out by the back door
my boot-heels are cooling
and I wait near your mind
to learn its thoughts
while your bountiful snore
aims itself toward the
peeled, curly wings
on the ceiling. Another project undone!

Someday I'll leave you here
with that half-crazy dog
to escape from the past through
a stream of perfume
patched blue jeans
sunflower seeds
candy cigarettes
and peacock colors
not to mention the heartless laughter of truth.

Funny how those
who know the least
about our life
think they have all the answers
about what we should be.
I am just one soul quivering
and inching forward
to my plaintive sleep still to come.

About Featured Poet

Lisa Lee Smith

Lisa Lee Smith grew up reading novels, poetry and the occasional cereal box, while letting her thoughts run wild around the western United States. A copy of Island of the Blue Dolphins *by Scott O'Dell remains on Lisa's crowded shelves, a reminder of those days when she fully realized a vivid imagination and a good book could take her anywhere in the world.*

After college and graduate school, Lisa followed her heart through freelance writing. About nine years later, she discovered Accentuate Services and joined the online forum.

In addition to the written word, Lisa believes that life with her husband, time spent with animals, the love of old movies and a view of snow-covered mountains are among the best gifts the universe offers. Uncontrollable laughter and overwhelming tears are right up there too.

Lisa treasures old photos, and she is forever grateful to the loved ones her soul will never forget.

Cries for Help

by Eric Patterson

Even though he knew he shouldn't do it, Tim turned his head and stole a peek at the woman across the room. She was intoxicating. Her silky brown hair lay against the back of her yellow sweater. Her skin, darker than his, was tan and smooth. She appeared to be of Arabic descent, maybe half, balanced with Caucasian. She was slender, with curves in all the right places.

Look over here, Tim thought. He knew she could feel him stare at her. He wanted her to see his spiked-up gelled hair that he'd combed that morning especially for her. *Come on, let me see those big brown eyes.*

He knew her eyes were as brown as his own. They had exchanged glances over the past couple of weeks.

The room was completely silent when the moment Tim had waited for finally arrived. She slowly turned her head in his direction.

Here it comes, Tim thought. *Don't be a chicken. Just keep staring, and see what happens.* Finally, their eyes locked. *Don't look away like last time.*

The woman's red lips curled upward while she continued her gaze. Tim smiled. His body grew hot, but he forced himself to continue the connection.

Piercing the silence, a loud voice interrupted their flirtation. "Okay, now that we've been able to pray silently for whatever was on your hearts, let's worship in song to honor and praise Jesus."

The congregation, including the brown-haired beauty, opened their song books while the organ music played.

That's just great. I need to find a new hunting ground.

He had tired of frequenting nightclubs to search for suitable women to date. He was almost thirty years old, and the women in the clubs all looked twenty-one, which meant he probably looked too mature for them. He figured church was the perfect place to pick up an unsuspecting female, one who wouldn't realize what he was really after. If only he weren't so damned shy around women, he might have stood half a chance.

Tim vacated the church before the sermon's conclusion. When he walked out the door, an old man stood hunched over with a white Styrofoam cup in his hand. His face was covered with gray stubble, and he reeked of urine.

"Can you help an old vet out with some spare change?"

Tim's right pant pocket bulged with coins, and they jingled with each step. He shook his head. "Sorry, don't have any."

"God bless you!" said the man to Tim's back.

"For what?" Tim mumbled, but the man didn't hear.

Tim pretended not to hear the blessing. Instead, he rummaged through his pocket, through the handful of loose change, and grabbed his keychain. He aimed it at his Honda, and the alarm chirped two short beeps, signaling the unlocking of the doors. He slid into his car, started it, revved the engine, backed out and sped away. He had nowhere to go but home, a small, one-bedroom apartment near the ocean, close enough to hear the waves crash on the shore.

When he was about to pull onto the freeway, he saw a car ahead with its hood raised. Smoke billowed in the air like the car was overheating. An old woman who wore large sunglasses was strapped in the passenger seat, and an elderly man leaned near the road and waved his hat at Tim. Tim stared but didn't ease up on the gas pedal.

When the old man realized Tim had no intention to stop, he yelled, "Go to hell, you selfish jerk!"

The words hit Tim hard. All the way home, he couldn't get the old couple out of his head.

After he arrived at his apartment, he tried to take a nap, but he couldn't stop reliving that reprehensible moment earlier that afternoon. He surely didn't want to go to hell, and he didn't want to be a jerk either. Maybe the old man was on the money. He wondered why he hadn't stopped to help them. He realized stopping would have obligated him to offer assistance. He wasn't willing to donate time to others. Tim wished to be a better person, one who would help people when they needed it. The problem was, he found no joy in helping others, no fulfillment, no pleasure. At the same time, he liked being egotistical and self-centered, if only because it sometimes did bring him pleasure, even if short-lived. Tim found himself wishing selfishly that he could enjoy helping others, and then there would be something in it for him.

He didn't pray often, except to become a partner at his law firm. He had wanted that desperately. Yet, that night, while Tim lay in bed, he folded his hands together as he'd done as a small child, and he prayed. "Hi, God. It's me, Tim. I know I haven't talked to you in a while, and I know I've been quite a sinner, but I want to change. It's just too difficult. I was wondering if maybe you could help me be a better person... you know, someone who helps the needy and less fortunate, that kind of stuff. I just don't think I can do it without your help. Amen."

The buzzing cellphone startled Tim awake. He opened one eye and waited for it to focus. The phone rested on top of his chest like an alarm clock on a nightstand, and he lay on the couch in the living room, not where he remembered falling asleep. Slowly, he flipped his phone open and answered, "Hello?"

"Tim! Where are you?"

"Home, Jeff, trying to get some sleep. What are you doing calling me at...," he pulled his phone away from his face so he could see the time, "eight in the morning? You'd better have a good explanation for this."

"Uh, how about you're late for work?" Jeff responded.

"Nice try, Jeff. You know I don't work on Mondays. I haven't worked Mondays for over a year—"

"It's Tuesday, Tim. Please don't tell me you're going to try that one on Richard. He's in no mood today. He yelled at Shelly this morning when she forgot to put sugar in his coffee, and you know what he said right after throwing a few f-bombs? He said, 'Where the hell is Tim?' That's why I'm calling you, buddy. You better get your ass in here now." Jeff paused then quickly said, "Oh, shit. Here he comes. Gotta go."

"Jeff?" Tim turned off his phone and threw it on the floor. He rose and walked to his computer to check the date. Sure enough, it was Tuesday.

What the hell happened?

Tim couldn't remember anything past lying down to take a nap on Sunday, after church. Somehow, he had lost a day. He scratched the back of his head and looked around the room, wondering how he ended up on the couch, too. He'd never been known to sleepwalk, and he hadn't been sick or drunk. He wondered if someone had broken in and drugged him, but the apartment seemed in order, nothing broken, stolen or out of place.

Tim raced to the door and searched for any signs of a forced entry. After finding none, he checked each window throughout the apartment. Everything appeared normal.

"I don't have time for this. I'm late for work. Shit!"

After a three-minute shower, he quickly dressed and rushed out to his car.

The sun had already started its day, climbing up the sky and warming everything its rays touched over smoggy Los Angeles. Hastily, Tim passed his favorite coffee shop without any hesitation. His little red convertible sports car flew down the road. After a short cruise on the freeway, he took the downtown exit toward his office building.

He pulled up to the red traffic light where he didn't intend to fully stop and noticed a bearded man on the curb with a cardboard sign in his filthy hands. While he turned the corner, he read the sign:

I could use any help at all

Tim usually ignored these men and their signs, but that time he felt compelled to stop. He skidded to a halt on the side of the road. Still in a hurry, he jumped out of his car, and while running toward the man, he thumbed through his wallet, searching for money to give to the vagabond. Out of breath, he reached the man and said, "Hi there. What kind of help do you need?"

The man, seemingly half-asleep, looked up at Tim's six-foot frame and said, "Like the sign says, any help would be good. How much can you afford?"

Tim stuffed a twenty dollar bill back in his wallet and then grabbed the whole stack of bills from inside. He folded the bills in half, grabbed the man's dirty hand and placed the wad of money in it.

"I can afford to give you all of it," replied Tim.

The money was like a splash of cold water in the face. The ragged man's eyes popped open and he stared at all the money.

"Thank you!" The stranger glanced upward, but Tim had already run back to his car. The man tried his best to stand without staggering too much. He said it again, this time more forcefully. "Thank you!"

Tim raised his hand as he sped away, acknowledging the man's grateful gesture.

Before he reached the office, Tim second-guessed himself. *What the hell did I just do? I just gave a complete stranger over four hundred dollars. What if he uses it all on booze?* Tim shook his head, trying to rattle the thoughts from his mind.

The elevator opened, and before Tim could step onto the office floor, his highly agitated boss, Richard, stood in front of him with his arms folded. Tim was dumbfounded. He froze. Before the doors could close all the way, his angry boss stuck his arm in the middle, forcing them to reopen. The elevator alarm bell rang, so Tim scurried out.

Richard checked his watch. "Do you know what time it is?"

"Yes, sorry. I, uh... overslept."

"You what?" Richard's face contorted into a scowl.

"Calm down, Dick," Tim replied. "You're acting like someone forgot to put sugar in your coffee or something."

Richard pointed at Tim. "I'm going to let it slide this time, buddy boy. Don't let it happen again. And don't call me Dick. Not even my mother has that pleasure."

He turned to storm away, but stopped and faced Tim again, saying, "And one more thing: If you have aspirations to make partner, this is not the way to pursue that."

Tim swallowed and then walked to his cubicle. His phone rang the moment he sat. He picked up the receiver.

"Remind me not to tell you about Richard's coffee mishaps any more," Jeff said on the other end of the line.

"You heard our conversation?" Tim asked.

"Conversation? Are you kidding? I'm surprised you can still walk after the butt-reaming you just took."

"Did anyone else hear?" asked Tim.

"The whole clerical staff heard, but don't worry about it. Meet me for lunch... Jimmy's Café at noon."

"Wake up, sleepyhead."

Billy's eyes fluttered open. He smiled when he recognized his mother's face.

"How's my favorite son, tonight?" Lisa asked.

"I'm your only son, Mom."

"Does that make me your favorite mother?" Lisa asked, her voice playfully teasing.

"Sure, Mom."

"Hey, guess what!" Lisa suddenly shouted.

"What?"

"I have a surprise waiting for you when you come home."

Billy slowly sat up in his bed. "What is it?"

"Well, the K9 unit officially retired a German shepherd today. He was shot last month but has been recovering nicely, and you know how I'm a sucker for taking in strays."

"Thanks, Mom." Billy reached to give her a hug, but the IV tubing connected to his arm wouldn't allow him to reach that far.

Lisa moved closer and leaned over her ten-year-old son, kissing him on the forehead. "I'll see you later, Billy. I have to get to work."

Billy sat taller in his hospital bed and said, "Like that, mom? Where's your uniform? This kind of looks like... well, it makes you look like a hooker."

Lisa adjusted her black-lace teddy. One of her boobs had almost slipped out, necessitating the retying of the belt of her trench coat that concealed her stunning figure. Her mouth opened wide. "A what?"

"You know... a prostitute."

"Yes, I know what a hooker is, but where did you hear that term?"

"My mom's a police officer."

"Very funny. It just so happens that I will be playing the part of a hooker at work tonight."

Billy's jaw dropped.

"No, silly," Lisa said. "I'm dressed like one so I can arrest someone trying to pay for the services of a prostitute."

"Do you mean it's illegal to pay for a prostitute?"

"That's right," Lisa responded. "Now, get some sleep. You never know when that phone's gonna ring. You need to always be well-rested."

She pulled his brown bangs aside and kissed his forehead again, leaving another dark imprint of a pair of luscious, red lips.

Billy looked at his mother's face. "Wearing all that dark eye makeup should be illegal, too."

"I love you, honey."

"I love you, too, mom. Be careful."

A plain-clothes cop dropped Lisa off at a corner where there were known to be plenty of prostitutes who worked the street. Dressed in tight, shiny black boots that ran all the way up her shapely legs and a silky black teddy loosely covered by her black trench coat, Lisa swaggered across the street toward the liquor store. Her long brown hair cascaded toward her cleavage. She stood outside the door, one foot against the brick wall, and waited. Because her knee was bent, the trench coat separated enough to expose the creaminess of one of her thighs.

"Nuh-uh, no way!" a woman shouted. She walked out of the liquor store with a brown paper bag in her hand. She was dark-skinned with long blonde hair, obviously fake.

Alarmed, Lisa stood tall. "What's the problem?"

"This is my spot." The black woman shook her finger in Lisa's face. "Ain't no white trash gonna take my spot from me."

"Relax," Lisa responded. "There's plenty of action on this corner for the two of us. And get your finger out of my face before I break it."

The woman didn't budge. Instead, she said, "Are you threatening me, bitch?"

Lisa didn't have the time or patience for this. The boots were unbearable, and the sooner she could make her arrest of some unsuspecting John, the faster she'd be back in the office writing up her report.

Lisa grabbed the woman's finger, spun her around, and rammed her head against the brick wall. "Why can't people just learn to share?"

The hooker fell hard to the ground. Touching the bloody gash on her forehead, she said, "You must have a death wish, bitch. Marvin's gonna mess you up. You know how much money he loses if I don't pull my tricks?"

Lisa extended her hand. "Here, let me take a look at your head."

Dismissing the gesture, the woman straightened her wig, picked herself up off the ground, and staggered awkwardly in her high-heeled shoes down the sidewalk.

Lisa pulled a mirror from her little black purse and checked her makeup. From the corner of her eye, she noticed a red sports car slowly creep by. Quickly, she flipped her mirror shut and walked to the curb. The passenger-side window was down so she leaned over and with her ruby red lips said, "Looking for a date?"

Tim gave a shy smile. "Oh, not me. I was just admiring the view. You're very pretty."

"You're not so bad yourself," Lisa replied. "So what da ya say?"

"Sorry," said Tim. "I don't do that sort of thing."

A rude voice interrupted their conversation. "That's the white bitch, right there."

Lisa turned her head and said under her breath, "Oh, shit."

The prostitute and her pimp were strutting directly toward her. The pimp wore a flashy yellow hat, and he was walking with a purpose.

Lisa panicked and said, "Come on, man, help me out."

Surprised by his own actions, Tim leaned over the seat and opened the passenger door.

Lisa jumped into the car and exclaimed, "Let's get the hell out of here!"

Tim pulled back onto the street. "Where to?"

"That depends," Lisa answered.

"Depends on what?"

Lisa turned toward Tim, licked her shiny red lips slowly and said, "That depends on what you want to do."

"You better run!" screamed the prostitute with her middle finger in the air.

"Friend of yours?" asked Tim.

"Hardly."

Tim withdrew his wallet and opened it shakily. He counted out two hundred dollars and held it toward her.

"Here," he said.

"What do I have to do to earn this?"

Tim's face turned red. "No, no, you have the wrong idea. I don't want to buy your services, although you could probably charge people just to look at how beautiful you are. You asked for help, so I want to help you. Will two hundred dollars keep you off the street for the rest of the night?"

"Are you for real?" asked Lisa.

"I don't mean to offend you," Tim said.

"Oh, I'm not offended," Lisa replied. "I'm shocked, and that's not an easy thing to do to me." Lisa pushed away his handful of cash. "Keep your money."

Tim looked bewildered. "But I thought you said you needed help."

"That's not the kind of help I was looking for. Pull over up here, please."

They drove through the entrance of a gas station. "Here you go. Be careful out there."

"You're one to talk," Lisa replied. "I'm not the one picking up total strangers."

"Not yet, you're not. By the way, I'm Tim." He thrust his hand out the window.

Lisa hesitated, sighed, and then grabbed his hand and shook it. "Lisa."

"Well, now. I guess you're not a total stranger any more, just a stranger... a very pretty stranger."

Lisa smiled. "Thanks for the ride... Tim."

"Be safe." He waved and pulled away from the curb.

Again, he questioned himself, the thoughts bouncing around in his head.

What the hell did I just do back there?

Did I really just try to give a prostitute two hundred dollars?

This is just too strange...

Then another thought rattled in his brain: *What the hell happened to Monday?*

Lost in thought while stopped at a red light, Tim caught a glimpse of a Hispanic woman stumbling in the dark toward his car. Her arms, which were flailing in the air, were what caught his eye. The light turned green, and he smashed down on the accelerator with his foot, not wanting to get involved with the frantic woman.

"Ayuda! Ayuda!"

Tim pretended not to notice her, at least not until she spoke in English.

"Help me! Help me!"

He knew what those words meant. Quickly, he pulled his car over to the curb.

The woman put her head in his car and yelled, "*Mi nino! Mi nino!*"

Not knowing what the woman was yelling about, Tim jumped out of his car and followed her while she raced back from where she had come. A few yards away, she dropped to the ground and pulled a boy's head to her chest. She cried and yelled words in Spanish Tim couldn't understand. The boy's white t-shirt was stained with blood. He appeared to have some sort of wound near his stomach, where most of the blood was concentrated.

Tim lifted the boy's t-shirt and saw the blood gushing out of a two-inch slash in his side. Hastily, he grabbed the woman's hand and placed it firmly on the stab wound while the boy groaned in agony. He helped the boy stand and motioned for them to follow him back to his car.

"Gracias! Gracias!" the woman repeated.

They screeched into the driveway of the emergency room entrance at the hospital. Tim ran around the car and cradled the boy. He carried him into the building. The woman was determined not to lift her hand from her son's wound. Again, while fighting through the tears, she uttered the same words: "Gracias! Gracias!"

Tim barged through the emergency room doors and yelled, "We need help! This boy's been stabbed, and he's bleeding to death!"

A dark-haired nurse with her hair pinned up rushed toward him and said, "Bring him this way."

The nurse led them to an examination room in the back. Tim placed the boy on the table and backed away to leave.

Before he could disappear, the nurse said, "The police are gonna wanna talk to you."

"I didn't see anything," Tim replied, and he turned away. "The mom was there. They can ask her."

He found himself questioning his actions again while he trudged down the corridor toward the exit.

What has gotten into me?

I'll help a woman and her dying son to come to the hospital, but I won't stay for the police.

Lost in thought, Tim passed a boy who tried desperately to get a drink of water from a fountain. He would have kept walking, but the boy yelled out, "A little help, please!"

Tim stopped and turned back toward the brown-haired boy. He wore a blue gown and had IV tubing attached to lumens coming out of his chest, just below the collarbone. He pushed a pole with a digital machine attached to it, and an IV bag hanging from the hook at the top of the pole. He also had a bandage wrapped around his leg, where slightly larger lumens dangled over the top of the bandaging. Tim hadn't seen anything like that before, so he didn't know why the boy needed it. He walked toward the boy, whose eyes were yellowed and his skin was dry and looked loose and thin. He had dark circles under his eyes as well.

"What do you need, kid?"

"A new kidney or two would be nice, but I'll settle for a drink of water."

While smiling, Tim thought about how amazing it was that this kid, who looked like he was dying, still had a sense of humor. Noticing the boy lacked the strength to do it himself, he pressed the button to force the water to shoot outward. The boy leaned over and shook while he strained to stay hunched in the same position.

Before he finished drinking, a sharp female's voice rang out from near the entrance door. "Billy! What are you doing out of your room?"

Tim gazed in her direction. The tapping of her black boots echoed down the hallway. It was Lisa, and she was still dressed to kill.

"Is that your mom?" asked Tim.

Billy stopped lapping at the water and glanced at her. "Yeah, but those aren't her regular clothes. She's not a hooker. She's a cop."

Lisa stopped in front of them and folded her arms, waiting for an answer from her son, while at the same time, concealing her cleavage, which was busting out of her coat. The belt around her waist was not adequately performing its job.

"A guy could die of thirst waiting in his room for someone to answer the buzzer," Billy said.

"Thank you for helping him get a drink," Lisa said to Tim, "but Billy knows he's on fluid restriction for his kidney condition. He's not supposed to be drinking this water."

"Ah, Mom, it was just a little sip," Billy said.

Lisa tried to give him a disapproving look, but her eyes sparkled with laughter and Billy knew she wasn't really mad at him. Billy smiled up at her, and then she finally looked up at Tim. Her eyes lit with recognition.

"Tim?" she asked.

"Lisa? Well, I guess we're not even considered strangers any more."

"You two know each other?" asked Billy.

Tim stared into Lisa's brown eyes that were highlighted with long black eyelashes.

"I was just telling your mom earlier tonight how she's the prettiest cop on the force."

Lisa looked shocked. "You knew?"

"No, Billy just told me."

"Billy, I thought I told you not to tell people I'm a cop!"

"You'd want him to think you're a hooker instead?" Billy asked.

"Billy!" Lisa said, laughing nervously. She reached out and grabbed Billy by the shoulders, changing gears and turning him around toward his hospital room. "Come on, Billy. Let's get you back to the room and let the nurse know you had some fluids that weren't on their list."

"Ah, Mom. She won't let me have any juice now," Billy whined.

"I'm sorry, Billy, but we don't want to take any chances, do we?"

Billy didn't answer. He looked down at his feet and shuffled them, pouting.

Tim felt awkward and didn't know what to do. He reached in his front shirt pocket and grabbed his business card.

"Hey," he said, interrupting the awkward moment. "Let me give you my card, you know, in case you need to reach me or something."

He held it out toward Lisa.

"What is it that you do?" she asked, while she took the card.

"I help people."

Lisa noticed the ATTORNEY AT LAW on the card under his name.

"Did you follow me here?" Lisa asked.

"I was here before you," Tim replied.

"Why are you here?" she asked, then realized she sounded like a cop, grilling a witness. "I mean, is someone you know sick or in the hospital?"

"Uhm, no," Tim said. "I was helping someone." A pause passed between them. "Anyway... it was nice bumping into you again, but I've gotta go."

"Okay," Lisa said. "I'll be sure to look you up should the need arise."

"In your line of work, I'm sure it will." Tim smiled. "Call me for any need, not just the legal ones." Tim turned around and cringed. He hoped Lisa didn't think that sounded as perverted as he did, in retrospect.

Tim could hear Lisa and Billy talking as he walked away.

"Are you off work now, Mom?"

"No, Billy. I'm just on my lunch break. You know I work the late shift."

Tim pulled into a bar he frequented. He needed a stiff drink to help him figure out the peculiar things he'd been doing. Maybe some strong spirits could also help reveal what had happened to him on Monday.

He straddled a stool at the bar in his usual place. "Hi, Bob!"

Bob, the bartender, looked like he hadn't shaved in a month. He acknowledged Tim by sliding him a rum and cola.

It was a slow night, only a couple of other people sitting at a table near the jukebox.

Tim pulled out the straw and chugged down his drink, the ice stacking on his lips. He slammed the glass back on the counter and said, "I think I'm gonna need some stronger stuff tonight, Bob. Let's go with 151-proof."

"Tough day, Tim?" asked Bob.

"Lost day, more like it."

Bob crinkled his eyebrows. "Care to explain?"

He handed Tim his stronger rum and Coke.

"Did I come in here on Monday?" Tim took a gulp of his drink and grimaced.

"Of course not, Tim. You're a working man. Frankly, I'm surprised to see you in here today."

"Let me ask you something, Bob," Tim said, "and be totally honest with me."

"Okay," Bob agreed.

"Would you say I'm a helpful person?"

Bob scratched his chin and hesitated. "To be brutally honest, Tim, you wouldn't help a stranger buy a drink who was short a lousy quarter, and I know because I've seen it happen."

"Exactly!" Tim cried out. "But something in me has changed, and I don't know how."

"What are you talking about?"

Excitedly, and halfway off balance, Tim jumped from his stool. "Ask me to help you do something... anything."

"No problem," said Bob. He spun around and grabbed a broom from the corner. "Here, go sweep the floor."

Tim waited for the feeling, the obligation to help like he had been experiencing these last few days. Nothing.

"No thanks."

Tim plopped down on the bar stool and thought, What's different?

"Ask me again."

"Sure," Bob agreed. "Please sweep the floor."

"No, no, you're not asking me for help. You're telling me to do something. Try asking me."

Bob blew out a big breath. "Will you please help me sweep the floor?"

Tim popped up from his stool and extended his arm. "Hand me that broom."

He took the broom and started to sweep the floor.

That's it! Help.

"Okay, one more request."

"What's this all about, Tim?" Bob asked.

"Humor me. Ask me to help you do something you know I will say no to. Make sure you ask and be sure to use the word help."

Bob pointed at the other two people near the jukebox. "Help me buy those two a drink."

Tim slapped ten bucks on the bar and said, "That's too easy. Try again."

Bob thought for a moment, and then he walked over to the corner of the room. He kneeled and gingerly plucked some pieces of a broken beer bottle out of the trash can. Nonchalantly, he walked back and set three shards of glass on the counter. "Can you please help me eat this glass?"

Tim listened to the absurdity of the question but then found himself picking up the glass, wondering the best way to eat it without cutting his throat. Slowly, he began to put the first piece of glass up to his lips.

"What the hell are you doing?" Bob asked.

"You said you needed help."

"No, I don't need help eating glass. What's wrong with you? You know what? I think you'd better leave. You're freaking me out. You okay to drive?"

Tim polished off his drink and said, "Yeah, yeah, no problem."

Lisa filed another report before she left the police station. She asked her partner to make a quick stop at the hospital so she could see her son once more before hitting another street corner. On the way, she saw a small red sports car that had been pulled over by a black and white police car with its twirling blue lights. She recognized the sports car as Tim's vehicle.

She hesitated and then said, "Pull over here, Joe."

"You sure, Lisa?" her partner asked. "Looks like a routine drunk driving stop."

He turned on his twirling light that was up by the dash to show the other police officer they were in an unmarked police car.

Tim stood outside his Honda and leaned against the door while the uniformed officer in front of him took his license and insurance information from Tim's outstretched hand.

The sexy vice detective jumped from the car and strutted her long legs toward the other cop. It was dark, but the blue lights lit up the area fairly well. "Officer Cline? Is that you?"

"Detective Jenkins, looking good tonight," Cline replied.

"Thanks." Lisa glanced over at Tim and could tell he was agitated. "Hey, what did you stop him for?"

"He was speeding, about twenty over," Cline answered.

"Uhm, why don't you let me take care of this one? He's a friend of mine."

Officer Cline hesitated a moment, then looked at his notebook where he hadn't written anything on the citation yet, and said, "All right, for you, no problem."

"Thanks, Cline. I owe you one."

Officer Cline jumped in his car and drove away, turning off his lights when he pulled back onto the road.

Lisa put a warm, comforting hand on Tim's shoulder. "Tim, you all right?" she asked.

"I think so."

Lisa glanced back at her partner who waited in the car and said, "Well, why don't you head home and get some rest? We'll let you go on the speeding ticket if you promise to go right home."

"Thanks, Lisa. You're pretty, and you're wonderful," Tim said. "You're pretty wonderful." He chuckled at himself.

"Have you been drinking?" Lisa asked.

"I had a couple, but I'm fine, really," he said. "I'll be fine. Thanks for your help."

There's that word again, but don't worry. No one asked for help this time.

Lisa patted his shoulder. "Drive safely."

"Lisa?" said Tim.

"Yes."

Tim gazed longingly at her from head to boot. "Will you go out with me?"

"Get home, Tim, and we'll talk about it tomorrow." She turned away, her trench coat swooping through the air.

When she climbed back in the unmarked police vehicle, Tim could hear Lisa say to her partner, "He's okay. Let's get out of here."

They drove away toward the hospital.

Tim wasted no time getting back on the road. He planned to go straight home, just like he had promised, but within a mile of driving, he noticed a car parked along the side of the road. The dome light was on. A couple of hundred yards ahead, he passed two people. One was carrying what looked to be a gasoline can. These two strangers didn't need to ask for help for Tim to realize they needed it.

A battle raged in Tim's head.

Should I help them or mind my own business?

Tim pulled his foot off the accelerator. He looked up and searched the rearview mirror to try to catch a glimpse of the people. It was dark, and he was drunk, so his eyes stayed glued to the mirror longer than they should have. By the time he heard his tires grind in the gravel on the side of the road, it was already too late. He turned to look out the front windshield and saw the telephone pole race toward him. He slammed on the brakes and closed his eyes.

Lisa looked through the window in her son's room and saw him sleeping peacefully. Mindful not to disturb him, she kissed her hand and placed it gently on the door.

"I'll see you when I get off work," she whispered.

While returning to the street corner, Lisa and her

partner recognized Tim's red car with its front end smashed up against a telephone pole. Smoke escaped what was left of the grill. The windshield had been cracked severely and had splotches of Tim's blood smeared on it.

Lisa's partner turned on his twirling blue light and pulled over on the opposite side of the road from the wreckage.

"What have I done?" Lisa cried. She shoved the door open and stumbled out of the vehicle. Awkwardly, she ran across the deserted street as best she could in her tall boots to see if Tim was all right. When she made it to the driver's side window that had shattered, Lisa looked inside and shouted, "Tim! Tim!"

She pulled on the door, but it wouldn't budge.

Tim's unresponsive face was a bloody mess with massive cuts and gashes. The air bag had deflated from several punctures. Tim was not wearing his seat belt, which explained why the windshield was cracked and his head was badly cut.

The sirens of the fire truck and the ambulance could be heard screaming in the distance.

"Help us!" Lisa screamed in desperation, as if the people in the emergency vehicles could hear her from all the way down the street.

Tim's ears must have still had some life in them because when he heard Lisa yell the word, help, he awoke and turned toward her. With blood on his lips, he gurgled, "How can I help you?"

Startled, Lisa shouted, "Tim! You're... you're awake! Keep talking to me. Where do you want to go on our date?"

Tim had already lost consciousness again before she finished her sentence.

After flashing her badge, Lisa was permitted to watch the medical team work on Tim through the large trauma unit's window at the hospital. The doctors furiously pumped Tim's chest with their hands. They gave him numerous injections. They tried everything they could, but in the end, there was nothing they could do to keep him alive. Because his driver's license stated he was an organ donor, the doctor made a notation on the chart and ordered an intern to contact the procurement team to get the patient on life support to keep his organs viable until next of kin could be contacted and he could be typed and processed by UNOS.

Lisa watched while the trauma team shook their heads and snapped off their gloves. Her nose burned as tears filled her eyes and her vision blurred.

The last she saw of Tim was when the procurement team came into the room and hooked the machines up to his still form.

Early that morning, when the sun was just peaking over the horizon, Lisa found herself in her police captain's office, volunteering to head to Tim's apartment to find his next of kin. She offered that it only made sense, since she was first on the accident scene. The captain wasn't initially keen on letting her go to the apartment and try to contact the landlord, because it wasn't her area of police work, but the pleading in her eyes caused him to relent and agree. Plus, she was just happy to get away from pretending to be a hooker. She also couldn't help but find herself sadly curious about the man who had asked her out on a date, but who, also sadly, would never be able to follow up on that request.

She quickly changed to her own street clothes and made her way to the address the department had on file for Tim.

The officer who had come with her spoke with the landlord at the front door. After he fumbled with a large set of keys, the landlord finally let them in. Once inside, Lisa glanced around and tried to get a feel for the man Tim had been. She wanted to see if she could find any phone numbers of friends or family in order to notify them of his passing.

Next to the cordless phone base and charger, she saw a small black book. When she picked it up to flip through the pages, realizing it was an address book, she noticed the voicemail light on the handset was blinking. She picked up the handset and pushed the voicemail button, hoping he hadn't set a password. When the phone connected to the voicemail, it asked for her password.

"Damn," Lisa muttered.

She was about to hang up, when she noticed the front page of the address book and a form filled out with Tim's name, address, phone number, and sure enough, five digits that were probably his passcode. She gave it a try on the handset, and was rewarded by hearing the following message, in a deep male baritone:

"Tim, hi, this is Dr. Reubens. I was calling to see if our hypnosis session on Monday has helped and how you're responding to the trigger word we used. I implanted a suggestion for you to not remember the trigger word, so it's possible you can't recall all of the session or suggestions.

"Just want you to know, I think it's great you're wanting to be a better person and find a way to better help others. As we discussed, you might need a couple more sessions before we get the trigger word and suggestions balanced just right for your life and lifestyle. Give me a call back if you have any questions, and I hope you'll schedule a follow-up session really soon."

Tears welled in Lisa's eyes to think of the man she had met, trying so hard to help others and be a better person, only to meet such a cruel fate.

"Why him, God? He was a good man," she mumbled.

When her cellphone rang, she jumped, startled, and then laughed softly to think she might have thought God was calling to answer her question.

She flipped her phone open and sniffled loudly before she said, "Hello?"

"May I speak with Lisa Jenkins, please?"

Lisa sniffed and wiped some of her tears away with her other arm.

"This is Lisa," she uttered. She pulled the phone away to check the time.

"Lisa, I'm calling from the hospital—"

"Is it Billy?" Lisa interrupted. "Is something wrong?"

"Oh, no, Ms. Jenkins, not at all. We received notification there might be a match for your son. You're not going to believe this, but it's right here at our hospital. I don't want to get your hopes up, since the family still has to sign the procurement paperwork, but the donor had a card and donor information on his driver's license. The initial workup shows he's a match for Billy, so we're optimistic enough the transplant team needs you to come in right now to get the paperwork started so Billy can be prepped."

Lisa was silent for a moment, her mouth slightly open, and she forgot to breathe.

"Ms. Jenkins," the woman on the phone said, "this is what we've been waiting and preparing for. This is it, ma'am. Let's save your son's life!"

Lisa finally took a deep breath in and the tears that had filled her eyes finally spilled over and down her cheeks.

"Yes!" she said. "I'm on my way, right now. Please, tell Billy I'll be right there."

For a brief moment, she stood there with cellphone in hand, still not certain she wasn't dreaming. This was what they had been waiting for, and now that it was finally here, she couldn't believe it was true.

Finally, she turned to the officer she'd come with and said, "I have to go to the hospital... my son—"

"Go," he said, knowing, as everyone at the department did, that her son was in the hospital and in critical condition, "it's okay. They just radioed that the next of kin showed up at the hospital this morning already, so we're done here. Go, be with your son, and I'll close this up."

Lisa didn't even take time to think before she pocketed her cellphone and took off out the door in a sprint toward her car. Only when she climbed inside and managed to crank the engine did she put the scenario together with Tim, the next of kin and her son.

Could it be? Lisa wondered.

She shook her head and threw the car into gear, racing to the hospital to be by her son's side. On the way there, through her tears, she laughed out loud and said, "Well, Tim, I guess, in a way, we're going to have that date after all."

About the Author

Eric Patterson has been writing for several years, mostly juvenile fiction, although he enjoys writing for adults as well. He is a high school teacher and the owner of Avid Readers Publishing Group, a print-on-demand publisher.

After self-publishing his first book, Something Lurking in the Bell Tower, *back in 2007, he decided to get into the business and start publishing his own books. Five years later, he has published over 200 books for authors all over the country.*

Eric is married and has a six-year-old daughter who is already writing books of her own.

Now Then When

by Joan H. Young

Running through the fallow field
chest deep in daisies
Callow carefree
Bare feet
crush new strawberries
so sweetly
scented–
        Now Then When

Braiding daisy chains into
her hair she sings
A maiden lost in
Thoughts
Unaware of innocence
From the north
a bird sings–
        Now Then When

Looking hopeful into eyes
of bridegroom who
begins that moment
to forget the prophecy
he loves me
loves me not–
        Now Then When

Crushing daisies searching for
one red strawberry
Furtive frightened
lips stained
forbidden fruit too ripe
too sweet
rotting–
        Now Then When

Fading wilted the garden
sighs with waiting
Meager efforts
No one
tends or cares for daisies
withering
gone to seed–
        Now Then When

Drowning in the reek of
funereal roses
Votive candles
Light the
path of knowledge Running
chest deep
in death–
        Now Then When

Lying 'neath the turf all smooth
the daisies mowed down
One small voice
no longer crying
out for pity
in the
cruel wind–
        Now Then When

Reborn

by M. Lori Motley

Her moral compass, which had served so well throughout her marriage, ceased to point due north the moment his fingers brushed against hers in the bank lobby. The touch zapped her with some force she had forgotten existed. It shook her world. Her poles reversed. The thought of "comfortably married, middle-aged housewife" fled her mind and was replaced with something much more primal and hungry.

His eyes broadcast a promise of pleasures she barely remembered: thrills of hot-fudge sundaes, sleepover parties and carnival rides all rolled into a pair of malachite eyes and a smooth palm under tanned fingers. She cashed checks, made deposits and reveled in the hot brush of his fingers over hers.

Weeks passed and the next step was inevitable. She had been a Girl Scout, but her only nod to "be prepared" was a hastily-bought condom tucked into the bottom corner of her purse.

Her conscience screamed at her when she approached the room her mind had dubbed The Den of Iniquity. In the dim daylight that filtered through green velour drapes of the motor lodge on Route 37, that voice in her mind's obnoxious cries were drowned out by a chorus of, "Oh god, oh god, oh baby", repeated in perpetuum through the long afternoon. The condom did its duty and then lay like a salted slug at the bottom of the plastic wastebasket next to the bed. It was exhausted long before they were.

The next morning, in the marble-countered suburban kitchen designed to ease a housewife's task of providing meals for her husband, she broke eggs into glass bowls and skewered thick-sliced bacon onto the skillet. She added pinches of this and that, each dried curve of fragrant leaf or coarse-ground flake of seasoning a penance. Bernard would come down the stairs in a few moments and...

She paused, fingers holding a sprig of rosemary poised over the hissing pan. The gourmet spread was guilt. It was an apology, but more than that, it was a confession.

She turned off the stove and dumped eggs, bacon and herbed biscuit in the garbage, then topped them with a crumpled paper towel and an empty bread wrapper. She stood, her fingers to her lips, and listened to Bernard's feet move down the upstairs hall toward the stairs.

The next time her sensible heels approached the green-draped room, she was still repeating, "Just a one-time thing," over and over again in her mind. Two hours later, her sensible heels under a chair draped with blouse, skirt and underthings, she thought, "That was the last time."

Her head rested on his toned and tanned arm. His fingers lazily traced the curve of her breast.

The last time, she thought, the image of Bernard's impassive face floated into her mind.

But it wasn't the last time. His hold on her was complete, his power over her practically mythic. Lazing in a bath, her fingers ran across her skin, she imagined him to be some legendary figure, a god perhaps, who seduced mortal woman with pleasures impossible to find on Earth.

Late at night, while Bernard snored softly on the other side of the bed, her fingers dipped lower to ignite a fraction of the fire his hands did. Her mind murmured, "Naughty woman... bad, bad girl... shame... sinner..."

As the weeks turned into months, the Catholic-school-teacher voice was easier to ignore.

"He's devilishly handsome," she whispered to her best girlfriend over coffee two months into the infidelity. Her cheeks still felt flushed from the day before's rendezvous, and her friend's nimbus of red curls shook with barely suppressed laughter.

"He must be the devil himself to tempt you away from your damned traditional morals. Does Bernie know?" Lacquered pink nails tapped a hysterical rhythm against the mug.

Her eyes gaped wide. "Oh, god, no. I doubt it," she added, a frown creasing her brow. "Bernard..." she peered at her friend pointedly. "Bernard doesn't notice much outside of his work."

Head tilted to one side, her friend peered at her.

"It's like a whole new you." Her smile grew again. "You're like a... a born again sinner."

Their laughter rang through the coffee shop crowds.

Perched on the corner of her marital bed, she stared down at the white-plastic wand and the two incriminating pink lines beaming up at her. Her palm rested on her flat belly and tried to imagine what the thing inside looked like. A worm perhaps. An ill-formed thing: boneless, faceless.

She did the only thing she could think of. Nights after Bernard came home from the office, she met him at the door in negligees, legs bare and breasts heaving with desperate hope. He ignored her, and she increased her efforts. She touched him, stroked him, hugged him and held him until he pulled away and snapped, "Get a hold of yourself," and retreated to his study on the other side of the house. She tried for days, weeks, and then gave up.

A rounded bump grew on her belly. She exhausted herself with worry while a thread of expectant joy crept through her being.

"Miranda," she said, lifting her shirt in front of the full-length mirror in the bedroom. "Or Mason, if it's a boy."

Her hand rubbed slowly over the swell, just as his had done the afternoon before. If he had noticed any change in her body, he hadn't said. His fingers traced fire over her skin the same way they had for months.

By the time the annual corporate function rolled around, her belly had grown enough to warrant a trip to the shops for new clothes. She chose loose-fitting sweaters and stylish swing jackets that could hide her changing body. While other corporate officer's wives would attend the theater in form-fitting elegant gowns, she would wear gathered lace and ruffles.

She dressed carefully on the night of the do, displaying her still shapely back to Bernard, if he cared to look. They dressed and then went downstairs silently to the waiting car. She held her beaded clutch against her stomach, knowing it would not be long before she would have to make some explanation for the thing growing inside of her.

She sat shoulder to shoulder with Bernard in the theater, surrounded by his co-workers and their wives. She glanced about at the other women: half were trophy wives, second marriages when the first ones had worn out. The other half were like her, fighting the slow approach of age. She wondered how many of them were faithful to their husbands.

They waited silently for the show to begin. Her mind

tried to cast itself away to the motor lodge, the den of iniquity, the green eyes and brown hands, but she would not allow it. She narrowed her gaze until it encompassed only Bernard's hand. She stared at it, mapping lines and creases, and wondered when it had stopped knowing how to bring pleasure.

The seam on her husband's jacket cuff bothered her. The stitching was even, perfected by the candlelit fingers of malcontents in some back corner of a sweatshop halfway around the world. The fabric gleamed along the edge, knife sharp and starched to stay that way for millennia. Its perfection was an affront to her state of mind.

The play began and her attention was drawn away from the bothersome sleeve. She sucked in breath and let it out again, a slow sigh of resignation. She stopped fighting the urge to think about him and let her mind loose to cavort away from the show to the memory of two-hundred-thread-count sheets, his hand inscribing fire down her spine and the low burn of pleasure and guilt.

The baby moved, the first physical insistence of its actuality, a slow roll punctuated with a sharp jab that made her hand fly involuntarily to her belly. She glanced away from the stage for a moment, downward toward her lap.

She looked back at the stage quickly, but already her husband's eye was on her, his brows knitting together in a practiced scowl. Staring forward without blinking, she watched the actors strut and stagger across the stage. She had forgotten the plot. Guilt, thick and hot, coated the fear that throbbed through her mind.

Another tiny appendage struck her inwardly, and a sound slipped past the stranglehold of her throat. His head whipped toward her again. His gaze shot downward to where her hand pressed and kneaded below her ribs and then up again to her wide eyes. His mustache quivered like the feathers on a slaughtered goose.

It was over.

In his dark glance, suddenly quite aware of her and interested after all those years of not caring, she saw irrevocable change.

They sat shoulder to shoulder and watched the rest of the play. His spine was straight, his mouth set as if against an ill-fitting bit that tried to steer him in a direction he did not want to go. Her eyes were on the stage, but her mind made up its own theatrical tragedy...

Even before intermission began, she was lying in the aisle, her silk gown rucked above her knees. At the first cry she could not bite back, a plump matron jumped up, claimed to be a nurse and rushed to her side.

The audience pushed back against the wall of the theater. The cast stood, arms akimbo, on the stage, the small ones craned their necks for the best view. Her husband sputtered and alternated between pacing furiously and standing rooted to the spot, gazing away from her in indignation.

"Just breathe," the midwife crooned over and over again. "Just breathe."

More than anything else she had ever wished for—a fluffy, white kitten; a comfortable husband, rooms full of stylish dresses and shoes—she wished she could just breathe. More than two years since her husband had touched her, but she knew denying the impending birth would be whimsy of the most ridiculous sort.

"Just breathe," the midwife said again, down on her knees in the dust.

Then the world washed blood red as the thing with the claws started scrabbling into the world. The thing squalled in the midwife's arms. Wide-eyed and gape-mouthed, the midwife stared at the thing.

Dust covered her husband's sleeve. It was the only part visible of him from his unconscious position between the rows of playhouse seats.

The actors and dancers yelped and shouted then

scattered away from the hole that splintered up through the floorboards. Shards of wood and gouts of flame flashed through the air. Something dark crawled out of the hole.

"A son." The voice sounded like it had come from something lurking in a dark alley halfway between Hell and oblivion. "Excellent."

The midwife joined the husband on the floor, and the creature plucked the newborn from her slack arms. It slipped below the floor once more, leaving a whiff of rot in its wake.

She lay back on the floor, dropping her head to the boards. The thought of knitting tiny things slipped like a weighted corpse into the well of her mind.

The production concluded in a burst of applause, shattering the horrific fantasy that played out in her mind. She returned to the dim theater with her husband by her side. She glanced at him, wondering vaguely what he would say to her once they were no longer in public. She wondered what he would ask her to do.

And then she realized she did not care. It did not matter what he said.

The thing, the baby, was still. Her fingers palpated gently on the growing mound under the ruffles and lace.

Without a glance, Bernard got to his feet and said, "Come."

She rose and, somehow, the guilt and fear remained behind on the theater seat. Her husband knew, and she could breathe again. Her eyes opened. Her mind opened. She felt reborn.

~~M. Lori Motley

Flames and Feathers

by Lisa Lee Smith

I'm saving all my precious time now
so I can really kill it later on
and melt myself into cool midnight
like blue bottle glass and song

I'm filling days between gray funerals
and you just keep haunting me
but I pray your voice won't stop yet
it's a blurry sound I can almost see

I avoid too many thoughts of Heaven
so I won't sprout white wings and sigh
but then I think of flames and feathers
burnt paper tigers and golden lies

I'm catching up with offbeat chances
and I try not to seem surprised
that you would let Death take you anywhere
it's what I never quite realized

I'm getting lost because I don't fit in
with anyone around here but you
and when it comes to rumors of saving grace
they are substantially far from the truth

I may not have a shot in blazing Hell
and the place might not have a shot with me
either way I'll just keep listening
for that missing voice I can almost see

I'm saving all my worthless time now
while I am still made of blood and bone
so I'll take your strings of broken promises
and go fly a damned kite of my own

> No matter where the brightest lightning strikes
> I'll go fly a damned kite of my own.

Amy

by Kim Kevason

Amy jumped out of bed and ran for the door. As soon as her tiny feet touched the icy-cold floor, she remembered where she was. She took three steps back toward her bed so she could slip her feet into a pair of furry pink bunny slippers. Amy ran back out her door and down the hall to room 102.

Sherry Anderson, the woman in room 102, was startled awake by the banging on her door. She opened the door but was not surprised to see little Amy looking up at her. Amy ran under her arm and into the room. She talked a mile a minute, and Sherry had a difficult time understanding her. Normally, Sherry found Amy easy to understand, but the three-year-old reverted back to baby talk when she was excited.

"And they will be there when we go bowling!" This final sentence was the only one Sherry could clearly make out.

"Wait, wait. Slow down. Who will be there?"

She picked Amy up and set her down on her bed.

"New mommy and daddy. Oh, and two brothers!"

"Amy, start again and tell me the story slowly."

Sherry sat on the bed next to Amy.

"Mommy said I'll meet my new family when we go bowling tomorrow. They have two boys and a dog and a big house and—"

Sherry had planned a bowling trip for the fifteen

children who resided at Sugar Ridge Orphanage, but she hadn't mentioned it to any of the children. If anything prevented them from going, she didn't want to disappoint all the kids. After being the house mother for nine years, she had learned not to mention special treats until right before the event happened. For these children, hope could be a cruel trick, even when intentions were good.

She interrupted Amy and asked, "How do you know we're going bowling tomorrow?"

"Because Mommy told me. She introd... introdu... introduded me to them and told me they was gonna adopt me, and I was gonna be their little girl."

Ms. Anderson knew it was impossible for Amy's mother to have told her anything, because Amy's parents had been killed in an automobile accident two months prior. Unfortunately, Amy did not have any family left who could take on the responsibility of caring for the three-year-old girl. Her grandmother was in a nursing home, and she had an aunt who would not return phone calls. Amy was a ward of the state.

Ms. Anderson was not only in charge of caring for the kids at the orphanage but was also in charge of trying to place them into foster homes. Not many families in the county wanted to open their homes to foster children after a horrible incident two years earlier. For the fifteen children, the orphanage was—and probably always would be—their home.

Sherry picked Amy up and carried her back to bed. She sat on the edge of the bed until the little girl drifted back to sleep. While Sherry walked back to her room, she prayed Amy's dream would come true. It would be a wonderful blessing if that cute little three year old with the Shirley Temple curls could find a new mommy, daddy, and two brothers.

That Saturday morning was just like every other Saturday in the McMathon household. Jeff cooked a pancake breakfast for his wife and two boys. Karen set the kitchen table while she sipped her flavored coffee. The boys, Paul and Justin, played with their dinosaurs and watched cartoons in the family room.

"So what's on our agenda for the day?" Jeff asked his wife.

He set a heaping pile of pancakes on the table. Jeff always made more food than the four and five-year-old boys could ever possibly eat.

"I know what I have to do, but I just don't want to spend the day doing laundry and grocery shopping." Karen felt like she was in a rut. The same old daily routine was getting her down. Plus, it was raining outside, and that always made her feel a little blue.

"Why don't we go look for new furniture? Or we can pick out paint for the living room?" Jeff suggested.

"No, I don't want to spend the day shopping. Plus, we don't really need new furniture."

"I know we don't need new furniture, but I hate that ugly couch." Jeff wrinkled his nose and he looked into the family room.

"I know you like changing things, but I want everything to stay the same for a little while. We just painted last fall, and I finally got everything decorated the way I like it. Can we manage to keep things the same for at least six months?"

Karen was half laughing, but she was completely serious. She felt the need to get control of balancing work, the kids' schooling, and the household before any other major changes took place, even a new couch.

Sherry worried because Amy would not take her eyes off the bowling alley doors. She knew how disappointed and upset a child could become when they expected a new family who never materialized. She had seen it many times with both foster and adoptive families. It would be even more traumatic for Amy, because the little girl still believed dreams could come true.

"Amy, it's your turn again." Ms. Anderson gently

nudged her.

Amy walked to the black line, set the ball down, and pushed the bowling ball down the lane. The ball rolled slowly down the alley. It bounced off the gutter guard twice and barely knocked down one pin. Amy wasn't paying attention to the bowling ball or the pins. She was staring at the door again.

It was the last frame of the last game, and Ms. Anderson was mentally preparing herself to explain to Amy that dreams were simply dreams. Sherry knew Amy would take it hard. When Amy had come to Sugar Ridge, she'd spent the first three weeks spontaneously crying at all hours of the day and night. Last night and that morning were the first times Sherry had actually seen Amy happy for any extended period of time.

"There they are!" Amy jumped off the bench and ran toward the shoe rental counter. "Mommy! Daddy!"

Karen saw a little girl with brown curly hair running toward them and yelling. She instinctively turned around to see who she belonged to, but saw no one else around.

Within seconds, the child had wrapped her arms around Karen's legs. Jeff looked down in complete confusion. He wondered who the little girl dressed in a purple sweatshirt could be and why she called his wife mommy.

"I knew you would come! I told Ms. Anderson you would be here! I'm so happy!" Amy squealed.

Karen bent down, and Amy wrapped her arms around her neck.

"See, Ms. Anderson, I told you they would come! Mommy said so," Amy said.

Karen had a confused smile on her face, but she didn't pull away from Amy's grasp.

Sherry reached the family and stumbled to explain the situation while she tried to pry Amy from the woman's neck.

"I'm sorry," Sherry said. "This is Amy, and she had a dream last night that she would meet her new family here. I'm Sherry Anderson, assistant director at Sugar Ridge Orphanage. Amy is one of our kiddos there."

Sherry extended her hand to Jeff and then Karen. They both shook it in a weak, stunned manner.

"Don't apologize," Karen replied, happy a child would see her family and want to be a part of it. Jeff McMathon didn't appear as accepting.

"Well, I tried to explain that dreams aren't real."

"It—it is real...," Amy stuttered. "Mommy told me. They are my new family! See, he's Paul," Amy said pointing at Paul. "And he's Justin." Amy pointed at the four-year-old boy, who was almost a full head taller than she was.

"Do you go to school together?" Karen asked her younger son.

"No." Justin shook his head with his mouth open while Amy gave him a huge hug.

"And you have a brown dog and live in a yellow house with a swing set in the backyard." Amy had added details she could not have known.

"You're exactly right!" Karen said. Now, she was surprised. She looked up at her husband, and they both had confused looks on their faces.

"Is this true?" Sherry asked. She would not, could not, believe it. There was no way Amy could have known those people would be there, and she didn't know how Amy could have known their names or any of the other details she had described from her dream.

"Yes, but I'm trying to figure out how Amy knows us." That was the first thing Jeff had said since Amy had approached them.

"I told you; Mommy told me last night that you would be here today and that you're my new family." Amy said it as if it were a fact known by everyone.

"Amy's parents died two months ago," Sherry explained. She didn't want to reveal too much of Amy's story to complete strangers. She was afraid that it would upset Amy and sound desperate to the family.

"Oh, poor child," Karen whispered.

She subconsciously ran her hand over Amy's hair. She turned to Amy and asked, "What else did your mommy tell you?"

"She showed me your house and told me I would have two big brothers named Paul and Justin and, and, and that you are the perfect family for me, and that I should be happy to be your new girl." Amy held fast to Karen's arm. "Oh, and she said that you would love me as much as she does... this big." Amy spread her arms out as far as they would go.

Amy's last sentence brought the tears Karen had been close to shedding over the edge, and they spilled down her cheeks. She looked up at her husband again, and this time he had a smirk on his face.

"Do you have business card?" Jeff asked Sherry.

Karen knelt to talk to Amy. "This is all quite a surprise. We are going to have to talk about this, but for now, it looks like your group is packing up to leave. Can I make you a deal?"

Amy's head nodded in a way that would make any adult dizzy.

"We will come to see you later this week so that all of us can talk some more, okay?" Karen asked.

"Okay," Amy said. She looked down. Her expression had saddened.

"Honey, even if these are the right parents for you, it takes some time to get all the paperwork together. I'm not saying they're the right ones, but we'll see," Sherry added.

She didn't want to get Amy's hopes up, but she had goose bumps running up and down her spine. Sherry had to make sure she wasn't getting her own hopes up, either.

Amy took Ms. Anderson's hand, and she led her back to the group. They packed up, and Amy blew the McMathons a kiss when she left.

They watched her skip out the door of the bowling

alley.

Paul was the curious one. He had an endless stream of questions, and his parents weren't prepared to answer. Karen and Jeff did not want their children to participate in the initial discussion. They needed to talk about it alone, first, and then they could include the boys.

"Where will Amy sleep?" Paul asked while Karen and Jeff put him to bed.

"Sweetie, we aren't sure if she will be coming to live with us." Karen tucked him into his bunk bed.

"Why not?" Justin asked.

"I told you guys we'll discuss it in the morning," Jeff replied.

To the kids, the answer was perfectly clear.

Once the couple was downstairs, Jeff spoke first, "What do you want to do?"

"It's not that easy." Karen was torn. Her heart broke for the little girl who needed love. She knew she could accept a dozen adopted children as her own, so that wasn't the issue. She didn't think she was ready for another child. Jeff and she had discussed having a third child, but the main thing that had held them back was that they were happy being a family of four. A third child would be more hectic, more costly, and more work.

Karen didn't think she was keeping up with the pace her family kept now. Adding a third child would turn her household completely chaotic. She just couldn't do it all.

"You're right. You would be responsible for most everything—school, laundry, cleaning—but you would get your girl, a daughter."

Jeff was more than willing to let Karen make the decision. He was fine with adopting a kid. His only issue was that they would end up having three kids in college back to back to back. They would definitely have to make some additional financial sacrifices, but he was fully prepared to make them if they all agreed Amy should be a part of their family.

"I never said I wanted a girl." Karen wondered why all men seemed to think their wives wanted a daughter. Maybe, she figured, it was because most men wanted to have sons, so they assumed women wanted daughters too.

"I'll admit that if we were going to adopt, I'd prefer adopting an infant. You just don't know what you are getting when you adopt an older kid." Jeff had that smirk on his face again. He knew if he made Karen argue on behalf of an older child, she might convince herself to do it.

"An infant is the last thing I need right now!" Karen rolled her eyes. "That's not even the issue. I just don't understand how she knew our names and all about our house and family. It's almost like a set-up."

Jeff laughed. "You never did understand the dream thing. Have some faith. Didn't you even consider that this is all part of God's plan? This little girl needs a family, and we are a family who can accept another child. It wasn't a coincidence that we up and decided to go bowling instead of furniture shopping."

Jeff gave his wife a hug. He'd always managed to bring his wife back to having faith. "Sometimes things happen exactly how they are supposed to happen and not how we want or expect them to happen."

"So what do you want to tell the kids in the morning?"

"It's up to you."

"No, it's up to us!"

This was not a decision Karen was going to make by herself.

"I'm perfectly fine with it, but if you really have your doubts, then I'm not going to push you into it."

Jeff knew which direction his wife was leaning, but he couldn't understand why she doubted herself.

"I will add that we need to find out more of Amy's history before we make a final decision... just to make sure we know exactly what we are getting into."

"Let's go see that director tomorrow. We'll have to get a sitter for the kids. I don't want them to get their hopes up just to be disappointed."

Jeff and Karen sat in front of Sherry Anderson's cluttered desk. The office contained a wall of filing cabinets adjacent to a wall of framed certificates. All Karen could think about were the children who needed homes represented by the files stuffed into those cabinets, their lives reduced to papers and forms.

They requested not to see Amy. Karen had promised the little girl they would come to see her later in the week, but she was afraid if they decided not to adopt her, any additional contact might be too traumatic for her.

Sherry entered with a thin file folder. "I have to admit, I'm a little surprised to see you guys so soon."

She smiled and extended her hand to the McMathons.

"We would really like to get more information about Amy before making any decisions," Jeff said. "She really threw us for a loop yesterday."

"You should've been me!" Sherry said. "She came running into my room at two in the morning to tell me this incredible story about how she was going to meet her new family at the bowling alley. She didn't even know we were going to go bowling. The whole thing is just incredible!"

Sherry opened the thin file and then folded it back to expose the papers inside. She held it out toward the McMathons.

"Here is Amy's file. Her parents were killed in a car accident. I only have a brief family history. Amy has an aunt. I only talked to her once. She never met Amy, and she doesn't want the responsibility of taking care of a child. I don't even know if Amy knows her aunt exists. Most of Amy's family history is from her aunt."

After they discussed a few more details, she said, "I'll

leave you to talk for a moment, and then we'll get back together and I'll answer any questions you have."

Sherry left the room and the couple opened the file to read about Amy. They learned her only family was her mother's mother and an aunt on her father's side. Neither were capable of taking care of Amy. The paperwork described Amy's family history, including a brief medical history and how each family member had died. There also was a doctor's physical evaluation and examination. This document showed Amy was a perfectly healthy three-year-old girl. The doctor had added a note that Amy was advanced both verbally and intellectually, and that there were no physical or emotional signs of abuse.

The majority of the file was Amy's psychological evaluation. It showed that Amy was very sad during each of her visits with the county's psychologist. Being so young, she did not have the skills needed to cope with such a complete loss.

One particular note jumped out at them; it said Amy was angry because her parents did not listen to her. Amy had told them she'd had a dream and begged them not to go on their trip because they were going to be put in a box forever. In retrospect, that dream made perfect sense to the adults, even though it probably didn't make any sense to Amy or her parents at the time. The McMathons assumed that was the best way a three year old could describe her dream.

Jeff completely understood these types of warning dreams. He'd had the same type of dreams since he was child. Jeff, however, had learned through the years that not all of them came true, because, he believed, people had the ability to change their destinies.

Sherry came back into the office and told the couple she had some other things they might want to know, before she answered any questions they had and before they made a final decision.

"Amy hasn't made much progress in healing from the

loss of her parents. She wakes up several times a week screaming. The dream she had about you was the first one that wasn't a nightmare."

Sherry wanted to make sure that the McMathons understood that raising Amy might not be simple; she did, after all, have some emotional issues to deal with that most children her age didn't have to work through.

"She rarely plays with the other children. She prefers to sit by herself and brush a doll's hair or work on a puzzle. I was trying to place her in a foster home, to help her get back to a normal, happy childhood. The psychologist won't release her to foster parents, because he is afraid that if it doesn't work out, it would be more damaging to Amy to be pulled from a family environment than to leave her here with all of us. He does believe a permanent placement, such as a family willing to adopt her, would be acceptable."

The couple sat on the other side of the desk looked at each other. Then they looked at Ms. Anderson and smiled. There was nothing she could say that would change their minds now. The decision was made.

There were more questions, and paperwork that would need to be filed, and forms to fill out. There was talk of home inspections, court proceedings, and attorneys. But in the end, the McMathons decided to adopt Amy, and Sherry was delighted.

Once the couple returned home that evening, Karen and Jeff knew they needed to have a talk with their boys before they began the process of fixing up the house for Amy to come home.

As they had hoped, Paul and Justin were excited. They insisted on going to see Amy as soon as they could, so the next morning, Jeff called and made arrangement to visit Amy at the orphanage. In the car on the way to Sugar Ridge, the boys told their parents they'd be okay with turning their playroom into Amy's room.

The weeks flew by while the family busied themselves

with paperwork, legal proceedings, and preparing Amy's room for her arrival. They painted the walls pale lavender and added a princess-themed wall border. The boys insisted Amy would love robots, so the family hung up pictures of robots the boys had drawn and colored.

The family visited Amy as often as possible during the week. The kids played and talked endlessly. Karen knew the novelty would wear off, and soon they would be fighting like siblings always do, but for now, she enjoyed watching the three of them get along like brothers and sister.

At each visit, Sherry helped Karen and Jeff with tips she'd learned over the years while working in social services. She hoped to help speed up the paperwork process to make the McMathons a foster home, so Amy could live with them while the adoption process finalized. It meant Karen had to take time off from work to personally deliver forms to the county instead of mailing them, and being available to fill out new forms and meet human services social workers at their home at a moment's notice. It would be hard work and inconvenient, but it would be worth it.

Jeff and Karen convinced Paul and Justin not to say anything about the adoption to any of their extended family members. They all agreed that adopting Amy would be a fun surprise.

Not long after the paperwork was filed and the home inspection had been completed, Ms. Anderson called the McMathon's house and asked when they could come and pick up Amy. Within three hours, the family was at Sugar Ridge, packing Amy's few belongings. Amy took her time saying goodbye to her friends and to Ms. Anderson. She was sad to be leaving, yet excited to be going home. Karen looked at the other children and wanted to bring them all home. Any doubts she'd had about her abilities to handle an additional child were completely gone, but she knew there was no way she could handle fifteen of them.

As soon as they made it home, the boys dragged Amy up to her new room. They showed her the dresser, the closet, and the shelves as if those items were the most valuable things in the world. Paul unpacked Amy's clothes and put them in the drawers. Karen and Jeff let the boys introduce Amy to Pickles, the family dog. Pickles sniffed then licked Amy's nose. She was officially accepted into the McMathon household.

The three children went to the basement, their new playroom to share, to play. Karen was afraid Amy would be overwhelmed with the boys' excitement, but she took everything in stride with a huge smile on her face and a sippy cup in her hand.

The family gathered in Amy's room to say prayers before bed. Everyone had a lot to be thankful for. Amy went first. "Now I lay me down to sleep. I pray the Lord my soul to keep. Thank you for my new Mommy and Daddy, for my brothers Paul and Justin, for our dog Pickles, and for my new room. Please bless my first Mommy and Daddy, and tell them I'll be okay, now. Amen."

Karen only had three days to plan Amy's party. They were going to do a cookout with the entire family and some close friends. Paul and Justin were excited to finally be able to tell everyone about Amy, but they were still sworn to secrecy for a few more hours.

Karen sent out email invitations that requested everyone to be at the McMathon's house promptly at one o'clock for a cookout and pool party. On the bottom of the invitation it said: *Come Meet Amy*

Jeff's sister was the first to call. "Did you get another dog?" Jeff would neither confirm nor deny the guess.

All Karen's mother said was that she was always coming up with creative party ideas and asked what dish Karen wanted her to bring.

About a half an hour before the party, Karen took Amy upstairs to get ready. Paul and Justin were not allowed to say anything to the guests when they arrived. Luckily, both boys were good at keeping secrets.

Karen pulled out the photo album again. She explained who each member of the family was and how they were related. Amy looked scared.

"It will be okay. I will be with you all day." Karen had her arm around Amy.

"What if they don't like me?" Amy looked like she was going to cry.

"I guarantee they will love you! We didn't even know each other three weeks ago, and now we are a family," Karen reassured her. "There will be a lot of people, and I don't expect you to remember who everyone is today. So, try to relax, and it'll be a fun cookout."

At a little after one o'clock, Karen walked Amy downstairs. The guests were on the back deck, the grill was fired up, and everyone was chatting.

Amy held up her arms for Karen to carry her. Karen picked her up and stepped out onto the deck. Everyone fell silent for a second or two. Then, as fast as they'd stopped talking, they started talking at the same time. Huge grins appeared across every family member's face, one by one, as they realized who Amy on the invitation was.

Paul, Justin, Jeff, and Karen answered a myriad of questions over the next several minutes. Amy was lifted from Karen's arms and passed from one family member to another, each giving her a huge kiss and hug. In no time, Amy was laughing and smiling. She gave bear hugs back to her new extended family.

Once things settled down, the kids went swimming. The cousins fought over who would watch Amy in the pool. Some of the adults decided to watch the kids swim, others were cooking, and a few snuck away from the party and piled into two cars.

As Karen set up the burger buffet, she noticed several people missing. No one at the party would admit to knowing where the guests had disappeared.

The adults had served the kids and were getting their own food when the missing guests returned. They had brought balloons, gifts, and a birthday cake.

"Well you can't have a birthday party without cake and presents, can you?" Uncle Phil asked. They piled all the stuff on top of the picnic table outside.

"But it's not my birthday?" Amy was confused. At least, she didn't think it was her birthday.

"It is to us!" Grandma happily told her, and she gave Amy a kiss on her head. "This is the day you've been born into this family, so it calls for a birthday party!"

With that, everyone sang Happy Birthday.

That night, Karen gathered dirty clothes in the kids' bedrooms. She reached under Amy's bed to get a t-shirt and her hand touched metal and glass. She pulled out a picture frame and saw a photo of a smiling man with his arm around a woman who held a younger version of Amy.

Amy walked into her bedroom and saw her new mom looking at the picture. She looked guilty and turned to leave.

"Amy, wait," Karen said. She patted the floor next to her.

Amy came back and sat next to her.

"Why don't we put this picture on top of your dresser?" Karen asked.

"You're not mad?" Tears rolled down Amy's face.

"Why on earth would I be mad?"

"Because you're my mommy, now."

"Yes, I'm your mommy now, but you don't have to forget or hide your first mommy and daddy. They love you very much. Just because you're a part of our family doesn't mean they are no longer a part of you."

Karen struggled to explain everything so the little one would understand. She sighed and pulled Amy closer to her, bringing her to sit next to her on the bed.

"Your mommy loved you enough to appear to you in

your dreams, to tell you about us... because of your mommy, we found each other. If she hadn't done that, we might never have met you.

"We have room in our hearts for you and for our boys too, so I know you have room in your heart for your first mommy and daddy and for us too."

Amy nodded. This time she was crying with a smile on her face.

Karen put the picture on Amy's dresser.

She told Amy to wait a minute, and then she went into her room and pulled out a picture Uncle Phil had taken at the party, with all five of the McMathon's gathered around Amy's birthday cake. She propped up the picture of their new family next to the first one.

Karen hugged Amy with all her might. She said a thank you prayer to God for Amy and Amy's first mommy and daddy.

◈◈◈

About the Author

Kim Kevason is a full-time wife and mom and a part-time nurse. She lives in northern Ohio with her husband, two children and their family mutt.

At a sleepover party, when she was a teen, Kim suggested it would be fun for everyone to write a chapter to a book. Her sleepover invitations dropped off considerably after that, but she still continued to write stories in her head throughout high school.

Her first short story, A Trip to the Haunted Castle, *was published in* The Harvest, *her school's anthology of essays, fiction and poems when she was in eleventh grade. She took a hiatus from writing to pursue her career and raise a family but rediscovered her love when she found encouragement and her voice at Accentuate Writers.*

Writing is not Kim's job; it's her passion. Kim has some spectacular stories to tell and Amy *is just the beginning.*

Foetus

by Catherine A. MacKenzie

a chance meeting
in the dark,
two strangers:
cells-
egg and sperm-
forming one,
a thimble of life

thriving inside,
growing,
yearning,
grasping air
as it yawns
and punches the barrier,
kicking,
wanting to exit,
not realizing its creation
veiled
in the cocoon

it hears the music
and listens to the words-
eavesdropping-
not knowing,
forming preconceptions
as it vibrates
in its camouflage,
demanding its first release

Crocus

by L.L. Darroch

frozen ground opens
bloom robed in purple glory-
diminutive strength

A Dance with Death

by Robert L. Arend

"Martha, what are you doing up this late?" Henry asked.

He furrowed his brow and narrowed his eyes, a confused expression crossing his face. He had not heard his wife get out of bed. Worse, in his mind, was that he couldn't remember leaving their bed either.

At the head of the staircase, Martha turned to look up into his eyes, which were as gray as his hair.

"I heard somebody call me from downstairs," she whispered. "I think it's Tony."

Saddened, more for himself in that moment than for Martha's decline into dementia, Henry took his wife's hand and reminded her, "Tony's been dead for years, Martha."

"No, no," she pleaded. She pulled her hand from his. "He's downstairs in the kitchen. He's calling for me. He wants his breakfast."

Martha turned away and descended the steps with more confidence and determination than Henry had witnessed in a long time. Resigned to a sleepless night, he gripped the rail and carefully followed his wife.

A single lamp provided light in the living room, but

Martha hurried left into the kitchen.

"Wait, Martha," Henry said, worried she would fall and break her hip again in the dark. He himself almost tripped while he hurried to the kitchen. When he touched the light switch, his finger passed through it and caused him to lose balance. Not until he fell backward did he realize the kitchen lights were already on, and his wife was not alone. Henry braced for the thud and pain, but his fall was more of a drift than immediate contact, like onto a cushion instead of a hard floor.

"Henry, quit making a fool of yourself." Martha scolded him from the kitchen table. "Get up and join us for breakfast."

And then there he was, sitting beside his wife. Henry couldn't remember getting off the floor or walking to the kitchen table.

Sitting at the table with them, he recognized Tony from the pictures Martha had preserved in her old albums.

"Don't mind Henry," Martha told her first husband. "He's been getting a bit clumsy in his old age."

Henry's face showed indignation, and for a moment, he thought about reminding his wife of her own age and forgetfulness.

"Glad to meet you, Henry," Tony said, stretching forth his hand to shake Henry's.

"Same," Henry said, more annoyed than puzzled by the dead man who sat across from himself. "Where've you been, Tony? Guess you weren't killed in Vietnam like the Army said. You desert? You been hiding all these years?"

"Henry!" Martha said.

Tony poked at the table and then raised his empty fingers up to his mouth.

"The Army told the truth, Henry," he said. His words were strained as though his mouth were full of food. "Fell on an enemy grenade to save my buddies."

"Don't mind Henry." Martha soothed her former

husband. "He sees your medal of honor every time he opens the top bureau drawer to get out the credit card. He's always been jealous I keep those memories of you."

Tony jabbed at the surface of the table again and pretended to put something in his mouth.

"What are you chewing," Henry demanded.

He was growing irritated with the pantomimed eating.

"Scrambled eggs," Tony answered. "Fantastic, Marty. Just enough cheddar and peppers to make them um-um-good."

"There ain't nothing there," Henry muttered. "You're eating nothing but air."

"What is wrong with you, Henry?" Martha asked. "If you don't like the way I fixed breakfast, don't eat yours."

Henry was almost amused when he watched his wife pretend to dip what he thought was pretend toast into invisible yolk on a plate of eggs. She put the pretend toast in her mouth and pretended to chew it.

He glanced down, but was disappointed to find his own plate of eggs, toast and home fries not there.

Tony pretended to wipe his mouth with a napkin.

Henry felt foolish for wondering if Martha had put her best cloth napkins on the table instead of the paper ones.

Then the ceiling lights went off and the floor became a kaleidoscope of whirling colors. Rock music—*Magic Carpet Ride*, by Steppenwolf—filled the kitchen. Henry was about to say he'd had enough and order Martha's dead soldier to leave when Tony took Martha's hand and pulled her through Henry to dance.

Well, you don't know what we can find
Why don't you come with me little girl
On a magic carpet ride

Martha wasn't old Martha any more; she was high school Martha, in knee-high orange boots and tight thigh-length white skirt. A wide crème-colored belt was loosely buckled around her gyrating hips.

Henry couldn't take his eyes off her young breasts, which taunted they might bounce out from under her tight but partially unbuttoned silk blouse.

Last night I held Aladdin's lamp
And so I wished that I could stay
Before the thing could answer me
Someone came and took the lamp away

Tony pulled Martha's body to his own and pressed his lips to hers for what Henry considered one of the sloppiest kisses he had ever been unfortunate enough to witness.

The floor lights turned to the white circles, signaling the spotlight dance. Henry found himself tapping Tony's shoulder to cut in. Tony retreated, perhaps more because of his dislike of the Vogues than out of courtesy toward Henry.

Henry tried to get Martha to dance closer, but her body was rigid, her expression a mix of fear and revulsion.

He tried to press his cheek to hers, but she tilted her head back.

When Henry tried to kiss her, she pushed him away so fiercely he was propelled through the wall into the dining room, where he bounced a few times before coming to rest on the dining room table. The music stopped. The room was spinning.

Henry could only close his eyes in hope he would awaken from the dream when he reopened them.

When Henry opened his eyes, he found himself in his overstuffed chair. From that corner of the living room, his attention was drawn toward the flames of the fireplace, and then to the woman and man who lay together on the sofa. Young Martha pulled Tony's shirt off, her blouse already on the floor beside her boots. Tony slid his hands behind her, and when he eased them back out, his fingers raised the straps of her bra. The bra joined the blouse and boots on the floor.

"Tony, we shouldn't," young Martha whispered, but her tone clearly indicated she merely spoke out of propriety and not desire.

Tony silenced her when he brought his lips to hers for another sloppy kiss, followed by dragging his tongue along her neck down to her breasts. His left hand drifted to her waist and disappeared under the band of young Martha's skirt.

Henry watched, enraged at their brazen display in front of him, but when he tried to get out of his chair, he found he couldn't move. He hated the excitement brought on by the sight of his wife's seduction by another man, yet it was the first erection Henry had experienced since his mid-fifties.

An end to the dream he believed himself to be in was perversely no longer urgent.

Her belt and skirt floated to the carpet. Tony's fingers tugged her panties down and off. Shyly, young Martha covered her most intimate exposure with her own hands, but Tony was having none of her pretense of resistance.

"Don't, Martha," Henry managed to plead. He bowed his head when she ignored him. When he looked through a blur of tears again at young Martha, she looked back at him, guilt written over her expression.

"No, Tony," she said, her voice firm and grim. "I've changed my mind."

Tony unbuckled his jeans. He either hadn't heard her or had decided to defy her.

Martha's scream shattered Henry's helplessness, but it took all of his strength to stomp over to the younger man and pull him off the sofa.

Looking stunned, Tony simply sank into the floor and vanished.

Martha was old Martha again. No longer nude, she was dressed in her flannel nightgown, but she was trembling. Henry sat beside her on the sofa and embraced her. He rocked gently with her.

"Henry," she said, and she pointed to the cherry wood clock on the top shelf of the display cabinet at a far corner of the room, "it's three o'clock in the morning. Why aren't we in bed?"

Henry tried to remember but could only shake his head. "I don't know. What about you?"

"I must have come down looking for you, I suppose," Martha said, her lips pursed.

They sat together and stared at the minute hand of the clock, following its jerky movement to the twelve. Henry felt a mild thrill to touch hips with his wife, his arm wrapped around her waist—a feeling he had not experienced in years.

He looked into her pale blue eyes.

She appeared younger than he recalled, face smoother, a few wrinkles instead of many. She no longer trembled but seemed at peace with herself and him.

He moved to kiss her. She invited his lips with her own.

"Now I remember why I married you," Martha said when their lips parted. "You're a great kisser. My first husband, though I loved him, used to kiss me like he was sucking on an orange."

Henry smiled and kissed his wife again. "Let's go upstairs."

Martha trembled again. "I don't feel sleepy at all," she said.

"Who said anything about sleeping?" Henry replied.

He hoped to calm her trembles by hugging her, but she gently pushed him away.

"Something's wrong. I can feel it. Maybe it's Timmy. Maybe he's been in an accident. I'm going to call him."

Both reached to the telephone that rested on the lamp stand—she to call their son, he to stop her—but both of their hands passed through the receiver. No matter how many times they tried to pick up the phone, it was like trying to grasp air.

"Henry, I think we're dead," Martha said when she tried to press her hand against the arm of the sofa, only to have her entire arm disappear into it.

"Then how come we can touch each other?" Henry asked.

Martha folded her hands over his. "Because we're both dead. We can touch dead stuff, but we can't touch life stuff."

"We've got to let Timmy know somehow," Martha said.

Henry nodded. "He just lives across town. We can probably walk there. Or you can stay, and I'll go."

Martha took her husband's hand. "We'll go together. The walk will do us both good. I can use a breath of fresh air."

When his hand dissolved into the doorknob, Henry braced himself and marched through the front door, pulling Martha after him. The couple learned they did not have to walk but could float a few inches above the surface of the living world.

When they realized movement was propelled by thought, their journey accelerated faster than the automobiles that drove through them with every crossing of the street. When Martha urged her husband to look up at the stars that crowded out all traces of night, she and he rose above the city, flying like Peter Pan and Wendy.

"There's Timmy's apartment building," Martha said. They immediately stood together in Timmy's living room.

Henry said, "Next time, let's skip the walk and just jump straight there. Those cars driving through me were a bit unnerving."

Martha nodded but said nothing. They thought their way up to their son's bedroom.

"Oh, my," Martha whispered, "he must be sick. That light around him is all curled and spoiled-looking."

"Who's that beside him?" Henry wondered.

"Don't recognize her," Martha said.

"They're both drunk," Tony said.

They turned toward the sound and Tony instantly appeared on the opposite side of the room.

"Our son just became a father," he told Martha. "He just won't know it for a while."

"The sins of the father shall be visited on the son," Martha said.

"Don't leave out the mother," Tony replied.

"At least I loved you," Martha said. "I was underage. You took advantage of me."

"I married you, didn't I?" Tony reached into his Army shirt pocket and withdrew a cigarette. "I wasn't ready to settle down, that's all."

He put the cigarette in his mouth, reached up in the air and found a lighter there. He lit the cigarette, inhaled, coughed, and then blew a cloud of smoke across the room at Martha and Henry.

"You signed up for the Army just to get away from me and Timmy," Martha said.

Tony pointed the cigarette at Henry. "If I hadn't died in Vietnam, you'd never have met him."

"Where did you get cigarettes?" Henry asked. "Are you allowed to smoke in Heaven?"

"Ain't been to no Heaven. No Hell either," Tony said. "There ain't nothing in life you can't have in death. You just have to want it, and it's there."

"Except Martha," Henry said, remembering how Tony had tried to take young Martha on the sofa. Henry put his arm around Martha's shoulders.

"The night's still young," Tony said. "Hold onto her while you still can."

Enraged by Tony's smart mouth, Henry clenched a fist and took a step toward him.

Martha pulled Henry back. "Leave it be, Henry."

Henry turned to face his wife. She appeared to have become younger, no more than thirty.

Martha's eyes were drawn to the bed.

"Timmy's girlfriend's awake."

"Tim, Tim, wake up!" The naked woman begged

Timmy to rouse and shook his shoulder. "I smell smoke. Something's burning!"

"She smells my cigarette," Tony said. "There are some things that can cross over between the dead and the living. For example, you wanted to let our son know you are dead," he told Martha. "Just think a phone in your hands. Better yet, I'll do it for you."

Startled, Martha nearly dropped the telephone receiver that appeared in her right hand.

Tony flicked the butt of his cigarette through the wall. "Now, think of Timmy's phone number."

When Martha pictured the numbers, her son's phone rang. Timmy groped for his cellphone.

"When he puts the phone to his ear, talk," Tony said.

"Timmy! Timmy! It's your mom!" Martha frantically hollered into her phone.

Tony lit another cigarette. "He'll hear a lot of static, but he should be able to just barely make out your voice.

"Mom? Mom, is that you?" Timmy mumbled.

"Time to hang up," Tony said.

The receiver in Martha's hand dissolved.

"That'll scare him enough to get him out of bed," Tony said.

"Where you going?" the naked woman said when Timmy hurried to get off the bed. "I don't smell that smoke any more. Must've dreamed it."

"I think that was my mother," Timmy said. He tried to get a foot through his briefs. He nearly tripped before he succeeded in pulling his underwear up. He paused while his left leg searched for a path into his jeans.

"Who the hell are you?" he asked his bed companion.

"Tanya," she said, clearly annoyed she had to tell him something she felt he should have remembered. She abandoned the bed and reached to the floor for her clothes.

Henry and Tony had found something in common: fascination watching Tanya dress. A side glance at Martha told Henry his leering did not amuse her.

Tanya covered her breasts with her bra. "I suppose you don't remember all those things you said to me when you were buying me all them drinks at Andy's Tavern—'You're my soul mate', 'I've been searching for you all my life', 'We're meant to be together'."

"Look, I know that was my mother. I don't have time for this," Timmy replied. He shoved his bare feet into his shoes. "She sounded like there's trouble. I've got to get over there."

Tanya wiggled into her tight jeans.

"Well, I'm going with you. You can drop me off at my apartment."

Buttoning her blouse, she ran out of the bedroom after Timmy.

"I don't have time to drive you home. Walk," Timmy said.

"It's dark, and I live at least ten miles from here," Tanya said. "I'll go with you to your mother's, and then you can take me home when you're done there."

Martha chased after her son. Tim had closed the apartment door behind him and Tanya before his mother could yell, "I don't want her to see me in my house!"

"I don't think he heard you, Martha," Henry said.

Martha gripped her husband's hand. "Let's get home, then, before they get there." She slapped Henry's arm. "And you, looking her up and down. Oh, but it wasn't okay with you when Tony was taking my clothes off while you just sat there and cried!"

"You remember that?" Henry asked.

"Of course, I remember," Martha replied. She closed her eyes, and she and Henry were instantly in their living room where Tony's attempted seduction had happened.

"You looked like you wanted him to have sex with you," Henry said. "Why'd you tell him to stop?"

Martha looked defiantly up into his eyes. She had become younger still—as young as the first day Henry had noticed her splashing out of the ocean onto the sand of Daytona Beach. The white bikini she wore that day, she wore again now.

The music of their first dance—*Make It with You,* by Bread—gently increased in volume. Henry embraced Martha. It was their song. It was their dance.

Dreams are for those who sleep,
Life is for us to keep,
And if you're wondering what this song is leading to
I'd like to make it with you
I really think that we can make it, girl...

They danced their dance, and all of their young love for each other, forgotten as they had grown older, found life again. Drawn to her irresistible lips, Henry kissed Martha in that gentle but hungry way deepest love required. His young Martha seemed oblivious to his aged face and body, gripping his shoulders and raising herself, wrapping her legs around his waist.

Henry dropped to his knees. While he removed Martha's bikini top, he lowered her to the carpet. The darkness of the fireplace gave way to the radiance of flames over a burning log.

The sight of his own erection was the first time Henry realized he was naked. The second time was when he spread his body over Martha's. His mouth cherished her firm breasts. Her long fingers jolted every vertebrae of his spine.

Once again feeling like a man with a purpose, Henry explored all of her with his lips and his tongue, until he could luxuriate in the moist blonde curls between her thighs.

And if I choose the one I'd like to help me through,
I'd like to make it with you
I really think that we can make it, girl...

Unable to wait any longer, Martha slid under her husband just when the doorbell rang.

"Who the hell—" Henry said.

"It's Timmy," Martha whispered. "I can't have my son see me naked!"

She pushed Henry off, but when she ran, she tripped over a glowing rope that trailed from the top of the staircase to the carpet of the living room and to the back of Henry's head. Unable to find her own luminous cord, she pulled herself, hand-over-hand, along Henry's, floating up the stairs in the path of its brilliant white light.

Timmy had abandoned the bell to pound his fist on the door.

Henry flew upstairs behind his wife.

In their bedroom, in their bed, covered by blankets, were their bodies. The glowing cord ended at the forehead of the snoring Henry.

Henry heard the crunch of the downstairs front door being kicked open, and someone or something pushed him. He fell forward onto his other self and rolled to stare at the far corner of the ceiling where Martha and Tony waved down at him. He sank into himself.

Henry opened his eyes when he heard a man crying. Timmy knelt at the other side of the bed, cupping and kissing Martha's face.

"What is it, Timmy," Henry said sleepily. "What are you doing here?" He pointed to the young woman standing beside his stepson. "And who is she?"

Henry looked at Martha and wondered why she had not been awakened by the commotion, too. He looked into Timmy's wet eyes, mentally pushing away the terrible truth.

"No, no, no, Martha," Henry wailed. He gently pulled his dead wife from his stepson's hand into his own loving embrace. "Martha, I thought we were going together. How could you leave me behind?"

In the far corner of the ceiling, Henry saw two glowing orbs. He raised his trembling hand toward them and cried, "Please, take me with you! Please! Please, Martha, I love you!"

One orb drifted down, hesitated, and then touched, Henry's right cheek like a kiss. The walls faded away when his heart stopped beating. The veil lifted between the dark and the light. Young Henry took Martha's hand while old Henry dropped back on his pillows.

"Where's Tony?" Henry asked, drawn to the blinding light up ahead.

"Stuck back there," Martha answered, "where he wants to be."

~~Robert L. Arend

The Tree of Life

by Catherine A. MacKenzie

The tree of life
Grows.
How far it goes
and where it goes
no one knows.
Branches separate
and spread,
outstretched like fingers,
splayed
and reaching to the sky
as if grasping for air
and life.
The buds sprout leaves,
growing
green and fresh,
living for a season
in the sun and rain,
then die when day is done
and fall to the ground,
pushed by the wind
and cold,
pulled by gravity,
lying there,
remains resting,
then scattered
as they're blown in the dust
searching for burial,
a final resting place,
earth to earth,
back at peace,
buried in the soil
waiting for rebirth
as the seasons
change again.

The Jar Girl

by Nancy Smith Gibson

Changpu cradled the infant close to her breast and stroked the tiny face with her finger.

"Wife, it is time," said Chuanli.

"One more minute. Give me one more minute," Changpu pleaded. Tears fell from her cheeks onto the face of the baby in her arms. She looked up at her husband and begged, "Have we tried everyone? Won't anyone take her?"

"We have tried every childless couple for many li. You know they all want boys. The month is up today, and she must be registered if we keep her. You know we cannot do that. We can barely feed our son, and this small girl will never grow up to be a strong worker. You have no more milk to nourish her. This is the best way. Her life will be in the hands of Shangdi. If He chooses to save her, He will send someone. If He chooses to take her into His Heavenly Palace, Shung Tian, He will do so. It is out of our hands."

Changpu held the baby to her cheek and whispered into her ear. "My sweet Lin-Lin. My Beautiful Jade. I love you. May God protect you."

With that, she handed the infant to Chuanli.

The lumbering caravan made its way over hills and

valleys, from village to town to city and on to more villages, towns and cities. Across the great land, they traveled, bringing the exotic, the foreign and the unusual to the lives of rich and poor alike. In the cities, they earned good money, because people flocked to see the strange, the extraordinary, the bizarre sights the traveling show presented. In the small towns, they earned much less; every little bit helped feed the people and animals in the caravan. In the countryside, they were lucky if they could scrounge up food for the animals, much less for the humans in the group.

On the other hand, the countryside sometimes afforded opportunities to add new oddities and talent to the assemblage of poor souls. They lived by showing their abnormalities to the public and hearing the gasps and moans of the crowds who observed the monsters God or the Devil had created.

From time to time, someone would approach the master of the company, Dingxiang—whose name meant stability and fortune—and would tell of a poor unfortunate person whose parents had not possessed the courage to do what should have been done at birth. The ill-fated individuals usually couldn't support themselves and were shunned by all God-fearing people.

Dingxiang sought out afflicted souls and, depending on the uniqueness of their malformations, he offered them jobs and a home with the troop. He offered them security and camaraderie; they would never again have to worry about where they would live or what they would eat, and they would be in the company of people who knew only too well how they felt about their misshapen bodies.

Although Dingxiang exaggerated somewhat about the quality of the housing, food, and surroundings to be enjoyed by the traveling group, it was, nevertheless, true these unfortunate souls would have a much better life than they otherwise would have had in the countryside, unless they were fortunate enough to be born into a loving family that could tolerate the sight of them.

Twenty or so wagons were spread out over several miles as they ploddingly followed the head wagon, driven by Dingxiang. They made their way toward the next town on their route.

"Husband," said Huiqing, "I am worried about Jiao. The death of her infant has made her so unhappy she is ill. She has taken to her pallet in their wagon. If she does not die of sorrow, she may take her own life. She told me there is nothing to live for. She has given birth three times, but each child has died within days. She yearns to be a mother, but cannot."

"Evidently, whatever caused her to grow long hair all over her body has caused her to be unable to produce a healthy child. What of her husband? Can he console her?"

"Alas, no. Chang tries, but nothing he does lifts her spirits. He spends his days driving the wagon, and he cannot be with her in her sorrow."

"Iiieee. If she dies, we lose our lion woman. And if we lose her, we may lose our man-as-tall-as-two-men also. What shall we do?"

They rode in silence, pondering the misfortunes that had beset them lately. The elephant that had been part of the caravan for over twenty years had died three months prior. It would be a year, perhaps two, before the procession made its way to an area where a new pachyderm might be acquired. The bear was quite old also. One never knew when an old creature might lie down and die. The big cage of monkeys seemed quite healthy, but one couldn't really tell with monkeys. Besides, they didn't draw a crowd like the more exotic animals. Thank God the tiger was healthy and in good spirits, although he was so tame he didn't growl and roar at the crowd as Dingxiang might have wished.

He took very good care of his menagerie. He understood, as some caravan managers did not, that his fortune relied on the well-being of the creatures, human and animal, the crowds paid to see.

Animals were easy to keep happy compared to the human members of the traveling show. The acrobats were fighting: Lei accused Kang of almost dropping him; Kang blamed Lei of not being in the right place at the right time; Duyi, being the top man in the final pyramid, worried about being supported properly and complained about both of them. Junjie and Da tried to stay out of the argument, but the act was suffering.

Jinhai, the three legged man, had only been with them for a few months and was still very happy to have left his old village and see the world. He was a good-looking adolescent. If he hadn't had three legs, he might have been popular in his home area, but as it was, girls shied away from him. He was enthralled with the daughter of one of the couples who traveled with the group and worked in the background. There was a small group of necessary workers who put up tents, repaired broken equipment, cared for the animals, and generally did everything the show people could not handle.

The two tiny people fought as well. She accused him of flirting with someone in the last town. Dingxiang could not imagine any normal woman wanting a two-foot tall man, but Ning—who was anything but tranquil, as her name suggested—chronically accused Fa of encouraging crowds of women to his bed. Their screaming fights could be heard all over the camp each evening.

The twins—who were joined into one person—were peaceful, at least, having years before settled any differences they might have had. They usually rode in the wagon with the armless man, Boqin, who was a master on the violin. They were all great friends and seldom tired of each other's company.

Guoliang—who Dingxiang used to bill as the world's largest man—had left their company in the last big city they visited. Travel had become too difficult for him, so he stayed with friends he had made there.

As they traveled along the rutted path, Huiqing put

her hand on her husband's arm.

"Iiieee, husband! What is that in the grass?"

Dingxiang pulled on the reins, drawing the oxen to a halt. He stepped down onto the wheel and then to the ground.

"It is an infant. A female," he said.

"Is she alive?"

"Yes, she lives. But she is very weak. Her cry is like that of a newborn kitten."

"Bring her to me. Perhaps she is the answer to our problem."

"Eh? What problem? What answer?"

"Jiao. She's dying for lack of an infant to nurture. Here is her salvation!" Huiqing took the baby from her husband. "Fetch my shawl from the back. I need to warm the child."

Dingxiang did as she asked, and soon the babe was wrapped warmly.

"Husband, let us wait here for the wagon of Chang and Jiao. It is the next one behind us and should be here shortly. The babe needs to suckle, and Jiao has plenty of milk for her." She held the child close, whispering to it. "Your parents could not keep you, and so they placed you for God's judgment to decide your fate. And God, in His wisdom, has given you in exchange for one whose life He took. Your life will save another's. Jiao will live because of you, and she will make a good mother for you."

A half-hour later the cart being driven by Chang approached and, seeing the lead wagon stopped, drew up beside it.

"Ho, Master Dingxiang, is there a problem?"

"No. There is a solution to a problem," said Dingxiang, climbing from the wagon and taking the bundled infant from his wife. "I have your wife's salvation."

Chang was silent as the wagon master ducked under the canvas that protected the meager home.

"Jiao, I have come to relieve you of your misfortune."

"Oh, Master Dingxiang, no one but God can do such a thing, and He has chosen to pile misfortune upon me."

"God can also give you good fortune. As He takes away, He can also give."

"First, He proclaimed that I be born like this, a monster to be feared and shunned. All good people turn away from my visage when they see me," Jiao moaned.

"But now, many hundreds of people pay good money to see you as what God has created. And you have married a good man who admires you and treats you well. It is better than many wives have."

"Iiieee. God also punishes my husband, as well as me, by sending children who die within hours of birth. A woman is meant to be a mother, but I am only teased with the prospect before it is snatched from me. I have no hope. I only wait to die."

"Jiao, God has given you a babe. Here she is. Her life is in your hands alone." He offered the bundle in his arms to the woman reclining on the pallet.

Pulling herself to her elbows, Jiao peered into the gloom of the canvas room. "What is this you mock me with?"

"A child. It is not to mock you. God has sent you a child. Some peasant family put this girl child by the side of the road, placing her life in God's hands. Surely they could not keep her, and, as is the custom in the countryside, she was put where passersby would find her. In this way, her fate was truly left to those who found her. God has sent her to you, to nourish and raise."

Jiao took the shawl-wrapped infant and uncovered the mewling baby. "Her cry is so weak."

"She looks half-starved. You need to give her nourishment."

Uncovering her hair-covered breast, Jiao nursed the child. A smile came upon the face even kind people could not find attractive. "Ah, little one, God has surely sent you to me. Drink deeply and live. Master Dingxiang and myself, we have saved your life, and now you save mine with your very existence."

"Just remember, Jiao, that I am the one who plucked her from the grass and brought her to you. One day I will make plans for her, and you are to let me have my way."

The woman was so intent on the child, she ignored his words. The only thing that mattered to her was that she had a living child.

"I will call you Meilin—Plum Jade—for you are as beautiful as jade to me. Husband," she called out, "come, see what God has sent us.

The years that followed were happy ones for Jiao and Chang, raising their daughter. Indeed, they were happy years for the entire caravan.

The troop gained the world's largest woman, Huian, who was as kind and peaceful as her name. Perhaps it was her nature that helped the company settle down and get along as they traveled the miles. Huiliang, the world's thinnest man, whose name also meant kind and good, also joined the group. Huiliang and Huian began their acquaintance riding in two separate carts. It took an especially stout contraption pulled by a team of strong oxen to transport Huian. Soon, however, they began to share a wagon, and shortly thereafter were married.

Meilin grew into a sunny, bright toddler, adored by everyone in the assemblage. She once again was called Lin-Lin, as she had been during her first month of life. Of course, no one in the present company knew this, not even Meilin herself. Dingxiang watched and thought, smiling to himself as he anticipated the crowds that would come to see her. When he told his wife of his plan, Huiqing berated him so much he almost felt ashamed. Almost, you understand, but not quite.

Finally, when Lin-Lin was about two years old, the caravan entered a fairly large city, and Dingxiang approached Jiao and said, "Remember when I gave you the child I told you I would have plans for her? And remember you agreed not to oppose my plans?"

Jiao did remember some words about that subject, but she didn't think she had agreed to forgo opposition.

"Iiieee, Master. You would not sell her body to the flesh-mongers would you? I will kill you before I will let you do such a thing!"

Dingxiang was incensed. "You think I would do such a depraved thing? I, a good man? No, I would never do such an act."

"Then what are you going to do with my child?"

"She is my child, also. I am the one who took her from the grassy grave where she was placed by her true parents and brought her to you. Shangdi, God, placed her life in my keeping."

Jiao bowed her head. "It is as you say."

"She is going to become a jar-girl."

"Oh, no, Master. Please do not do that," she cried. Jiao pleaded and cried but he could not be dissuaded from his plans.

Dingxiang took the child with him as he navigated the narrow back streets of the town. Finally they reached what was obviously the shop of a potter, for it was filled with pots and bowls, urns and plates, vessels as large as a man and those as small as your thumbnail.

"This is the child I spoke to you about," he said to the shopkeeper.

"Iiiiee, she is as you said," replied Nianzu. "I have the vessel ready for her. Come into my workroom."

There on the worktable were two pieces of an urn, placed on their sides. "Come place her in this larger piece," said Nianzu.

Dingxiang lifted Meilin onto the table, and then grasped her under the shoulders and knees. He carefully placed her into the jar. With some difficulty each arm was placed into pottery tubes on either side of the vessel. Her right arm curved until it touched her hip. Her left arm extended out, then up. When she was placed to the potter's satisfaction, he picked up the other section of the jar and fit it to its counterpart, making an entire pot, open on the top, where Meilin's head extended, and less the bottom, from which her legs stretched. When everything met Nianzu's liking he took a bowl of clay and melded the two pieces together.

"It is done. Pay me the rest of my coins," said Nianzu.

Dingxiang counted out the remainder of the payment and started to pick up his jar girl.

"It would be wise to have me or another artisan look at this every few years, in case she grows so big as to cut off the blood flow. You should not have to change jar size for some time. The jar children I have seen adjust, even thrive, in their jars. This one will, also, I am sure."

When Dingxiang returned to the caravan everyone gathered around to see what had been done to Meilin, and he found himself explaining to those who had never seen nor heard about a jar girl.

"She will grow into the shape of the jar, which is that of a teapot. There are several cup girls traveling the country, but she will be the first teapot girl in history. She will be famous." He stopped and looked around at the crowd. Somehow Dingxiang expected them to be happier over this. Instead, they all looked with sad eyes, and he even saw tears trickling down cheeks. He anticipated Jiao would be upset, but not the others... not the burly man who wrestled with the tents and the wagons, not the brawny man who cared for the oxen, not the muscular man who cared for the tiger, the monkeys and the new elephant. They looked on with sadness in their eyes, and then they turned and walked away, shaking their heads and muttering.

"Shangdi gave her life to me," Dingxiang said to himself. "He guided my way to find the babe before the wild animals did. If not for me, she would not have a life. I have done the best for her, insured she will be able to earn her way through life."

Time went on, and everyone got used to seeing Meilin

in her jar. Jiao fed her every meal, and lifted a mug of water to her lips when she was thirsty. She kept her child as clean as possible, and even though she could not cuddle her as she had the first months of Meilin's life, she made sure the child was surrounded with love. Mighty Chang, the man as tall as two men, lifted Meilin onto her pallet each night, placing the jar on its side for sleep. The child could not move either arm, and so she was limited in what she could do. While Jiao tended and loved her, Chang showed his love by stopping the cart when he saw a wildflower blooming and picked it for Meilin to hold in her tiny hand. He pointed out the birds in the grass or trees as they passed, and told her stories to keep her entertained. Dingxiang encouraged her to eat, and told others to give her sweetmeats when they had them. In that way, he said, she will grow round, like a teapot.

Finally, when Meilin reached puberty, Dingxiang announced it was time for the jar to be removed. It would be done, he said, when they reached the next town with a jar potter. That way, if it was determined Meilin should be placed in a larger jar (she was presently in her third jar) the potter could do the job. But it was possible, Dingxiang said, entirely possible, that Meilin had reached her full growth and could stay without a jar.

Everyone waited with mounting excitement as they entered the gates of the next city. And it was as Dingxiang said. Meilin was a perfectly formed teapot, with her right arm as the handle and the left as a spout. He dressed her in the finest of robes—kimonos made of beautifully flowered silk woven in designs that indicated her high status. Her hair was thick and shiny, like a raven's wing. The teapot girl was the finest jar girl ever seen. Everywhere they went, people came to see her and marvel over what God had wrought.

Dingxiang concocted two stories to explain this amazing thing. At first he said she was the daughter of an eminent man, a maker of teapots for the Emperor. His ancestors had made teapots for thousands of years; it was so much in their blood that when this man fathered a girl child, who could not work in the family business, Shangdi had seen fit to send the man a girl shaped as a teapot, in order that she might glorify the tradition of the family. The crowds marveled over such a thing.

Soon Dingxiang grew tired of saying the same thing over and over. So sometimes he said that Meilin's mother was a concubine in the home of a noble man. One day, as she was bringing tea to the mistress of the house, she dropped and shattered a very expensive pot. Her mistress became enraged and beat the pregnant woman with a cane. When the child was born, well, the result was witness to the concubine's trespass.

The years passed and the troop traveled the length and breadth of the country, showing the people the wonders God had given mankind to puzzle over. One year was particularly rainy, and the caravan of wagons sloughed through mud everywhere they went. They were struggling to reach the next town, where they hoped to secure housing in a building instead of sleeping in wet wagons, carts, and tents, when they approached a bridge over a raging creek. One by one, the wagons made their way across.

"Hold on tight," Chang said as their oxen started across. "Hold on tight, wife. Hold on tight, Lin-Lin. Pray Shangdi takes us safely across."

But his prayers were in vain. As they reached the center of the span, the bridge gave a mighty groan and tipped sideways, dumping the contraption and its occupants into the raging water. The oxen immediately used their mighty strength to pull what remained of the wagon to the bank, but Chang, Jiao, and Meilin were tumbled and tossed in the rapids. Each of them was swept along, pushed here and there by the currents, until finally Meilin was able to grab hold of the branch of a tree which had been uprooted by the torrent. With difficulty she hooked her right arm around the stout limb, insuring she would at least remain in that spot unless the tree came loose and floated along with the flood.

She'd hung there for some time when she realized a woman was floating toward her, clinging to a piece of lumber. Reaching with her left arm, which was permanently extended outward like a spout, she seized hold of the woman and held on tight until the woman pulled herself to where she could also grasp the tree. They both clung there for what seemed like days, but was in reality hours. Gradually, however, the water abated, until they were left mired in mud on the side of the creek.

When they had recovered enough to speak, they sat up and appraised the situation.

"Iiieee. You saved my life," said the woman. "If you had not reached for me and held on tightly I would have perished."

"Surely God placed me there to save you," replied Meilin.

"You are still clinging to the tree which was our salvation. Can you let go now?"

"I cannot. I am a teapot girl. My limbs are in this position forever. Without help I cannot release the tree."

"Then I shall help you," said the woman.

"I thank you for your help," said Meilin.

"It is I who thanks you. I owe my life to you. Shangdi sent you to save me. My life is in your hands. I will help you forever."

At that moment, Dingxiang arrived. His cart had made it safely across the creek before the bridge washed out. When he was farther down the road, he heard the cries of Chang and Jiao as they washed along the rapids. After helping them to shore he walked back along the bank looking for Meilin. When he saw she was alive, he ran to her and hugged her. Not only was he glad his investment was not lost, he genuinely loved Meilin, as did everyone in the traveling group.

"And who is this?" he asked.

"I am named Changpu," the woman answered. "This kind girl saved my life. Surely I would have perished if not for her."

"My name is Meilin, Plum Jade, but everyone calls me by my baby name, Lin-Lin."

"I once had a daughter named Beautiful Jade. I called her Lin-Lin, also." She looked shyly at the ground. "I humbly request that I be permitted to serve Lin-Lin as her servant. She needs someone to help her in her daily activities, and I would like to do that to repay her for saving my life."

"Do you not have a family? A husband and children who will miss you?" asked Dingxiang.

"My husband is dead, and my son did not like the life of a poor farmer. He abandoned me and went to the city to live. I have no one."

"Then perhaps it is best if you come with us. It is true Meilin needs help with everything, and her mother suffered a broken leg in her rush through the flood."

"Iiieee. It is as we said. God truly sent her to save my life and sent me to serve her. Shangdi sees all and arranges all to His liking."

And as they trudged along the path to join the other members of the troop, Dingxiang could be heard telling her, "She is the famous teapot girl, you know. Shangdi sent her to be the most famous in all the land."

Author's note:

Victor Hugo, in his book The Man Who Laughs, *told of Chinese dealers who took a small child and put him in a grotesquely shaped porcelain vase without a top or bottom. At night they laid the vase on its side, so the child could sleep; in the morning, they set it upright again. They kept the child in it for years, while his flesh and bones grew according to its shape. Then they smashed the vase. The child comes out—and, behold, there is a man in the shape of a mug."*

~~From "Very Special People" by Frederick Drimmer. Bell Publishing Company--1985.

About the Author

While cleaning out the shelves to make room for yet more books, Nancy Smith Gibson came across an old volume about those special historical people who were once called freaks. From the famous Siamese twins to the Elephant Man, the world once celebrated the unusual among us. It was in this tome she discovered the ancient Chinese practice of placing a young child in a jar in order to make the child grow into a certain shape, and this story was born.

In the circle of life, what part does one of these misshapen people play? In "The Jar Girl", Jade saves the lives of two women who are part of her life, her mothers.

For Posterity

by Katherine Shaye

Ideal *(n.) Conformity to an ultimate standard of perfection or excellence; a value or principle one actively pursues as a goal; the regulations and standards instituted by The Clinic.*

"Honey, it's time."

Harold swung his eyes up from his spreadsheet to the clock above the fridge. Sure enough, it read nine thirteen, right on schedule. That's what made his wife, Lola, so great: punctuality.

Setting aside his unfinished work, he pushed up from the kitchen table and followed her into the hall. His fingers flew to the single knot in his sweatpants and freed the bowed string. The couple stripped simultaneously, clothes hitting the hardwood with soft thumps, marking a path to the bedroom. They crossed the threshold separately, Harold already pumping himself into a state of readiness.

On the bed, Lola had the pillows stacked up, a pedestal for her bottom. Elevating the hips meant a twenty-three percent increase in their chances. Lola fell into the sheets, situating herself just so. Following her lead, Harold climbed between her thighs to perform his duty.

Thrusting at her, his docile Lola, Harold couldn't help but admire her crystal-blue eyes, burning sapphires that would someday shine out from the faces of his offspring. The thought warmed his heart with that same effect potential fatherhood had on all men. The chance to see his genes passed on to the next generation caused his hips to quicken their pace.

Diligent training meant that within a few careful strokes he had expelled himself fully, ending their routine. Extricating himself, Harold backed off the bed to give Lola plenty of space to assume her post coital position. Swinging her legs and hips upward, she leaned her toes against the back wall in a shoulder stand. Fifteen minutes in this pose meant another seven percent increase in odds.

"Can I get you anything?" Harold asked. "Water, juice, crackers?"

Lola smiled serenely. "Water would be nice."

Hydration was essential for strong uterine health. Lola was always responsible about her liquid intake. Seventy ounces daily for optimum health, and Lola never missed a drop.

Harold started for the kitchen, but paused in the doorway.

"I'll bring you an apple as well, shall I?" Never could be too careful with nutrition. Proper maintenance ensured another three point seven percent increase.

"Hmm, I suppose that would be nice as well," Lola said, her cheeks flushed pink with blood. Harold noticed that it complemented those baby blue orbs, and donned an appreciative smile before journeying after his wife's sustenance.

The break room smelled of lemons, a sharp tang left behind by the all-natural cleaning products used to sanitize the clinic's offices every two hours. Lost in his thoughts, Harold stared down at his mug of tea, a ginger stain on the gleaming white countertops.

"Still no luck?" Fenwick asked, clapping a sympathetic hand on Harold's shoulder. His grip was firm, shaking Harold from his brooding.

Harold lowered his eyebrows, confused. "How did you..."

Fenwick gestured at his coworker's face. "You don't have that bundle of joy glow that everyone gets."

Harold knew that look well. All parents had it the moment they tested positive.

"Still negative," Harold grumbled, eyes resuming their intent focus on his mug. "It's been five months."

Trying to be supportive, Fenwick adopted a half-hearted smile. "There's still time."

Newly-mated Potentials had six months to complete implantation.

The thought did little to comfort Harold.

"Not much," he mumbled to his tea. If he and Lola were unsuccessful in this last cycle, the Clinic would step in. Their fertility examinations would be re-administered, and he shuddered to think what might happen if one of them failed. Among other more dire consequences, they would have to separate.

This saddened Harold. Lola was such a competent wife.

"I'm worried," he said, gaze swinging up to Fenwick's appeasing smile. "What if it's my fault?"

The fear had been plaguing him for weeks. After their first three attempts at conception had failed, Harold had redoubled his efforts to stay virile and up his count. Vitamins, exercise, nutrition... he'd been adamant about his daily schedule, keeping himself in absolute peak condition.

All he knew for sure was that it couldn't be Lola. His past month of extra effort still paled in comparison to her regimen. If she were any more fertile, she'd have been sprouting little ones on her own.

"There's nothing wrong with you," Fenwick assured him, his voice less than convincing. "Just give it a little more effort this month. You'll be celebrating before you know it."

Slightly mollified, Harold let Fenwick lead him back to his desk.

Upon reaching Harold's office, both men paused in the doorway to admire a new hire walking toward them, wide hips swaying back and forth in a determined rhythm. She passed them a polite smile as she strode by, her pace never slowing.

"Look at those hips," Fenwick whispered, practically salivating. "She could easily drop ten with those. And can you imagine a whole flock of little ones with that fiery red mane?"

Fenwick was living a pipe dream. The Clinic monitored and arranged most pairings for the highest level of genetic compatibility. It was a rarity to allow the Potentials to choose. However, that didn't stop unmated Potentials, like Fenwick, from lusting over the possibilities.

Harold and Lola hadn't met until the day they moved into their Clinic-sanctioned home, both having reached the requisite twenty-four years of age. They had received word of their pairing as mated Potentials through various outlets: Harold an email at work, Lola a phone call to her mother's home. Arrangements had been made within the week, and both were scheduled to move in the following Monday. Never as fussy as Fenwick, Harold had been satisfied to find simple Lola waiting on his doorstep when he arrived.

"Directive 213C."

Fenwick blinked several times, reluctant to draw his attention back to Harold and the office.

"Directive 213C," Harold repeated while Fenwick stared at him perplexed. Though they had both worked for the Clinic for the past seven years, Fenwick wasn't nearly as familiar with the Codex as Harold was.

"The regulation concerning recessive genes," Harold explained. "Red hair like hers can only be paired with others of her kind. To preserve the gene code."

Fenwick eyed the woman more intently. Sure enough, when she turned the corner away from their offices he glimpsed an extended Marker tattooed on her right temple: 23-626.

The first number was an indicator of genetic viability. Everyone had those, numbering from one to twenty-three, tattooed at birth in the same place on the right temple. Harold and Lola both bore twenties.

The second figure by the woman's eye was special, unique to some quirk in her DNA. It would place tighter restrictions on her mating assignment.

Fenwick of course knew all this, but preferred to play the dreamer.

"I guess it's for the best," he said with a shrug. Scratching the twenty-two at his temple, he quoted the company line, "The Clinic has humanity's best interests at heart."

It wasn't uncommon for Potentials to covet the rarer genetic traits. In the end, it would mean privilege and prestige for all of their descendants. Although they were far from exceptional commodities, blue-eyed youngsters scurried through Harold's mind increasing his worries of separation from the woman who could provide them.

That night Harold slept with Lola in his arms for the first time. She'd argued at first, claiming that if she didn't sleep flat, she would ovulate crooked, but gave in when Harold convinced her that they could switch sides the next night. Hand curled over her belly, he yearned to feel the absent kicks of life.

The next few days at work didn't ease Harold's anxieties. Every eye in the building seemed to center on him, knowing and pitying the horrible truth of his predicament. He walked the halls with his gaze glued to his toes. It didn't matter if he was trying. The Clinic ruler had two measurements, success and failure. When the relief of Friday afternoon arrived, Harold almost reached the speed limit in his rush to drive home.

The respite of the weekend withered away when Harold turned onto his street and found strange vehicles crowding his driveway—strange because he'd never seen them in his neighborhood before, not because he didn't know to whom they belonged. The hulking steel giants of the Clinic Hospital staff were recognizable to all.

Harold was halfway across the lawn before he remembered he'd left his car on. Not stopping to remedy the issue, Harold barreled through the front door calling out, "Lola?"

At first, there was silence, broken only by the soft beeping and whirring of machinery. Then Lola's singsong voice floated down the hall, "In the bedroom, Harold."

Following that voice, Harold crept toward his bedroom. A sliver of light shined through the cracked door and Harold nudged it the rest of the way open with his foot.

Plugged into a dozen different machines, a nude Lola lay splayed on the bed while three Clinic Health practitioners prodded at her. A dark-haired woman on her right held a needle to Lola's bare arm searching for a vein. At one point, Harold had thought he might like to have dark-haired children, but both he and Lola were fair-headed, so he'd abandoned that dream months ago in favor of a new fixation.

The woman's tongue stuck out in concentration and she shoved a tuft of hair behind her ear. Two other female practitioners ran back and forth between Lola and the machines, marking clipboards and adjusting knobs, but Harold's attention was all for the brunette at his wife's elbow. The tiny thirteen on her temple had consumed his entire focus. Harold had never met a Desolate in person before.

Once, at six years old, Harold had asked his mother why she wouldn't let him play with the Desolate children when he went to the park. She'd told him it was because they were unclean. It wasn't until twelve years later, when he began his work at the Clinic, that he learned what she meant. A Desolate was anyone unable or unfit to have his or her own children.

Harold hadn't even known they held jobs within the Clinic Health department. Usually Desolates labored in more menial, hazardous occupations too risky for Potentials.

Most Desolates were classified by their Marker, denied their procreation rights because their DNA grades were less than fifteen. Others were Potentials who contracted diseases or had accidents that left them sterile. Either way it meant the same thing: no children.

All these facts tumbled through Harold's mind while he stared at the dark-haired Desolate. Noticing his scrutiny, the practitioner let her hair fall back down over her face. Lola let out a tiny squeak when the needle finally sank into her skin.

He rushed to her side. "Are you all right?"

Lola's beatific smile beamed up at him. "Just fine, you old worry wart. Pinched a little is all." Harold slid his hand into to hers anyway, perhaps only to comfort himself, and stared at his wife. Like twin pools of soothing ocean, Lola's eyes grounded Harold, holding his dread at bay while the three practitioners bustled around them both.

"Mr. Tielson?"

A voice from the doorway startled Harold from his calm. He hardly conversed with anyone who didn't refer to him by his given name. Turning, he found two new practitioners awaiting him in the hall.

"If you would come with us, please," said the same voice, belonging to the taller of the two. The second practitioner gestured ‘come here' with two fingers, and Harold hurried forward, still stressing over the dire implications of this unscripted visit.

Once he had scooted through and closed the bedroom door, Harold loosed his concerns on the two men in sober white scrubs before him. "We are supposed to have another month, another cycle to try again. This has to be a mistake. It's all far too soon."

"Addendum 4A to Directive 34," the taller practitioner droned. Eyes glazed, his face suggested that this wasn't his first time making these explanations. "Primary implantation period will be reduced from six months to five, in order to catch failed partnerships sooner, and promote quicker reproduction. If you'd like to see the paperwork..." He flipped back pages on his clipboard.

"No, no, I believe you," Harold said raising a resigned hand, too distracted to make a fuss. What he couldn't believe was how an Addendum as major as this had taken him by surprise. He worked directly for the Clinic. There should have been a warning, a meeting, an email, a Post-it... something.

"Where would you like to conduct your tests, sir?"

"Excuse me?" Harold shook his head trying to focus on the question he hadn't quite heard.

"Your wife is being monitored in your main bedroom. Is there another where we can administer your tests? It will be easier if we get everything done at once."

The nursery beside the kitchen came to Harold's mind, but there was no more than a crib and a few toys in that bedroom. Harold shook his head again. "No. The living room will work. It has a couch."

He led them there and turned to face the two men when he reached the couch. He began to sit, but stopped when the tall practitioner grabbed his arm. "We'll need you to strip down first, sir."

Harold followed his instructions without complaint. While he did so, the practitioners set up their equipment. The periodic chirps and beeps reminded Harold of Lola's machines in the other room. Once naked, he lay on the couch, his mind still racing.

"That woman in there," he said, "with my wife... she's a Desolate?"

Not looking up from his work, the tall practitioner nodded. "Yes, sir, she is. She was with us before

Addendum 3G to Directive 67 raised Marker requirements from thirteen to fifteen. She's very good at what she does. There's no need to worry about your wife, sir. She's in good hands. Focus on your own tests."

"Is there something I can do that would affect the outcome?" Harold asked hopefully.

The practitioner paused for a moment, considering.

"No, sir, but focus anyway. Worrying will only raise your blood pressure. Now sit up and take a deep breath for me."

The man slid a cold stethoscope across the width of Harold's back.

Harold couldn't get enough air into his lungs.

"They've taken Lola," he wheezed, raising both hands to his forehead and rubbing the ache that had settled there. "I don't understand it. They've taken her to the hospital, and they won't tell me anything."

His loafers scuffed trenches back and forth into the carpet.

Fenwick studied the memo detailing Addendum 4A and its agenda.

"It looks like you were in the first wave of retests. This information was only issued this morning." He pointed to the time stamp marked 8:03 am on the bottom corner of the page. "Maybe they didn't want to worry you in advance."

When Harold continued to pace, Fenwick shot an arm in his path to stop him.

"You could go visit her," he said.

Harold cocked his head to the side. "You can do that?"

He'd never known anyone who'd gone to a hospital for anything other than pregnancy.

"Sure. I mean, I think so. My aunt's first husband was Desolated in a car accident when I was little. She visited him in the hospital while they were still trying to save him."

Jacket in hand, Harold was through the door before Fenwick even stopped talking.

"Cover for me," he called over his shoulder, his mind already on the road to the hospital.

Swollen bellies crowded the waiting room, each woman perched in a chair, radiant and cheery. Their eager husbands snarled at onlookers, waiting to clobber the first person who dared jostle their precious cargo. Harold eyed the pregnant women, envious of their hovering husbands. In his imagination, he and Lola sat in those plush leather chairs awaiting their first checkup, his child barely beginning to push at the flat plains of her stomach.

The crackle of the hospital intercom snapped him back to reality and deflated his fantasies. Ignoring all the beaming parents, Harold eased his way through the lobby to the front desk. A clean, scrubbed nurse stared out at him from the window, clearly uninterested in whatever his problems were.

"What trimester is your wife in, sir?" she asked, cinnamon gum smacking between her lips. Harold wondered absently if tooth rot could ever be hereditary.

"My... my wife isn't pregnant," he said to the counter. It might have been a hallucination, but the lobby behind him seemed too quiet. Venturing a glance up Harold added, "Her name is Lola Tielson. She came in on a Clinic van last night."

This proclamation gained a raise of eyebrows from the bored nurse, out of pity rather than concern. She knew the type of cases that rode in on the Clinic vans.

Reaching across her desk, she retrieved a clipboard and ran a finger down the list of names muttering Tielson under her breath.

"Room 635," she spouted, already looking past him to the next patient in line. "Down the hall to your left."

Perspiration beading at the nape of his neck, Harold ticked off door numbers as he quickstepped in the direction she indicated. 520... 525... 530...

His pulse hadn't stopped racing since the practitioners had announced they were taking Lola away the night before.

"What are a few more tests?" Lola had cajoled him, rolling through their front hallway strapped to a gurney.

Blocking the front door, Harold grasped her arm. "I don't know, but I don't like it."

He couldn't shake the fear that if he let her leave, Lola wouldn't be back.

She slipped her hands free and patted him on the head. "You worry too much."

Perhaps not enough, Harold thought, his feet propelling him down a never-ending hallway. The uninterrupted bleeping of machines pouring out of each room was almost familiar to him in an unnerving way. Goosebumps sat erect on his arms despite both his long-sleeved shirt and jacket. *590... 595... 600...*

Harold had worked hard. He'd accepted Lola into his life without question, valued her for everything she could bring him. Together, they'd endeavored to create a perfect child, a shining, burbling, idyllic version of themselves, unimpeded by any defects. They'd done everything right, and still they'd failed. Now the only thing Harold had allowed himself to develop any affection for was being taken away from him. He burst into room 635, not sure there'd be anything to find.

The air inside reeked of lemons, every surface scoured clean too often, like the Clinic break room. White sheets, white frame, white gown. Harold stared at his wife resting in the hospital bed, her chest rising and falling in a slow rhythm. Lola brought the only color to the room.

Burning brightly against their deadened background, her blue eyes lifted to greet her husband.

"Harold?" she said, "What are you doing here? You should be at work."

"I came to see you," he said, closing the distance to her bedside in three steps. "How do you feel?"

"Tired, mostly." Lola swept stray hairs away from her face. They stuck to her head, plastered with grease and sweat. "I still have anesthetics in my system from the surgery."

Harold paled. "Surgery?"

Brow creased, Lola tried to bat at her covers with a frail arm. She only succeeded in brushing them back and forth, but persisted until Harold stopped her. "Lo, just tell me what you want."

Bottom lip curling to an almost smile, Lola sighed.

"I wanted to show you my incision." Her tired arm trailed across her hips. "It's a long one, right here."

Biting his lip, Harold tried not to show how much this disturbed him. Men with big scalpels had been slicing into his wife, and no one was telling him a thing. "Have they said what's wrong?"

Lola gave a tiny shake that Harold assumed was a shrug.

"Nothing definitive yet." She coughed and licked dry lips. "They're doing their best to figure it out."

"You need water," Harold said already walking back toward the hall.

Lola coughed again and rasped, "Proper hydration is an—"

"...eleven percent increase," Harold finished, warming when she grinned. "I'll go find you something."

What Harold really needed to find were answers. Leaving the glass of water on her bedside table, he left his now sleeping wife in search of the nearest practitioner.

The first one he found told him Lola Tielson wasn't in his department; the second, not in his specialty; and the third was positive that Lola Tielson was not even in his hospital. Two nurses couldn't access the information, and the last practitioner couldn't disclose it.

Every employee he interrogated stared at him with blank eyes, flatly refusing him any information: We're still running tests, sir. You will be briefed as soon as possible, sir. Let us take care of everything, sir. The Clinic has your best interests at heart.

"You look awful," Fenwick said, following it with a swig of Harold's morning tea. "Did you sleep in those clothes?"

"I spent the night at the hospital with Lola," Harold said, eyes fixed on the wall in front of him.

The hospital had given him no new information before he left, so when Fenwick asked for an update, his answer reeked of bitterness. "They're supposed to call if anything changes."

"Well, that's good." Fenwick smiled, chipper until Harold glared at him, and he added, "At least they're still working on it. That means there's a chance."

Whipping out a folder, Fenwick brandished it in front of Harold like a trophy. "I've got news to cheer you up, friend."

Harold didn't even bother to feign interest. Unperturbed, Fenwick dove into the packet, reading it aloud like a sports announcer. "The R&D department at Clinic building 278—that's us, man—has recently concluded their study on the genes affected by the hereditary disease known as cystic fibrosis. They have isolated its components and believe that, with proper manipulation, this disease can be eradicated from the population within seven years' time." Slamming the folder shut, Fenwick slapped it against his knee. "Hot damn! Can you believe it? Those geeks downstairs are finally onto something."

Harold's lackluster response drew a frown from Fenwick. "I know this stuff with Lola is bad, but Harold, this is good news for everyone. We're getting closer to the Ideal. Don't you want to bring your children into a world where they won't have to worry about what diseases or deformities their kids might have?"

"What? Yeah, of course, I just..." Harold tried to imagine his future kids... strong, healthy, blue-eyed offspring.

Finishing off Harold's tea, Fenwick clapped a hand on his shoulder. "Get some rest, man. It'll all be okay soon. You'll see."

Harold headed home after work to change before he returned to the hospital. Seeing an unfamiliar car in his driveway, he perked up, thinking maybe a friend had brought Lola back from the hospital. There was someone waiting for him on the doorstep.

Sprinting across the lawn, Harold felt his heart rate speed until he found himself face-to-face with a woman very much not Lola. A Miss Geraldine Portman greeted him at his door.

"Soon to be Geraldine Tielson," she corrected with a coy smile. A tight chignon kept her hair drawn back, displaying the shining twenty-three on her temple in permanent black ink.

Unmoved by her pedigree, Harold said, "But Lola is already my wife."

"Oh, that's been taken care of." Geraldine whipped out a stack of documents from the depths of her giant purse: divorce papers and new marriage license. She winked a muddy brown eye at him. "All they need is your signature."

Accepting the papers she brandished, Harold flipped mutely through them.

Geraldine had no trouble filling the silence by herself. "I'm not on schedule yet, so we have about a week for you to get used to my cycle. I'm not sure how different I am from your first wife. It may not even take that long."

Harold couldn't process her words, still staring at the pages of legalese without comprehension. "But Lola is still in the hospital. They're running tests. Th—the surgery..." Harold trailed off.

Being ever helpful, Geraldine relieved Harold of his house keys and opened the front door. "Didn't they phone you? She was diagnosed and transferred this afternoon."

"Transferred? Transferred where?" Foot hovering above on the threshold, Harold watched the strange woman stroll through the hall and invite herself into his bedroom.

"The Desolate Ward," she called from seemingly a million miles away.

Nothing else registered in Harold's brain. Not one word of Geraldine's consistent chatter made any impact after those three damning words. He lay in bed next to Geraldine, solid proof that Lola and all she offered were lost to him. He tried to reconcile himself with that idea, but the nagging question of where his beloved blue eyes were resting that night kept him tossing for hours.

He posed the question to Fenwick the next morning.

"What do you mean where do they go? They live in the buildings on the other side of the river. They go to work every day. They go home. Not much else," Fenwick said, his attention focused on the Tetris game in front of him.

"Not the ones who are born that way, the... new ones, the ones like your uncle." Harold lounged in the doorway as though the question was only of casual interest to him.

The nonchalance didn't fool Fenwick. He pried himself away from the computer to eye his friend warily. "This is about Lola, isn't it? They finally diagnosed her as a lost cause, a Desolate."

Crass. That's how Harold would have characterized the term Desolate. It was so dead, devoid of hope or feeling. It carried no indication of the character of a person who bore such a label.

"That's not the point," he said, not meeting Fenwick's stare. "I need to know what happens afterward, for my own peace of mind. Where do they go?"

"Harold, you can't..."

"I'm not planning anything, Fen. Just tell me what you know. Please?"

Fenwick squirmed a bit but eventually gave in. "It was a long time ago, but I think my aunt said that in this district, after a new Desolate goes through processing in the ward, they're transferred to the warehouse down on Loki Street. That is, until they can be set up with a new job and apartment on the other side of Isis River.

"It's supposed to be a holding camp. I can't say for sure, because I've never been down there myself..."

Harold hadn't listened much beyond warehouse on Loki Street but he nodded along as Fenwick continued to describe the place where the Clinic held Lola.

Harold left work that day with every intention of heading home. Geraldine had promised to make her famous pot stickers, which he was under strict instructions not to miss "for all the oil in Alaska."

As usual, he locked his office, rode the elevator down to the garage, and walked to his parking space. Then his feet carried him straight past his car and out to the street. Crisp air cut across his cheeks when he reached the sidewalk, making his eyes water and his hands curl tighter in his pockets.

Cars whizzed by in the fading sunlight, many headed home to a mate and a well-cooked meal, much like he was supposed to be doing. Instead, Harold walked. Turning left from the Clinic building, Harold walked toward Isis River.

The buildings in his district were monstrous, all sleek chrome and mirrored siding, towering over the streets like watchdogs. Several had cameras on the corners painted bright sunshine yellow, lest anyone forget their presence. Collar turned up against the wind, Harold weaved down the street cognizant of each lens that turned to observe his progress. Forty-five minutes later, he was not surprised to find himself standing in front of the warehouse on Loki Street.

This close to the river, the burning stench of alcohol assaulted his nostrils. A vice of the Desolates. Harold wrinkled his nose against it.

The Clinic forbade all body pollutants. Regular contamination by any drug was at the very least a forty percent decrease in viability. Then again, Desolates didn't have those concerns.

Intercut by an eight-foot chain-link fence, Harold had a clear view of the holding warehouse. Its thin metal walls, barely able to hold back the winter chill, were coated in layers of built up grime. Compared to the surrounding buildings, the warehouse was the stray mutt in a dog show. Milling around the decrepit doors, a few Desolates gathered to exchange some sort of conversation Harold wasn't close enough to hear.

When the doors opened to usher in the straggling Desolates, Harold ducked into the shadows. Something told him his presence would not be welcome. A man in a stiff uniform counted off the heads of all those who flowed back into the building.

Sun setting behind the horizon, Harold used its last remaining tendrils of light to search for a way through the fence. No options readily presented themselves. He could neither scale the fence with its barbed wire at the top, nor pick the padlock that secured the gate.

Hidden in the shadow of the neighboring building, Harold cursed himself. He'd never broken a rule a day in his life. Nothing in his experience had prepared him to break into a warehouse full of Desolates.

It was a stroke of luck that the dark uniform didn't follow the Desolates into the building. Instead, he let the door fall closed behind him and made his way out the front gate. Mere feet away, Harold pushed farther backward into the darkness.

A flicker of light bloomed in front of the man's face, casting shadows on the sunken contours of his cheeks. Moments later, he billowed out a pillar of smoke.

Watching this, Harold blanched. Even secondhand smoke meant a thirty-two percent decrease.

With every puff of that cigarette, Harold's stomach knotted tighter. Lola couldn't stay in that place.

There was a moment, somewhere in between springing from the shadows and lashing out at the strange man, that Harold had the good sense to think, What the hell am I doing?

But by then, it was too late. Harold's fist connected with the man's Marker, and the man crumpled to the ground. His lit cigarette rolled to a stop at the toe of Harold's boot. Harold stomped it out before sneaking through the gate.

Inside the warehouse was as dingy as outside, the cloying stench of mildew overpowering all else. Harold was not two steps into the building when a commanding voice stopped him. "Excuse me, sir?"

Harold spun to meet the gaze of another uniformed guard posted behind a desk entirely too small for him.

"What are you doing in here?" the guard asked. He leaned forward on his fists. "Civilian Potentials aren't allowed in this building."

Harold blinked at the man, his brain paralyzed in shock. "Uh... your man. At the door. He was um... attacked. By a Desolate I think." The lies flowed from his lips easier than Harold would have liked. "One of the bigger ones sneaked up on him and, uh, clocked him good. Used his keys to get out. I thought you should know. Last I saw, the Desolate was headed for Richter Street."

"Shit." The guard was out from behind his desk and almost to the door before he remembered Harold. "You stay put. I'll need you to fill out a report," he said.

He slammed the door shut behind him. The lock clicked into place, followed by the sound of retreating footsteps. Harold was alone, aside from about a hundred Desolates who were asleep on cots. The few who had perked up when the guard spoke settled back down, uninterested in the new addition to their ranks.

Bent low, Harold weaved through the cots, eyes roving over each occupant. Most were bundled deep into their blankets attempting to escape the cold. Harold had to choose between examining each cot thoroughly and moving through them quickly. The guard would only be distracted for so long.

Getting as close as he dared, he peered over shoulders and under arms at all the sleeping faces. When he came to a tiny supine figure, hips and shoulders aligned even in sleep from months of strict practice, Harold beamed.

Face half buried in a grimy pillow, Lola slept in a seeming cocoon of tranquility. Harold dropped down by her cot, tentatively running a hand over her hair. Lola bolted awake in surprise. "Harold? Oh, no!"

"Hush, I'm here," he said. "I've come for you."

Sitting up, Lola's head tilted in confusion. "Come for me? I don't understand."

Harold clarified. "I've come to take you home."

"You mean you aren't Desolated?" She exhaled a huge breath and reached a hand out to squeeze his shoulder. "I thought they'd sent you here after more testing, like me. I was so worried when they told me about the virus. It would have been such a shame to ruin both of us."

Harold drew back from her touch. Her relief stemmed from the knowledge that the disease hadn't claimed another Potential, not that he, Harold, was all right. Misinterpreting his solemnity, Lola reassured him. "Don't worry. It's something we contracted ages ago. That's why it took so long to track. The damage was the only trace the disease left behind. The good news is that you're okay. You can still get a new wife."

Harold shook his head, adamant. "I don't want my new wife. I want you. That's why I came. To take you back."

Lola's blissful expression dimmed as she said, "You can't take me anywhere. I'm a Desolate now. I belong here."

"Don't say that. You belong with me." The scuffle of footsteps sounded outside the door and Harold's voice dropped to a whisper. "Now come quick before we're discovered."

He moved to pull her forward, but she resisted.

"Harold, I can't."

The creak of the door hinges brought Harold's attention to the front of the warehouse. The fallen door guard hobbled in with the support of his fellow sentry.

Harold felt his chance slipping away. He'd come without a plan. There was no secret escape tunnel or special getaway car, but if he couldn't even convince Lola to slide off her cot, the rest of the rescue wouldn't matter.

"Lola, please. Come with me," he said. "We have to go now."

He tugged harder, and Lola responded with stronger resistance. Fingers clamped to her arm, Harold took one last look into those deep blue eyes, still blazing despite the dimness of light.

"Go home, Harold," she said. "I'm no use to you now, and you don't belong here." Hearing the conviction in her voice, Harold knew there would be no persuading her. His non-plan had failed him.

Following the only course of action he had left, Harold released the woman he'd known as his wife, stood up and turned to give the guards his statement, never looking back.

When Harold opened his door, another new woman stood on his doorstep. "You must have the wrong house," he said, "I already have a new wife."

Geraldine's bubbly giggle echoed down the hall. "Stop being silly, Harold, and let Christy in." Pushing past him, Geraldine greeted her friend in the entryway with a huge hug. "I'm setting everything up in the living room. Straight down the hall on the right."

While the woman named Christy slid into the house, Geraldine remained on the front step greeting a bevy of other young women. After hugging each one of them in turn, she ushered them all toward the living room for snacks and shut the door behind herself. Harold observed all this in a mild state of apathy.

"What's all this?" he asked, more because it was expected than out of genuine interest.

"My book club. It's the third Wednesday of the month. Staying involved in a social network is a thirty-two percent increase. You remember."

He didn't remember, but that didn't really seem to matter.

"I'll be in the kitchen," he said to the back of Geraldine's head while she followed her friends through the hall. The sounds of their chatter burbled out of the living room like a pot boiling over on the stove, unable to contain the sheer vastness of its contents.

With a sigh, Harold made his way to the kitchen and settled in for a few hours of work. After a while, he was able to tune them out entirely, save for the occasional excited shriek. It was a shock when Geraldine's sharp voice addressed him from the hallway.

"Harold, it's time."

Glancing up from his work, Harold found that the clock read nine thirteen. She'd synchronized their schedule perfectly.

Geraldine's brown irises peered around the corner at him. "Are you coming?"

For a long moment, Harold considered that question. He stared at his new wife and the gleaming twenty-three beside her right eye. He contemplated her flawless skin and her upturned nose, her delicate fingers gripping the doorframe. He took in all of her, standing there, waiting for him and eventually decided to return to his work.

"In a minute."

~~Katherine Shaye

13 Reaper Street

by Jo Brielyn

The long drive from Beaver Falls, Pennsylvania to Long Island, New York gave plenty of opportunity to reflect over the events that had led to her move. Too much time. Not usually one to dwell in her thoughts for long, she found the pain of the quiet nighttime drive comparable to enduring open-heart surgery without anesthesia. She scanned radio stations, searching for something—anything—to occupy her mind and drown out the uncomfortable silence that surrounded her.

Soon, the Jeep resonated with sounds of saxophones, piano riffs and the deep hypnotic intonations of Carmen McRae that floated from the speakers.

"Ah... that's better. Now, come on, Babe. Quit acting like a child. It's not like we've never moved before."

The music appeased the voice of doubt in her mind. Everything was better when set to music. Music was what moved her, what drove her. When nothing—and no one—could get through to her, music did. Music communicated with her in a way spoken or written words never could. Her mother never had seemed to understand that about her.

Neither had Shawn.

She had met Shawn during her sophomore year at Penn State University. She'd sat two rows over from his seat in Advanced Psychology. Although they both were aware of the other, for the first few weeks, their only interaction was flirtatious eye contact or quick smiles across the room.

Then, one day, she found Shawn waiting for her in the hall when she left the classroom.

"Hey. Uh, I... I was wondering if you'd like to study together for next week's psych exam." Shawn ran his hand through his jet-black hair and scuffed his running shoes on the tile floor while he awaited her response.

Her insides danced. She'd secretly daydreamt about him since the first time their gazes had locked across the classroom.

She bit back a giddy grin and simply said, "That'd be nice. I could use the help."

"How about we meet this Friday in the library? Say about seven o'clock? Maybe we could get a bite to eat afterward."

"That sounds great, as long as it's not at Jimmy's. My vegetarian roommate's convinced me to swear off eating meat for a while. I'm afraid I won't be able to resist one of Jimmy's famous bacon cheeseburgers with all the works." She rolled her striking green eyes playfully at him. "Imagine that: An Irish girl who doesn't eat meat! My mom would flip."

"Unthinkable!" Shawn threw his arms into the air dramatically and let out a deep, throaty laugh. "No problem. I'm sure we can find some place that serves food a little less tempting."

As it turned out, the food hadn't been the only temptation that evening. The couple had accomplished little studying at the library. Each study question turned into playful banter that left them in fits of laughter. After the first hour, they tossed the psychology books aside and decided to focus on getting to know each other better.

They spent hours in a dimly lit corner booth at Gianni's Bistro while they shared a large vegetable pizza and cold beers. The food, alcohol, and conversation flowed easily between them. As did an undeniable physical attraction.

"Mmm. Who'd have thought pizza would still taste this good without pepperoni and sausage?" Shawn poked her arm with his fork and flashed his prize-winning grin. He abandoned his own seat to slide into the booth beside her. "See that, Red. You're good for me. I would've never tried it on my own!"

She grinned at his pet name for her. Absentmindedly tucking her long auburn hair behind her ear, she said, "Yeah. That's what I'm here for, to get you to try new things."

Sarcasm had always been her way to deal with uncomfortable situations. She'd learned that trick from her mother, the queen of irony, a long time ago. She had been suddenly sucked into an unfamiliar whirlwind of feelings, and it scared her. She delighted in the tingly sensation that shot throughout her body when Shawn scooted closer and caused their thighs to touch, but the newness and intensity of her own feelings made her uneasy. She couldn't help but feel like she was quickly losing control.

Shawn's flirtatious gaze met hers, seductively scanned her body, and then landed again on her face.

"I'm definitely game for trying anything with you. You name it, we'll try it. It'd be my pleasure." He gave her a wink that melted her in her seat. He lowered his voice and added, "Hopefully, yours, too."

She was at a loss for words, something that didn't happen to her often. She struggled to control the rapid pounding of her heart while she allowed her gaze to meet Shawn's. His coal-black eyes were so deep, so captivating, they magically sucked her in and drew her to him. His hand moved from her shoulder and weaved its way into her hair. Lingering for a moment to fondle the base of her neck, he pulled her to him and enveloped her lips with his. The kiss began tenderly and then increased with such a passion, a demand, that she soon forgot everything else around her. Almost before she knew what she was doing, she'd slipped her hand into his and was being led from the restaurant.

That was day the passionate facet of Red truly emerged. And when she realized she would be Shawn's forever.

Forever. What had once seemed like an exciting and romantic notion had turned out to be more like a death sentence. Always to be plagued by the passionate arguments, accusations and questions. Endlessly feeling punished for an uncertain crime. Forever imprisoned by the memories she fought to keep contained.

The speeding Mustang swerved into the lane only inches from the front of her tiny Jeep and jerked her out of her thoughts. Her grip tightened on the steering wheel, knuckles whitening, as sports cars, luxury sedans, mini vans, semi-trucks, and taxis all whizzed past by like the Jeep was parked on the highway. She let out a sigh of relief when she finally spotted the sign for Mineola up ahead.

She quickly spotted a hotel called the Regal Inn, which appeared anything but regal, and searched for a place to park the Jeep. At least it didn't look busy. She left her Jeep in the far corner of the parking lot and hurried cautiously through the dark. A rustle in the nearby bushes startled her and a squeak escaped her lips. When the little gray squirrel ran out, she bit her lower lip in frustration. She used to be fearless, always the daredevil in her group of friends. Not any more. Lately, it seemed like every little sound and movement made her jump out of her skin like a scared little girl.

It didn't pay to be too trusting. Nothing was as it first appeared.

Once settled in her hotel room, she felt the strain of the day slowly dissipate. Of course, that was only after she'd turned on every light, double-checked the door locks, peeked behind the shower curtain, checked under the bed, and closed the drapes.

It was better to be careful than sorry.

She took a quick shower, changed into pajamas, and surfaced from the bathroom a new woman.

Before long, she was surrounded by the contents from the grey case. Newspaper clippings, scribbled notes, photos, and computer printouts flooded the Queen-sized bed.

"My life is a mess. It's time to piece the clues together. Come on, Detective. Do your work."

Speaking the words into the emptiness charged her adrenaline. Sleep would not come tonight. Resigned to that certainty, she slid the reading glasses onto her nose and set to work rummaging through the stacks of papers. A myriad of questions, and hopefully some answers, were hidden in the documents in front of her.

Six hours later, the answers were no closer to being discovered and her head was fuzzy from lack of sleep. She'd been in so many places lately it was difficult to even remember where she was.

"Oh, yeah. We're in New York. Let's go check out the area."

She dressed in her favorite blue jeans and t-shirt, and pulled a Penn State sweatshirt over her head. Agile fingers quickly wove her long hair into a French braid. Ten minutes later, with only a few touches of mascara, a quick brush of blush over her porcelain skin, and a swipe of lip gloss, she exited the hotel room.

It took only about ten minutes to find the place. The sign read "Encore Music" in faded red letters. She smiled at the clever play on words chosen for the used instrument and music shop. The bells on the door jingled loudly, announcing her arrival when she stepped inside.

The distinct smell of second-hand instruments and sheet music filled the air. She paused in the center of the store, breathed in the musty scent and let out a sigh of contentment.

Yes, this is the place...home. Finally.

She wandered around the shop unnoticed until her eyes fell on the shiny black Baby Grand in the corner. She ran her hand appreciatively along the sleek top of the piano and then took a seat on the bench placed in front of it. Her fingers instinctively tapped lightly on the keys and she began to play. Everything else became a blur as she continued to play harder and faster, faster and harder. Every ounce of passion and power in her body was released through her fingers as they flew skillfully over the keys. For those few minutes, all of her confusion, fear, anger and pain disappeared as she was swept away in her own musical rapture.

"Wow. That was incredible. Where'd you learn to play like that?"

She snapped out of her trance and turned toward the voice. It belonged to the middle-aged man standing beside her. His long, blonde and gray streaked hair was pulled back in a messy pony-tail. He shoved his hands in the pockets of his faded and ripped blue jeans and stood waiting for her response.

"Oh. I'm sorry. I...I didn't mean to disturb anyone. This piano just kind of...well, just kind of drew me to her." She rose from the bench and awkwardly adjusted her stance, unsure of what to do next.

"Are you kiddin'? You didn't disturb anyone. I don't think I've ever heard that piano...no, make that any piano...sound like that before." He stuck out his right hand toward her. "I'm Dylan. This is my place."

I've seen you before.

She blushed and looked down at her feet. Then she grasped the outstretched hand in front of her and gave it a gentle shake.

"Hi, Dylan. My name is...uh, um. You can call me

Aria."

"Aria, huh? How about that? What a perfect name for such a talented woman. I guess someone knew you were destined for greatness." Dylan flashed a slightly crooked, yet charming, smile. "By the way, what was the name of the piece you were just playing? I don't think I've heard it before."

"Um. I don't know what it's called. It's just something I heard in my head that wanted to come out." She hesitated for a moment and then continued. "Hey. Since you're the owner, maybe you could help me with something."

"Sure, I'll try. What do you need?"

"Well. For starters, I could use a job. I was thinking maybe you'd have a list of bands that are looking for musicians. I'm new to the area and need to find a job as soon as possible." She stopped herself, afraid to give away any more personal information about herself, no matter how harmless he seemed.

"Hm. Let me think. I might have something for you. Your piano skills are obvious. Can you, by any chance, play any other instruments or sing?" Dylan shoved his wired-framed glasses against his nose while he searched the bulletin board behind the cubicle where the cash register was housed.

"Yes. I sang in the school chorus from the time I was in fourth grade. During my first two years of college, I was also a member of an all-girls band. I sang the lead and played the keyboard. I can also play the guitar, saxophone, and drums. Pretty much, if it makes music I can figure it out. It just kind of comes naturally to me. I guess you could say it's what I live for."

"Heck. Why am I looking at these, then? I could use you right here in my shop. Anyone who knows that much about music would be a huge help to me." Dylan twisted around and faced her again. "What do you say, Aria? Would you be interested in lending a hand around here? I'd be willing to work around any other gigs you find. I may be able to even hook you up with a few of my connections. Come on. Won't you be an angel and help an old guy out?"

Perfect. Absolutely perfect.

She couldn't believe her good fortune. Things never seemed to fall into place this easily for her. A small voice in the back of her mind warned that maybe it was too easy but she ignored it. After all, what's the worst that could happen? He hadn't asked a lot of questions about her past. God knows she wasn't crazy about giving too much information away. What could be more perfect? Besides, if it didn't work out, she could just walk away.

"All right, Dylan. You make it hard for a girl to say no." She pulled out the chair beside the cubicle and sat down. "Now, let's talk salary."

Dylan rubbed his nose with the back of his callused hand in an attempt to conceal the smirk that crept across his face. That'd been easier than he'd expected. She'd settled so quickly.

She pulled the Jeep to a stop in front of the house and admired the large two-story brick home from the road. Another glance at the piece of paper where the address was scrawled, 13 Reaper Street, verified it was the right place.

Wow. Is this really the place? If the apartment is anything like the outside, this place is going to be great. Luck is finally changing.

She paused on the landing at the top of the old stone steps and reached out to ring the doorbell. Even before her finger reached the button, the door flew open wide and she was grabbed by the arm and yanked into a tight embrace.

"Welcome. I've been expecting you. Ooh, look at what a beauty you are with all that red hair! I always wanted to have red hair but Mother Nature thought I'd be better as a mousy brown head. I guess I'm just too old and set in my ways to change it now. But, never mind that.

Please come in. I'm Liz." Liz's words ran together as she tried to get out everything at once without pausing for a breath. An image of the hospital's big charity auction Aria had once attended with her mother came to mind. Liz's fast paced chatter reminded her of an auctioneer.

Whoa. This woman must be lonely. It's like she hasn't talked to another person in days.

She looked nervously behind her and then stepped inside the large foyer. "Uh. Hello, Liz. You can call me Aria. I appreciate you meeting with me this morning. I'm anxious to see the place."

"Oh, then how about we take a look at the apartment?" Liz motioned toward the wooden staircase at the far right side of the foyer. "It's right up these stairs. You know, my Joe and I lived up here when we were first married. My father had the whole upstairs of the house converted into a separate apartment when we were engaged. My parents wanted to help us out but still allow us our own space. Newlyweds need to have plenty of that you know... privacy." She gave Aria a mischievous wink.

Not eager to discuss her own less than pleasurable experiences as a newlywed, Aria was relieved when they reached the top step. When they stepped into the apartment, Aria was both grateful for the distraction and pleased with her new surroundings.

"Gosh, I'm sorry for the mess, hon. I didn't have the chance to get up here and tidy up. I do hope you'll overlook that and see the potential in the space." Liz scurried into the room and began pulling off the sheets covering the furniture and shook her head when her hand swiped at the thick coat of dust on the nearby table.

"No, really. It's fine." Aria wandered from room to room, shaking her head in amazement at her sudden strokes of good luck. First, she'd landed a job at the music store last week and now she'd found the ideal apartment complete with furnishings and a friendly landlady.

"So, what do you think? I just helped my daughter and her husband redecorate the place this past year. Then she decided to break her mama's heart and move away to Connecticut. I guess I always thought Annie would stay here forever, like I did. Like my boy, Vince, has. But she didn't want that...she didn't want this." She swept her hands around the room.

For the first time since Aria had arrived, Liz was silent. Aria wondered which was more difficult to endure, her incessant babbling or the awkward silence.

"The place is great. I'll take it, Mrs. uh...er." Aria let the sentence drop when she realized she'd never even learned Liz's last name.

"Nonsense. Never mind all that formal talk. Just call me Liz. We're going to be living together, after all." Again she was caught off guard when she was abruptly pulled into Liz's tight embrace. "I can't wait!"

"Oh." She giggled uncomfortably. The hug was more affection than she'd received from anyone in a long time and she was still inwardly shaken from it.

Liz patted her shoulder affectionately and smiled. "Now, when do you want to move in? It's available whenever you're ready."

"I'd like to move as fast as possible. I'm not crazy about staying in hotels. I don't sleep well. And I don't have much to bring...only a few items from my hotel room. The rest is still packed in my Jeep. Is today too soon?"

The new place was truly more than she could have imagined finding. It was comfortable, quiet, and away from the busy side of town. Of course, things would be even better if she could get a restful night's sleep.

She'd been lying in bed for almost an hour and felt no closer to sleep than when she first laid down. The unfamiliar objects in the bedroom formed into mysterious figures which tormented her as she lay in the darkness. Even worse were the nightmares that lurked in her mind and threatened to revisit should she allow herself to give in to sleep. Nights were always the worst. Pulling the pillow close, she sang softly and prayed for morning to come quickly.

Too-ra-loo-ra-loo-ral, Too-ra-loo-ra-li, Too-ra-loo-ra-loo-ral, Hush, now don't you cry!

"No, please...please. Don't hurt me. I'll do whatever you want. Please." She begged her assailant to stop.

He hovered over her, leering and laughing cruelly as she crouched in the corner of the room. The wild, wide-eyed look he gave her confirmed her worst fear. Her appeal for mercy wouldn't save her from his wrath. In fact, it only seemed to further enrage him.

"Oh, so now you'll do what I want. Sorry, but it's too late, little girl. Guess you're not such hot stuff now, are you? What happened to the cute little smile and wagging hips? Am I not good enough for that?"

"I...I don't know what you're talking about. Why are you doing this? Please just go." She spoke without raising her eyes to meet his. She couldn't bear to see the hatred and evil brewing in his eyes.

"Not until I'm finished with you." He squeezed her arm and yanked her onto her feet. His rough hands dug into the flesh on her neck as he one-handedly lifted her off the ground. "You've told your lies about me for the last time. Say goodnight, Babe." The hands tightened around her neck, constricting the air supply and preventing her from hollering out for help. The room spun with such force she had to close her eyes to block it out. That was it. She'd made a costly mistake. Now she would die.

Dylan parked his Volkswagen in the side alley of the building and headed for the door. There were no other cars around and inside of the building it was still dark. He leaned against the door but it didn't budge. He rubbed his sore shoulder, frowned, and checked his watch. It was 8:58 a.m., exactly two minutes before opening time. He wondered where she was. She should already be there by now. Since the first week he'd hired her, Aria came early to the store every day. She'd asked for his permission to come before hours and practice prior to unlocking the door for customers. So, where was she now? It wasn't like her to be late. He just hoped she wasn't in some kind of trouble.

When her eyes opened, she found herself inside a hard white box. Unpleasantly cold water surrounded her naked body and sloshed around her head. A wave of panic clutched her heart as she fought to regain her consciousness and desperately tried to remember where she was.

No, please, no. Not the box again.

While she became more alert, the blurry scene around her slowly came into focus—black tiled wall, knife on the edge of the sink and clothes strewn on the floor. She soon recognized where she was, but there were so many unanswered questions nagging at her.

Oh, God. Not again. How did I get here? How long has it been? And why… why can't I remember doing a blasted thing after going to bed?

She stepped out of the white porcelain bathtub and wrapped herself in the towel lying beside the sink. She shivered more from shock than from the chill when she walked through the hall of her new home. With her heart pounding wildly, she did a quick search of the apartment. The front door was locked, the windows closed and latched, and everything else still in place.

So what happened last night?

It was after 11:30 a.m. when she stumbled into Encore Music. Dylan was in the middle of a long, boring explanation of the qualities of a Selmer versus a Keilwerth saxophone to a novice musician. When he caught a glimpse of her, his words dropped mid-sentence.

"Oh, man. Aria? Are you all right?" Dylan politely excused himself from his customer and came to her side. "What happened to you? I was worried when you didn't show up."

"Who? Oh. I mean, yes, I'm fine. Sorry you were worried. You know, most of my friends call me Red." She rested her manicured hand on his arm. "I simply overslept, that's all. I didn't even hear the alarm go off this morning. Please forgive me for being late."

"Red? Oh, okay." He frowned slightly and gave her a quick once-over. "Listen. Are you sure you're okay? You don't look...you just don't seem like yourself this morning."

She forced herself to smile although inside the anger raged and threatened to erupt.

Ha. Like you know who I am. I swear, I'm so tired of people saying that. What the hell does that mean?

"Is that your way of saying you don't like the way I look today? Well, thank you." There was no denying the sarcasm dripping from her words. "I already told you. I'm fine."

"I...I...uh. Oh crap. No, that's not what I meant. You look beautiful...even more stunning than usual." Dylan hung his head to hide his blushing cheeks. "I just meant something's different. You look distracted. You can't blame a guy for worrying, can you?"

Actually, she could. She didn't want anyone worrying about her or feeling like they needed to take care of her. She chose her words carefully before answering. "I'm a big girl. Thanks for caring, but I'm fine. Now, enough about me, okay?" Ready to rid herself from his questions, she gestured across the store. "Actually, I think you might want to get back to that customer over there by the saxes. He's looking like a whipped puppy dog looking for a place to hide."

"Yeah. You're right. The guy is definitely out of his

element here. Just promise me you'll come to me if you have a problem, if you need to talk. I've been told I'm a pretty understanding guy."

"Of course," she said knowing it would never happen. Life had proven the only person she could truly trust was herself.

Some days even that was uncertain.

She paced the perimeter of the small apartment. Something bizarre was going on and it was time to get to the bottom of it. It was out of hand. It was affecting her sleep, her work, her music, everything. She'd been through the whole thing over and over and still it didn't make any sense. The facts didn't add up no matter how she pieced them together. It was like completing a jigsaw puzzle only to discover one vital piece was missing. She needed to find that stupid final piece. She had to discover it soon. But what exactly was she missing and where could she find it? If she didn't find it soon she was going to lose more than that. She was going to lose her sanity.

After wandering into the bedroom, she closed and locked the door. Underneath the piles of shoes accumulating in the back of the closet, she found it. She shoved the reading glasses back into place and set the grey plastic case beside her on the floor. From inside her shirt, she withdrew a silver key attached to the chain worn around her neck. She gently placed the key into the hole and turned. The answers she was searching for were in here. They had to be. She braced herself and lifted the lid.

"Hello! Aria, are you home?" Liz's shout from inside the apartment caused her to jump with surprise. "It's Liz. Hello? Are you here?"

"Uh, I'll be right there. I...I was just changing out of my work clothes." She thought she'd locked the front and she hadn't heard a knock on the door either. Irritated by the unexpected interruption but not wanting to offend her landlady, Aria choked back the snide remark that sprung to her tongue. It wouldn't do any good. Besides, Liz meant no harm. She was just a lonely woman who'd treated her almost like a daughter since she'd moved in upstairs. In fact, she'd become more of a mother figure than her own mother had ever been to her. She didn't deserve to be a target for her frustration. She quickly closed and locked the box and shoved it under her bed. She'd have to return it to its hiding spot later. "I'm almost done, Liz. Give me just a second and then I'm all yours."

"Take your time. I'm in no hurry. I'll be here when...Oh, there you are." Liz broke into a grin as the bedroom door swung open.

"Hi. What can I do for you?"

Liz stood beside the chair and grinned slyly at Aria. "I have a suggestion. How about you join me for dinner tonight? Just the two of us so we can get better acquainted. I could use some company tonight."

Aria smiled at the kind woman. "Actually, dinner with a friend sounds like just the thing to relax me and take my mind off things. I'll come... on one condition. You have to let me help cook and clean up. Do we have a deal?"

"Are you serious? Of course we do. Cooking and washing dishes are two of my least favorite things to do anyhow. Sadly, it's been ages since I've had anyone share my kitchen. This'll be fun." The elderly woman giggled with excitement like a young school girl.

"You know what else is kind of pitiful? This'll be the first date I've had since I moved to the area. Who'd have thought it'd be with my landlady?" Aria gave her a playful squeeze on the shoulder and followed down the stairs to Liz's home. "I'm not much of a gambler but I'm betting it'll be better than most of the dates I've been on in the past."

They sat in Liz's living room, sipping coffee and

savoring the last few bites of the store-bought cheesecake. The kitchen was clean and the leftovers were packed away in the fridge. They'd retired to the living room for, as Liz phrased it, the 'chitchat.' Aria wasn't exactly a chatty kind of girl, but the rest of the evening had been so nice, and she didn't have the heart to disappoint her sweet elderly friend. She'd been fortunate so far and Liz had spent most of the time telling stories of her own. Aria was pretty sure her talkative companion hadn't even noticed she hadn't shared many of her own experiences. That was fine with her. In fact, that was exactly what she wanted. The less she dredged up about her own past the better. Not much of her former life was really worth remembering as far as Aria was concerned. She was much happier focusing on the present and planning for her future. She had no desire to look back on the things she couldn't change.

"So, anyway. I hope I'm not boring you by going on about my Joe, God rest his soul, and my children. They all just mean so much to me. I couldn't imagine how unsatisfying my life would've been without them in it. I hope you don't mind me asking this, Aria, but it seems to me like a beautiful, talented woman like you would have hordes of young men knocking down doors and walls to get to you. So, why aren't you married or, at least, dating? Have you ever been in love before, dear?"

The questions hit Aria with the force of a speeding semi-truck colliding with her heart. She was thankful for the darkness in her corner of the room. Hopefully, it helped to mask the pained and stunned look on her face.

"Um...well. Honestly, Liz. I'm not with anyone because I choose not to be. I have no desire to be in a relationship right now. No relationship means no one is analyzing my every word and action."

She hoped her answer would be sufficient enough for Liz to overlook her failure to answer the second, more personal question. Slowly rising to her feet, she stretched her arms up over her head and let out a loud, drawn-out yawn.

"Aahh, excuse me. I guess I'm not much of a party animal any more. Here it's only a little after eleven and I'm beat. Thanks for the evening, Liz, but I'm gonna have to get to bed. If I don't go now, you might be carrying me up the stairs!"

"Oh, yes, of course. I forgot you worked a full day. I'm sure you're exhausted." She walked Aria to the bottom of the staircase. "I should be going to bed soon, too. Thank you for joining me tonight. I enjoyed your company. Goodnight. Sweet dreams, Aria."

The sweat beaded on her forehead as she took one final look at the building and then walked away. She darted her head from side to side, searching through the shadows for signs of movement. Did that sound in the corner of the alley mean someone else was outside the house? No, it was probably only a stray cat scrounging for food, she reasoned. Or, maybe her stressed out mind was simply playing a cruel joke on her. No one was here. More importantly, no one knew she was here. Still, she wanted to get out of here and the sooner the better. She increased her pace and broke into a sprint across the road. Once inside her car, she wasted no time in starting the engine, eager to speed away from the building and everything in it. And everyone. She needed to escape, to get as far away as possible.

"Thought you'd imagined me, didn't ya? Well, you were wrong." The grungy, brown skinned man taunted from the backseat. "I was there. I know who you are. I saw what you did."

"Huh? What... What are you talking about? Where did you come from? I know my car was locked. How did you get in?"

"Ha. Are you kiddin'? I don't need keys. Anyway, how I got in your car is the least of your problems. I've been watchin' you." He yanked the back door open. Before climbing out, the man spat out the final words that sent her heart racing. "Choke on this thought, Red. I was there. I saw you. I know what you did."

No. It's not possible. No one was there. I'm sure of it. So, who is he and what does he know?

She quickly reached over with trembling hands and locked the car doors. She could still see her unwanted visitor sneering and gesturing obscenely at her through the window. She threw the car in gear and squealed out of the parking lot.

The threatening words lingered in there air long after she was gone. "I was there. I saw you. I know what you did..."

As she looked around through dazed eyes, it was apparent she was no longer in her bed. Somehow she'd ended up on the couch in her living room, still dressed in the t-shirt and running shorts she'd worn to bed the night before, only now they were soaked with her sweat.

Thank, God. It was only a dream. But what is going on? she thought. *I remember going to bed last night, so what am I doing out here? I don't know what's happening around here but this is starting to freak me out.*

She looked apprehensively around the small apartment. Everything seemed to be in order. Still, it was impossible to shake the nagging feeling that something was wrong... desperately wrong.

Answers. I need answers... now.

She double-checked the door lock, pried the kitchen chair under the doorknob for extra measure, and headed to the bedroom. After locking that door, too, she lowered herself on the carpet in front of the closet and heard the haunting voice again.

"I was there. I saw you. I know what you did."

Huh? Saw what? What did I do?

She whipped her head toward the door. It was still closed and locked. She looked toward the window. It was still sealed and the blinds were shut. She jumped up and peered out between the slats. Nothing. She crouched on the ground and looked under and around the bed and closet. Still nothing.

Geez. I must be losing my mind! It's bad enough I'm waking up in strange places and blanking out on things. Now, there are voices, too? I think I need to get out of here for a while before I lose my mind.

She pulled on her black sweatpants and a red t-shirt that said "Whatever" in big white letters, grabbed her running shoes and bolted for the door. She needed to get out of the apartment. She yanked open the door and collided with the large stranger at her door.

"Are you all right, ma'am?" The police officer steadied her with a firm grip. "My name is Sergeant Walters. This is my partner, Sergeant Jamison. We'd like a word with you."

How? Why? What are they doing here? Oh, God.

"I was just on my way out. What can I help you with, officers?"

"Well, maybe you could start by explaining why you are living in a house and the owner has no idea who you are or how you got here."

"I...I don't understand. Liz, Liz, she knows me. I just had dinner with her last night." The room began to spin around her.

"Now that's interesting." The female officer, Sergeant Jamison, interjected as she entered the apartment. "Especially since the owner is a Mr. Michaels who hasn't lived here in over fourteen years. Not since it became a crime scene. Who is this Liz lady, anyway?"

"Michaels? No, Liz lives downstairs. I was with her last night." She groped along the wall until finding the edge of the chair and collapsed into it. "What's going on?"

"That's what we're trying to find out." Walters followed her into the dark living room. He flipped the light switch but nothing happened. He nodded to his partner. "I should've known. No power."

Jamison took over. "Ma'am, I don't know what game you're playing but there's no way you ate dinner with anyone downstairs last night or any night. The house is vacant, except for the rats who've taken it over." She looked back toward the door. "This might be a good time for you to come in, Mrs. O'Brien. Maybe you can help make sense of this."

"Very well. Thank you, Officer."

"It's you! What are you doing here? I thought I told you to stay away the last time. Get out! Get out now!" She lunged and swung wildly at the woman in front of her.

Catherine O'Brien held up her hand to halt the charging police officers and calmly blocked the shot. "Are you done now, Red? I'd like to speak to my daughter."

"I'm done, all right. I'm done with you just like I was done with that no good, Shawn. He's dead and you're next."

"No. He deserved what he got. Not even the police will dispute that. Deep down Eileen knows that, too." She lightly patted her daughter's chest. "She's still in there somewhere."

"Ma'am, would you mind filling us in here? All we know is there were reports that someone's been seen coming and leaving the house." Walters shook his head in confusion. "How did you know your daughter was here and what's wrong with her?"

Catherine glanced at her daughter who had wandered away and was now curled in a fetal position on the couch. "She always returns."

Dylan charged into the room. "Catherine. I'm glad you made it. How is she?"

"Shook up, but she's okay now. I'm glad you called." Catherine turned her attention back to the puzzled police officers. "You see, my Eileen knows firsthand of the crime you mentioned. She was the young girl abducted and held hostage in this house almost fifteen years ago. She was only ten at the time. My baby was trapped here, enduring only God knows what, with that awful Joe and Liz Shew for almost a year before she got away. God, they kept my child locked up in a box like an animal."

"Oh, wow. I'm sorry, ma'am. We had no idea she was the victim." Jamison frowned in disbelief. "But why would she return to this place?"

"After the whole thing, Eileen was never the same. My poor baby was the one who stabbed them both to death while they slept. Someone got lazy that last night and didn't lock her up. I guess they thought they'd broken her by then. It was her only chance to leave and she took it.

"Anyway, the trauma from it all made her a tormented and very sick little girl. Her father and I soon noticed we were dealing with multiple people—not just one little girl. According to her doctors, it was her way of blocking out the pain and memories. At last count, there were at least six alters making appearances. With medication, Eileen is present most of the time. Without it...well, without it the strongest alters seem to dominate—ones like the passionate, sometimes violent, Red; and Babe, a scared ten-year old girl.

"When Babe takes over, she comes back here to where it all began. She hallucinates that Liz is still here. Only, for some reason, she's her friend. We've never been able to figure that one out. She usually only stays for a few days, maybe a couple of weeks, until she pieces the facts together.

"We keep a small case in the back of her Jeep. Inside are all the things she needs to remember who she is and where she belongs. Only, this time, she didn't return. That's when Dylan called me to come."

"And the Shawn person she mentioned? Is he really dead?" Jamison asked.

"He never existed. After all she'd been through, Eileen was never able to have a romantic relationship with anyone. So, instead, she created one in her mind – the first date, the romantic courtship, the wedding, the rocky marriage and even his fateful demise. None of it happened, except in her head."

Sergeant Walters cleared his throat and turned to Dylan, who was crouched on the floor in front of Eileen. "And you? Where do you fit in to all this, sir?"

"Me?" He reached out and brushed the hair from the broken woman asleep on the couch. "I moved here and bought the music store back when Eileen started making her trips."

"Why would you do that?" Sergeant Jamison asked.

"She needed me even though she never remembered me." Dylan carefully hoisted her into his arms and walked to the door. "I made a vow a long time ago that she'd never be here alone again. I'm her father."

About the Author

Jo Brielyn is the co-author of Combat Fat for Kids: A Whole-Family Approach to Optimal Health, *which is set to release in December 2012. She works as a contributing writer for Hatherleigh Press and has currently completed thirteen nonfiction books about health and wellness.*

Jo is an author and poet whose works have appeared in two other Twin Trinity Media anthologies: Elements of the Soul *and* Elements of Time. *She is also a devoted mom and wife, freelance writer, vocalist with the band 24:seven, former youth leader, veteran of the United States Air Force and self-proclaimed coffee addict.*

Jo Brielyn is currently completing her first novel, a humorous tale for middle-grade children.

To learn more about Jo, please visit her website at JoBrielyn.com. Jo now resides in Central Florida with her husband and their two young daughters.

Rest in Peace

by Jo Brielyn

I stand now at your gravesite,
Still shocked that you are gone.

The mourners near are weeping,
Some who never knew you at all;

For if they truly knew you,
They'd understand like I.

You'd be upset to see the tears
On a sunny day like this.

Instead, you'd ask for laughter,
For jokes to bring a smile.

"Don't mourn for me," you'd say to them,
"But hold each other close.

"Look to the sky and sing a song
"And dance together, too.

"But most of all, show that you love.
"Don't waste a moment here on Earth.

"My time here now is over,
"Yet yours still lingers on.

"So live each day without regrets.
"Don't leave it left unsaid."

I can't hold back the laughter now
As I remember you.

I think of all that we have shared and
Of a friendship strong and true.

A butterfly lands on my chest
Then flutters against my cheek.

I'm honored you still think of me
And give one final kiss.

I love you, too, my precious friend.
Now, go and rest in peace.

In loving memory of my childhood friend, Rodney W. Pike II. I am blessed that you were in my life, although our time together was much too short. Your mischievous grin and spirit live on in my memories. You will never be forgotten, my friend.

Printed in Great Britain
by Amazon

59322401R00148